PENGUIN CANADA

THE DUTCH WIFE

Eric McCormack was born in a small village in Scotland. He moved to Canada in 1966 and attended the University of Manitoba. Since 1970 he has taught English at St. Jerome's University, Waterloo, Ontario, specializing in seventeenth-century and contemporary literature. His debut collection, *Inspecting the Vaults*, was hailed by *The Kingston Whig-Standard* as "provocative, disturbing, humorous, harrowing, imaginative and shocking." His previous novel, *First Blast of the Trumpet against the Monstrous Regiment of Women*, was nominated for the 1997 Governor General's Award for Fiction.

Also by Eric McCormack

Inspecting the Vaults

Paradise Motel

The Mysterium

First Blast of the Trumpet
against the Monstrous Regiment of Women

THE DUTCH WIFE

ERIC MCCORMACK

PENGUIN
CANADA

PENGUIN CANADA

Penguin Group (Canada), a division of Pearson Penguin Canada Inc.,
    10 Alcorn Avenue, Toronto, Ontario M4V 3B2

Penguin Group (U.K.), 80 Strand, London WC2R 0RL, England
Penguin Group (U.S.), 375 Hudson Street, New York, New York 10014, U.S.A.
Penguin Group (Australia) Inc., 250 Camberwell Road, Camberwell, Victoria 3124, Australia
Penguin Group (Ireland), 25 St. Stephen's Green, Dublin 2, Ireland
Penguin Books India (P) Ltd, 11, Community Centre, Panchsheel Park, New Delhi – 110 017, India
Penguin Group (New Zealand), cnr Rosedale and Airborne Roads, Albany, Auckland 1310,
    New Zealand
Penguin Books (South Africa) (Pty) Ltd, 24 Sturdee Avenue, Rosebank 2196, South Africa

Penguin Group, Registered Offices: 80 Strand, London WC2R 0RL, England

First published in Penguin Canada hardcover by Penguin Group (Canada),
    a division of Pearson Penguin Canada Inc., 2002
Published in Penguin Canada paperback by Penguin Group (Canada),
    a division of Pearson Penguin Canada Inc., 2003

(WEB) 10 9 8 7 6 5 4 3 2 1

Copyright © Eric McCormack, 2002
Interior image © Barnaby Hall/Photonica.Re-use.

All rights reserved. Without limiting the rights under copyright reserved above, no part of this
publication may be reproduced, stored in or introduced into a retrieval system, or transmitted in
any form or by any means (electronic, mechanical, photocopying, recording or otherwise), without
the prior written permission of both the copyright owner and the above publisher of this book.

*Publisher's note: This book is a work of fiction. Names, characters, places and incidents
either are the product of the author's imagination or are used fictitiously, and any
resemblance to actual persons living or dead, events, or locales is entirely coincidental.*

Manufactured in Canada.

NATIONAL LIBRARY OF CANADA CATALOGUING IN PUBLICATION

McCormack, Eric
    The Dutch wife / Eric McCormack.

ISBN 0-14-301342-4 (bound).—ISBN 0-14-301319-X (pbk.)

I. Title.

PS8575.C665D87 2002   C813'.54   C2002-901941-9
PR9199.3.M42378D87 2002

Except in the United States of America, this book is sold subject to the condition that it shall not, by
way of trade or otherwise, be lent, re-sold, hired out, or otherwise circulated without the publisher's
prior consent in any form of binding or cover other than that in which it is published and without
a similar condition including this condition being imposed on the subsequent purchaser.

Visit the Penguin Group (Canada) website at **www.penguin.ca**

For Nancy and Jody

 INTRODUCTION

Look at the world, with its thousands
upon thousands of years of wars,
plagues, famines, murders, public
and private brutalities, injustices,
parricides, genocides. One would have
to be a supreme cynic not to believe
there must be some great pattern,
some great plan behind it all.

—PABLO RENOWSKI

− 1 −

GENTLE READER: I'd like to tell you about an incident that happened ten years ago. I was visiting an old friend who was the Director of a U.N. medical agency in Central America—in a little town along the equatorial southwest coast of San Lorenzo. One morning early we went down to the market. At the busiest fruit stall, the stallkeeper was a big man, naked to the waist. He had a twig, a few inches long, somehow stuck to the surface of his belly. While he was talking to my friend about the freshness of the cantaloupes and the oranges, his fingers would occasionally go to the twig. He'd give it a little slow twirl, the way you wind a wristwatch.

We chose our bag of ripe fruit for breakfast. On the way home, I asked about the twig on the man's belly.

"Ah, so you noticed that?" my friend said. "He was reeling in his worm."

"His what?" I said.

"It's a parasite he has inside of him," said my friend. "A worm—a Guinea Worm. The only place they used to be found was on the Guinea Coast of Africa, so they're called Guinea Worms. They're all through the tropics now, in unpurified drinking water. They grow inside the victim till they're about four feet long. Sometimes they burst through the skin and stick their necks out. If you can wrap a little twig round them, they can't pull themselves back in again. But you have to be patient. Every time the tension slackens, you wind a little more, then a little more. It's the same principle as reeling in a fish with a line that's not very strong. If you tug too hard, the worm snaps and

3

all your work's for nothing. It just slides back inside and keeps on growing. To get one of them out can take weeks or years. Sometimes, just when one worm's almost out, another one pops its head up. Some people live their whole lives pulling the things out of themselves."

My friend told me all this in the matter-of-fact way doctors talk about such horrors.

"Is there no cure?" I said.

"Not while the drinking water's contaminated," he said.

"What an awful thing!" I said.

"It's hard for outsiders to understand how these people put up with it," he said. "But some families down here have had the worms for generations—they're almost like an inheritance. Those who are infected get married and seem to get on with their lives just the same as anyone else. Take a look over there."

We were passing a ramshackle house with a tin roof. A man and three women were sitting in the doorway, chatting and laughing in the shade of a poinciana with huge, blazing flowers. Some children were playing in the red dirt. I tried not to stare, but I could see clearly that one of the women had a twig attached to her bare belly and was fiddling with it while she talked. Two of the children, a boy and a girl, each had a little twig attached to their bellies. They smiled shyly and waved to us as we walked by with our bag of fruit.

THAT WAS THE FIRST TIME I'd ever heard of the Guinea Worm. Then, by one of those weird coincidences, just a few weeks after I came home someone mentioned it to me again. He was an elderly man and he spoke about it in the course of telling me about the life of his mother. Equally interesting was that several times he called her "a Dutch Wife"—which turned out to mean much more than I would ever have suspected. The story he told made such an impression on me that it's the substance of this book.

ONE DAY WHILE I WAS WRITING it, I happened to be driving downtown when a black car with darkened windows swerved in front of me and cut me off. There was hardly any other other traffic around so it seemed deliberate. At the next set of lights, I got alongside the black car and peered in. But with those windows, it wasn't possible to see who was in there, only the reflection of my own face staring back. When the lights changed, the black car made a left turn and that was the last I saw of it.

But that incident got me to speculating how that's the way it is with certain stories. They seem to be *more* than just stories: they *must* mean something, and *ought* to mean something, or are maybe *on the brink of* meaning something—maybe about *yourself,* rather than anything else. They're like a key to a door, then to a door beyond that, then to a door beyond that, and so on.

Anyway, that's precisely the way the story that follows is for me. I haven't been able to figure out all of the *why*s of it. Maybe you can.

BY THE WAY: that elderly man who told me the story was a great book lover. He once said he missed seeing the phrase, "Gentle Reader," in books. So I'm using it here in his honour.

And I'm begging you—GENTLE READER—not to blame him for *this* book's many deficiencies. They're mine, all mine.

– 2 –

SO, I'D JUST COME BACK to Camberloo after a few months abroad, ending with that side trip to San Lorenzo, and now I was looking for a place to rent. My wife wasn't with me—she was on loan for a while to the West Coast branch of her law firm—and I was staying at the Walnut Hotel on my own while I found a new place for us.

I was being helped in the search by Victoria Gough. She was a real estate agent who'd found apartments for us over the years when we returned from extended trips. I suggested that this time it might be a nice change to rent an entire house. After three days of looking, she phoned to say she'd come up with something.

I met her in the lobby of the Walnut.

"I think I've found just the place for you," she said. "It's not an entire house, but it's one side of a really big semi. It's near the downtown. It's furnished. And it's within your price range." She was an energetic, wrinkled little woman and her green hat and red dress made me think of a carrot. "It's not far," she said. "We can walk."

THAT WAS A SULTRY JULY DAY with thunder in the air. We walked along North Princess, a street full of those big old Camberloo houses among trees that are themselves so massive they might be survivors of the original forest that covered these parts. Most of the houses are now offices for lawyers and accountants. Some look as though they might have even less respectable uses.

After ten minutes walking in the heat, we headed east along Baron, a side street so narrow the trees make a canopy over it. Near the end was a mansion that looked to me as big as an Old Folks' Home.

"That's it," said Victoria.

As we came nearer, I could see that it wasn't actually one huge mansion but two semi-detached houses. Each side had a driveway and a path, leading to separate front doors at the west and east corners. There were turrets at either end and ancient oaks.

"I have the key," said Victoria.

We went along the west pathway and she opened the heavy panelled door. The musty odour of time welcomed us.

"Enter," said Victoria.

During the next ten minutes, as I inspected the place with her, some things especially caught my eye. Downstairs, there was a gloomy living room with a brocade sofa and dark-brown wainscotting and mahogany furniture. Adjoining was a dining room where the table alone would have taken up my entire room in the Walnut. On the walls, I could see the ghostly traces of pictures that had been removed. At the back of the house was an old-fashioned kitchen with a bulky electric range and matching refrigerator.

I told Victoria I loved the spaciousness downstairs. Then we went to check the bedrooms. We climbed a staircase that was so bevelled and warped in places, it might have been the work of a woodcarver rather than a carpenter. The windows at the top let in only a muted light through ivy. A landing gave on to four high-ceilinged bedrooms. They were big—palatial, in fact, to someone used to apartment life.

The bathroom off the main bedroom really took my fancy. It was green tiled and had one of those luxurious old-fashioned showers with a dozen spouts all round the walls to let the water come at you from every angle. Even the toilet was dramatic: it stood on a little dais with brass handrails around it.

Curiously, above the green hand basin, at eye level, a clock was set into the tiles. I'd never seen a clock in a bathroom before. This one was all rusted out now: the hands had fallen off and lay like stick insects trapped behind the glass.

From the landing, we climbed another, shorter but just as uneven staircase to a huge, dark attic. In the corner I could see that the turret, which looked so impressive from the street, was really only a hollow ornamental structure supported by criss-crossing beams.

WE WENT BACK DOWNSTAIRS and I looked around more carefully. I opened an inset door off the living room and saw—to my great delight—a library. It was almost as big as the living room, with a writing table and a leather armchair by a fireplace. I went in and took a quick look at the books. Some were very old and I didn't recognize the authors. Others were classics you know you ought to read.

I just stood for a few minutes, looking around. I could swear I felt that odd sensation you sometimes get from old books—as though they're aware they're changing owners. And, like all libraries, the room was comforting—breathing softly, like some large, kindly animal.

How could I resist it?

"What a great house," I said to Victoria. "I'm surprised it's available."

"Not many people want to rent these big houses nowadays," she said. "They're so hard to heat in winter. But I really think you'd enjoy it. And if you think it's too expensive, I'm sure we can negotiate a lower price." She seemed very keen on my taking it.

"Do you know who the owner is?" I said.

She blinked once or twice. "Well, there've been a few owners. It's being handled by a lawyer."

I could have asked more but I was thinking: What does it matter, anyway? I looked around the library again. It was so enticing. I saw myself, on a winter's day, sitting in that leather chair with the fire roaring, a glass of Scotch in hand, reading some old book I'd always avoided, like Gibbon's *Decline and Fall of the Roman Empire*, or maybe one of those Henry James novels that seem to go on forever.

"I'll take it," I said.

"Good." Victoria sounded relieved. "I'll get the lease ready." Just as she said that, a huge clap of thunder sounded outside, and within a few seconds a summer rain was battering against the windows.

MY WIFE CAME BACK from the Coast for a week to help with the move. She loved the house too, though she was a bit worried about the size and the problems of keeping it clean.

We brought our own things out of storage and she retrieved our cat from her parents, who'd acted as cat-sitters while we were away. The cat was a grey, stripey, optimistic kind of a cat named Corinna (my wife's always had cats; she believes the world would be a better place if everyone had cats to practise loving on before moving on to people). Corinna seemed delighted with the house too and roamed everywhere.

Except for the basement. She wouldn't go down there. In fact, she'd even give a wide berth to the basement door under the staircase. Her fur would stand on end and she'd fluff out her tail to make herself look ferocious as she passed that door. Who knows what goes through a cat's mind? We used to laugh at her, but I must admit I myself went down there only once or twice to check the ancient plumbing system or the fuse box. The door was made of some kind of heavy wood, unpainted on the inside, and it had scratch marks on it, as though one of the previous owners had kept a dog in there. The caged light bulbs in the basement ceiling were feeble, and the crude cement walls and the earthy smell were hard to reconcile with the elegant mansion above.

I even dreamed about the basement.

The night after my wife went back to the Coast, around midnight, I heard a noise and got out of bed. I went downstairs and crouched in the darkness outside the closed basement door. I could hear some creature behind it, stealthily climbing the creaky stairs. It reached the landing and the doorknob slowly began to turn. My heart was thudding. When the door opened, a beautiful creature (I was certain it was beautiful though I couldn't see it in the dark) stood there, looking at me.

I jumped at it and pushed it back down the stairs. Then I slammed the door shut and crouched again, waiting. I was quite certain that if that creature ever managed to get out of there, it would destroy me.

That was the dream. I had it that night, and then again, in almost exactly the same form, the next morning—as though it straddled the border between waking and sleeping and needed to be passed either way. I had some variation of that dream, night and morning, at least once a week for my entire stay in the old house.

– 3 –

AS I'VE SAID, my side of the house was only one-half of the entire building. The dividing walls must have been very thick, for I never heard any sound from the other side. I imagined it must have the same big, gloomy rooms and the same forbidding basement. Victoria Gough had told me a retired History professor lived there.

During the first few weeks, I often sat at a rickety picnic table in the back yard, trying to write. I was working on a novel and it wasn't going well. Several times, through the gaps in a high, straggly hedge, I caught a glimpse of our neighbour doing some gardening.

One day in particular, I was sitting there with pen and paper, just staring into space or admiring the trees with their lush foliage and the variety of birds that seemed to live in them. I suddenly had a sense I was being watched and looked up—and there he was, just turning away from a gap in the hedge. He was a thin man with a pinched face and a prominent jaw. He must have been well into his seventies.

He looked vaguely familiar in the way many elderly people do.

When I phoned my wife that night after dinner, I mentioned seeing him. By then, I'd had a glass or two of wine and I suppose I felt philosophic. I said how odd it was that just as babies often look alike, so do the elderly. I speculated that, in the case of babies, life hasn't had a chance to place any distinguishing marks on them; whereas, in the case of the very old, the years have stripped away most of the distinctions. "Time seems to beat them down," I said, poetically, "leaving them all alike again. Like hills that were once mountains ranges."

"Hmph!" was all my wife said.

ONE MORNING, TO AVOID DOING MY QUOTA of writing, I even resorted to pulling some weeds from a flower bed in the back yard. I happened to look up and saw my neighbour standing at a gap in the hedge and looking down at me. The sun was directly behind him so his fine white hair was tinged with gold. We were only three or four feet apart and could hardly avoid speaking.

"Good morning," I said. I held out my hand to him through the gap and introduced myself.

His hand was bony, but his grip was quite strong.

"How do you do?" he said. "My name is Vanderlinden. Thomas Vanderlinden." He had a soft, tenor-ish kind of voice and such alert blue eyes you might have believed there really was another, much younger man hiding in that old body. He asked me how I was enjoying the house. I told him I loved it—except for the basement. I gave him a humorous account of my nightmare.

He didn't seem amused.

"Oh, well," I said, "I know dreams don't interest most people."

"That's quite all right," he said. "Do you happen to have read any of the works of Vociferus O'Higgins?"

I laughed. "No," I said, "I'm sure I'd remember anyone with a weird name like that."

He didn't laugh. "Not many people have read O'Higgins," he said. "In fact, his books haven't been published for three hundred years."

I had a feeling I was in for a lecture.

"O'Higgins was a great student of dreams and insomnia," said my neighbour. "His major treatise was *Spiritus Nocturnus*. Sixteen forty. In it, he claimed even God used to enjoy dreaming until He created this world. When He saw how it turned out, it gave Him such nightmares, He was afraid to let Himself fall asleep any more."

"Wouldn't that have been a dangerous kind of idea to publish in those days, what with the Inquisition and that sort of thing?" I said, just to show I knew something.

"Very dangerous," he said. "But then, O'Higgins wrote a lot of dangerous things. And indeed, he was burned at the stake for them, eventually. His work's full of quite ingenious thinking for a man of his time. One of his theories was that dreams are the soul's memories of the body."

I was puzzled by that.

"He seemed to mean," he said, "that when you're asleep the soul—which is supposed to be pure—remembers the body as a dangerous, chaotic place it's been forced to inhabit. But, according to O'Higgins, it actually longs for the body with all its flaws."

I nodded politely. "Was that what they burned him at the stake for?" I said.

"Not at all," said Thomas Vanderlinden. "What they objected to mainly was another section in his book. In that part, he posited that religion itself was dreamt up by the weakest human beings—those who need to believe in a divine order in all things. They have to keep finding evidence for that order everywhere, so that they can congratulate themselves for being right. On the other hand, the strongest human beings need no religion. They believe chaos is at the root of everything and they find unlimited evidence of it and are convinced that those who can't see it are nothing but fools." He smiled a tight little smile. "That was the idea they burned him at the stake for. And they burned every one of his books they could find. Only one or two copies survived."

I was trying to think of something to say that would make me sound intelligent. "How absurd," I said, "for someone to be burned at the stake over that kind of thing."

From the way Thomas Vanderlinden looked at me, I couldn't be sure he agreed with me. "Time for my lunch now," he said abruptly, and disappeared from the gap in the hedge, leaving me standing, quite astonished at this entire conversation with a man I'd just met.

I SAW HIM IN THE GARDEN frequently after that and we'd invariably talk. But never small talk—he had no interest in that. I guessed he missed having an audience of students for his scholarship and I'd become a substitute. He admitted to an excessive love of reading. "It's probably a kind of drug," he said. "Have you read any of Balthazarus of Rotterdam? Late sixteenth century?"

Of course, I hadn't.

"Balthazarus believed that the sensation—or lack of sensation—of being immersed in a book is actually thought, thinking itself," said my neighbour. "Perhaps it's that disembodied feeling that makes reading so addictive."

"Ah," I said.

On another occasion, he defended his enthusiasm for curious ideas he'd find in old books: "Most modern scholars think these old notions are like the light from stars—impressive enough, but dead nevertheless." He looked at me with those unblinking blue eyes. "But even if that's true, I always think there's no harm in admiring the ingenuity of the minds that invented them. Wouldn't you say so?"

Naturally, I agreed.

"Certainly, no one would deny the world has progressed in the last few hundred years," he said. "But, I wonder: has it progressed in the right direction?"

I was glad to see he really didn't expect an answer from me.

ON ANOTHER OF THOSE SULTRY MORNINGS as I was making some coffee I heard a loud wailing. It was an ambulance and it pulled up at my neighbour's pathway. Not long after, I saw him being wheeled out on a stretcher.

As soon as the ambulance left, I went over to his door and pushed the old brass bell-button. A little nunnish woman of middle age with a brown, round face answered. I'd seen her once or twice walking along the street.

"Is everything all right?" I said. "Is there anything I can do?"

"The professor's been taken ill," she said. "It's happened before but this time it's bad."

"I'm sorry to hear that," I said. "By the way, I'm your neighbour."

"Yes, he's mentioned you," she said.

I was about to ask if she was his wife, when she said: "I work for Home Makers. I just clean the house and sometimes cook. It's lucky I was here when he felt ill."

There was no more to say so I was about to go.

"He left me a message for you," she said. "He hoped you'd visit him in the hospital."

"He did?" I was surprised, considering the short time I'd known him.

She assured me that was the message.

"He'll be in Camberloo General," she said.

"Then maybe," I said, "I'll drop by some time."

I didn't really intend to.

– 4 –

TO GET TO THE POINT of all this: one afternoon, three days after Thomas Vanderlinden was taken away, I happened to be driving along Regent Street past Camberloo General when I made up my mind—on a whim—to drop by and see him.

I found him in one of those little private rooms, propped up in bed. He was hooked up to various machines and had an oxygen mask on. He turned his head when he heard the door and took off his mask, like a scuba diver, surfacing. "How kind of you to come," he said.

His voice was quite strong, but I could see that he was indeed very sick. His already thin face was strained, and though his eyes were alert enough, there was a certain look in them— I suppose of someone who's seen the shadow of death.

"How are you?" I said.

"Oh, fine, fine," he said. "It's so nice of you to visit me. I know you must be busy." He was aware by then that I was struggling with a novel.

Hanging on the wall beside him was a wooden cross, for this hospital had once had religious affiliations. He saw me looking over at it.

"I can't help seeing it when I'm lying here," he said. "I know it' s meant to have an edifying effect, but it makes me think more of a kite about to take off."

That was the first time I'd heard him say something I was sure was meant to be funny.

On the bedside table, I noticed, there were no flowers, no cards. "Do you have any family?" I asked quite innocently as a conversation opener.

He didn't blink, but it was as though a spare eyelid, like a lizard's, descended.

I suspected then that I was his only visitor.

ON THAT DAY, and on my subsequent visits—I went there exactly seven times—Thomas Vanderlinden mentioned his illness only once, and that was really just to illustrate a linguistic point. "Sixteenth-century physicians would have called what I have 'Gripe in the Guts,'" he said one day. "Such colourful phrases are no less useful than the technical language used by today's specialists. That's because language of any kind is severely limited. '*Words are the shadows of things; and shadows can never show the light.*'" He gave me the impression he was quoting some well-known, indisputable axiom.

Of course, I'd never heard of it.

AT THE END OF MY VISITS, which usually lasted a couple of hours, he often looked worn-out, for he did almost all the talking. But overnight, he'd have a little resurrection, and his eyes would be bright again when he welcomed me the next day.

One afternoon just after I'd arrived, his doctor, a tall, balding man named Doctor Moleman (curiously, he had three prominent moles on his right cheek), came in to examine him. He shook his head at the sight of his patient, propped up, talking animatedly.

"Now, now, Professor Vanderlinden," he said. "You should be resting, not exerting yourself."

I went out in the corridor till Moleman finished his examination. When he came out, I asked him if it would be better if I cut my visits short.

"No, no," he said. "He knows very well I only tell him what a doctor's expected to say. Let him talk as much as he likes. It won't make any difference."

That sounded ominous, and Thomas Vanderlinden must have noticed that I felt uncomfortable when I went back into the room and sat by the bed.

"When I was young," he said with a little smile, "I used to consider death as something exotic and distant. But now it seems to me fairly domesticated, like a pet animal. I'm quite prepared for it."

I knew he said that to reassure me. Through all my visits, he seemed less concerned about his own health than about keeping me entertained.

– 5 –

AS I'VE HINTED, one reason for my willingness to spend hours each day at the hospital was this: I welcomed the distraction from my own work. Writing a novel isn't as easy as some people think. You get yourself up out of bed each morning, eat some toast, drink some coffee and go to your desk, ready for action. But that's only the preliminary. Now you have to reassemble that fictional world and—hardest of all in the mornings—wake up your characters. Often they can be even more sleepy-headed than you are and stubborn as cats. Some days, they won't remind you what they were doing yesterday, or they might even change their names to confuse you. And so on. Yes, the whole endeavour can be quite irritating at times.

On top of that, this particular novel I was working on was giving me a lot of trouble. It was called *The Kilted Cowpoke* and it was about a group of Scottish farmers who'd immigrated to the Wild West in the early part of the nineteenth century to become ranchers. They did all the usual cowboy things: herded cattle, battled against wild Apaches and Comanches, were involved in stampedes and shoot-outs and so on. I built in a typical Western plot about dynastic squabbles: the patriarch dies and his two sons, who've always loathed each other, fight over the division of the land. The mandatory love-element was in the plot too: the heroine admires the older brother, but her heart goes out to the younger.

Misfortune and mayhem result.

But what made the story interesting for me was that I was trying to allow the characters to keep their authentic Scottish trappings: for example, they wore kilts and sporrans (the little purses that hang in front—I put their six-shooters in there). More important, for the sake of realism I made them speak in Scottish Lowland dialect: they called the steers "coos"; the older brother always referred to the younger as "the wee crapper"; the ranch foreman told a captured Apache: "Ah'm gonny rip aff yer herry cheuch!"; the heroine pleaded with her lover: "Och, c'mon, laddie. Dinnae brek ma herrt, wulye?" And so on.

A major problem was this: when I read out parts of an early draft to my wife she could barely stop laughing at the dialogue—even at what I'd intended to be the most moving parts. So I was faced with quite a conundrum: how to have the characters speak a perfectly respectable and ancient dialect, without turning tragedy into farce.

In the midst of this struggle, it was a relief to go to the hospital and visit my neighbour—he insisted by then that I call him "Thomas." With an extra-large coffee from Tim

Hortons to keep me alert, I'd sit contentedly at his bedside for as long as he wanted me there.

– 6 –

ON MY THIRD VISIT, I'd barely settled myself when he handed me a silver-framed photograph he'd taken out of the bed-table drawer. "That's my mother, Rachel," he said. "Rachel Vanderlinden."

The photograph was a black-and-white head shot of a young woman in a high-necked blouse wearing a little pillbox hat with flowers. She had a handsome enough face, with confident eyes and the same longish jaw as Thomas. It was certainly a face full of character.

"Before she came to Camberloo, she lived all her life in Queensville," he said. "Do you know it?"

"Of course," I said. It was an old town, on the shores of the Lake, two hundred miles north of Camberloo.

"Her father was a judge there till his death," he said. "But he also served on the circuit courts around Camberloo, in the summers. So he bought a house down here, too. That's where this photograph of my mother was taken. She was expecting me, at the time. She told me that in the first months, it felt quite gigantic, like having a sore in the mouth. She said she didn't experience the pregnancy so much as it experienced her."

I gave him the photograph back.

"She's been dead for more than twenty years now," he said, looking at it for a moment. "I still find that fact hard to believe. I used to feel guilty at letting other things interfere with the memory of her. But they do, they do. '*For memories melt like teardrops into oceans of oblivion.*'"

That sounded like another of those well-known quotations, so of course I nodded.

"When my mother was as old as I am now," he said, "she began to have heart problems and couldn't get about much any more. She said she had something very important to tell me." He looked at me, making sure he had my full attention. "And indeed what she told me was quite surprising. It was about the man I'd always known as my father." He breathed. "She told me he wasn't her husband." He looked at the photograph again, immersed in it and silent for a long time.

Of course, I didn't find his revelation all that startling. Who would, nowadays? But I wanted to humour him. "Did she explain?" I said. "I mean about him not being her husband?"

He looked up at me, almost as though he'd forgotten I was there. "Oh, yes," he said. "Indeed she did. She said it all started, long ago, while she was still living in Queensville . . . *late on a Saturday afternoon in early Fall.*"

THAT WAS HOW THOMAS VANDERLINDEN'S STORY began. Over the course of my visits, this quite ordinary-looking old man told me some of the most extraordinary things I'd ever heard—so much so that I began keeping notes, a thing I rarely do. Though I don't need notes to remember the little smile on his face when he first told me about his mother's confession. Or how he lay back in his hospital bed, narrowed his eyes and fixed them on that day in the distant past, as though it were a comet trailing dust and ice.

PART ONE

RACHEL
VANDERLINDEN

Once out of the water, they
no longer resemble anything.
And so it is outside of dreams . . .
—Antoine de Saint-Exupery

. . . LATE ON A SATURDAY AFTERNOON IN EARLY FALL, Rachel Vanderlinden waited for her husband, Rowland, to come home from abroad—he'd been gone from Queensville for more than three months. He'd sent a telegram to say he'd be arriving by train from the East Coast that day. She needed, once and for all, to talk to him.

She was standing at the kitchen window looking across the lawn to the Lake: the waves were still rough with whitecaps from the storm. Last night, even this big stone house had felt as though it might be ripped away. But the wind was moderate now and the window was slightly ajar. Through it, she heard a sad noise and looked skyward: a huge formation of geese was flying overhead, bringing scraps of the north with it. She shivered and went to the stove and poured some more coffee.

She was sitting at the table, leafing through the *Gazette,* when the doorbell rang: three long, distinct rings. That was always the way Rowland rang, announcing his arrival before letting himself in.

She sat still, breathing evenly, waiting for her husband, the returned traveller, to enter. She needed to be calm.

The bell rang again. Again three long, distinct rings.

Perhaps he'd lost his key, she thought.

She got up and walked slowly out of the kitchen, along the polished wooden hallway to the front door. Passing the full-length wall mirror, she checked herself: a young, brown-haired woman in a green dress, of medium build, with a longish face, the shadows under her eyes well disguised with make-up. She glanced quickly into those familiar green eyes, trying, as always, to catch them by surprise, testing to see if they would ever accidentally betray something about the mystery of herself.

Not today. She looked perfectly calm, as she would need to be.

She went to the door, took a last deep breath, and opened it.

A stranger stood there, a sturdy man in a brown cloth cap, which he took off. He had a bent nose and scarring above the eyebrows. The eyes themselves were a washed-out blue, giving a mildness to what would have been a hard face. He didn't seem sure of himself.

"Yes?" said Rachel Vanderlinden. She thought this stranger might be one of those beggars looking for a meal in return for mowing the lawn.

The man mumbled something she couldn't quite make out—he had an accent of some sort, Scottish perhaps.

"I beg your pardon?" she said.

He shuffled his feet. His black boots were dusty, his brown corduroy suit was worn and tight. He clutched his cap and cleared his throat. This time, when he spoke, she could make out the words "your husband" quite clearly.

Her heart stopped. "My husband?" she said. "What about him?"

The blue eyes now looked directly into hers. "*I,*" he lingered on the word, "am your husband." His smile was partly a frown.

"What?" she said, scrutinizing his face. "What are you talking about?" She was beginning to be afraid.

He ran his fingers through untidy fair hair. He had the hands of a working man. "I'm your husband," he said again.

"I'm just back from England." As though reciting words he'd memorized, he said: "I arrived in Halifax last week. I sent a telegram." He waited, then said again: "I'm your husband."

The man stood, awkward, waiting. He seemed to think he'd delivered some message in a code she'd understand and expected a reply.

And in that instant of waiting, she all at once did understand. Her heart beat faster, her mind was in a ferment.

He watched her for a moment, then he said: "This is stupid. I'm sorry to have bothered you." He turned away and started down the pathway to the street.

She was relieved. She wouldn't have to say anything. She would just let him go.

Then, as he was opening the gate, she changed her mind. "Wait a minute," she called.

He stood at the gate and looked back.

She looked at him for a long moment. She had to clear her throat. "Come inside," she said.

"Are you sure?" he said.

She thought for a moment. "Yes," she said.

And he came back up the pathway and into the house.

THEY'D BEEN SITTING IN THE LIVING ROOM for almost an hour, he in one of the plush armchairs, she on the couch at an angle to it. Her black cat, Lucy, had sniffed him over cautiously and now lay across his knees, purring as he petted her with his rough hand.

"I need a while to think," she'd said when they sat down. "Please don't say anything and please don't look at me." He had kept his eyes away from her, though she could watch him as he sat, biting his bottom lip now and then, knowing that she was looking him over and thinking. She had a lot to think about.

The clock on the mantel chimed six slow chimes. She rose from the couch and went and sat in the armchair opposite him. "All right," she said. "You can look."

His pale blue eyes showed he wasn't quite sure yet what she meant.

"I'm so glad you're home," she said.

His eyes widened.

'Would you like some coffee before dinner?" she said.

He seemed pleased. He nodded his head. "Yes," he said. "I would like coffee. That would be great."

". . . Rachel," she said.

Again he nodded his head. "Yes," he said. "All right . . . Rachel."

In this manner, an agreement was made.

SHE POURED HIS COFFEE with a steady hand and they drank together silently. Then the man who said he was her husband asked if he could wash himself. She showed him the bathroom off the main bedroom, and while he showered, she went to the closet and found a complete set of clothes for him. She left them on the bed.

She went back down to the kitchen and started preparing dinner.

She was busy with the steaks when he came in. His hair was slick from the shower, and she could smell the soap. The shirt she'd left out was a little tight across the shoulders.

"Feeling better?" she said, making herself breathe steadily. "You look better . . . Rowland," she said, trying the name out.

He sat down at the kitchen table and watched her at the stove. "You look marvellous, too, Rachel," he said after a while.

She didn't turn round, but she smiled.

HE ATE HIS DINNER HUNGRILY. She was too nervous to eat much because one matter was of the utmost importance to her and she knew she must deal with it right away. "Are you . . . home for good now?" she said.

He lowered his knife and fork and looked at her squarely. "I hope so," he said. "I really do."

That was the answer she wanted to hear and she was satisfied. "Good," she said. "Is the steak all right?"

"Delicious," he said. He began eating again and there was silence. After a while, he drank some water and cleared his throat and looked at her. He seemed to want to play his part in the conversation too. "So, you've had some bad weather?" he said. "I saw branches down all over the place."

"This is the season for storms," she said.

"Ah," he said. Then, "I didn't realize the Lake was so big."

She shook her head and said nothing.

He didn't know what to think of that, so he tried again. "This house," he said, gesturing around him. "It's so comfortable. How long have you lived . . . ?"

She looked at him imploringly and he stopped. He obviously couldn't see that even the most ordinary of topics was a potential minefield.

"Sorry," he said, frowning. "I don't . . . ." He was at a loss for words.

"Why are you asking me things that you, of all people, already know?" she said. "Do you understand . . . Rowland?" She didn't know what else to say. She hoped he'd realize how careful he'd have to be if she was to go through with this.

Perhaps he did understand. Certainly, he nodded his head slowly. "Aah," he said. "Aah."

DINNER MORE OR LESS successfully completed, she took him back into the living room. She put a match to the fire then poured them both a liqueur and offered him the humidor. He picked out one of the cigars, lit it and exhaled contentedly.

For an hour they sat exchanging the safest of small talk, he smoking, both sipping. The clock on the mantel chimed ten. She thought he must be wondering: what now? She herself had wondered about that.

Then she put her glass down firmly. She knew it was up to her. It was astonishing but true—everything was up to her!

"Well, I suppose it's time for bed . . . Rowland," she said, looking him in the eyes, keeping her voice steady.

"Right," he said, and put down his glass.

In the bedroom, she watched him take off his clothes. He didn't turn away as she looked him over but stripped in a businesslike way, with no sign of embarrassment when he caught her eyes. He had the body of a man used to physical work.

He got into the bed, pulled the covers up and watched her. She switched off the room lights, leaving only the half-light coming from the bathroom. She undressed quickly, not looking at him, knowing he was watching. She came into the bed beside him. They, whose fingers had never touched before, embraced immediately, their bodies cool against each other's, pressing against each other from head to toe.

"Rowland," she murmured. "Rowland."

He'd been stroking her back and he paused. She thought he was going to say something, that he was going to spoil everything. But instead he sighed and held her close.

In doing so, he set her free.

DURING THOSE FIRST DAYS, they actually did a lot of talking. To a stranger overhearing, their conversations then would have sounded like the banal talk of people who knew each other too well. But for her, these conversations were utterly exhausting, based on the careful exclusion of anything that would spoil the illusion.

She left the house only to buy food, and when a week passed she knew a decision had to be made. Sophie, her housemaid, was due back from her holidays. Explanations would be required. There would be gossip. It would be simpler to leave, for a while, at least.

She packed and they set out together the next morning in the Daimler. They were headed for the house in Camberloo, two hundred miles to the south, where hardly anyone knew her.

The long drive was uneventful, except that whenever he saw the mangled body of a groundhog or a squirrel on the highway, he'd ask her to pull over. He'd get out and lift the body off the road and lay it gently on the grass verge.

"What a slaughter," he'd say, over and over again.

She would have tried to dissuade him. She would have pointed out that the bodies probably had ticks and fleas and lice, and that he'd get blood on his hands. But he was so upset—"Poor little creatures!" he'd say—that she was ashamed of her fastidiousness and said nothing.

THE CAMBERLOO HOUSE had been bought by her father when he'd presided on the bench of the circuit courts, in the ten years before his death. They had lived there for six weeks each summer, but she barely knew anyone in the town.

Now, as she brought the Daimler to a stop in the driveway, the front door opened and a man and woman came out to meet them, with three very young children trailing behind.

"The Zeljats," Rachel said. "They keep an eye on the place." She took a very deep breath. "Well, let's see what happens."

Zeljat opened the car door for her. He was a slight man with a black beard and black eyes with a glint in them. His wife was a small, brisk woman with a hook nose. The children clustered around her. A black-and-white collie came bounding from behind the house towards the car as Rachel stepped out.

"Maxie!" she said to the dog, which was wagging its tail violently. "I haven't seen you in years!" She looked at Zeljat. "How long has it been?"

"Not since your father died," he said. "Three years." He was staring inquisitively now at her passenger, who had got out of the car and was standing in the driveway.

"You remember Rowland, don't you?" she said offhandedly.

If Zeljat was surprised, it was hard to tell. He just narrowed those black eyes a little, said nothing and gathered the baggage. Maxie came over and sniffed at the newcomer cautiously. He bent over and petted the dog, till it relaxed and licked his hand.

Rachel Vanderlinden smiled at that. "Good, Maxie!" she said with delight.

As though the dog had settled everything.

THEY WERE HAPPY IN CAMBERLOO, even though, after the first week, the weather turned wet, for the Fall was advancing. The nights were marvellous. In the mornings, they'd go for long walks in their rain-gear, and in the afternoons they'd sit in the living room beside the fire, reading. Or, at least, Rachel would read. He treated books as objects of veneration, but preferred picture books of birds and animals, even shopping catalogues. After an hour or so, he'd become restless. Often, he'd watch for Zeljat, who lived in a row house about a half hour's walk away, to arrive. Then he'd put on rubber boots and go into the garden to help with pruning and preparing the ground for winter.

"Does Zeljat ever ask any questions?" she asked once.

"No, not really." He shook his head. "He said I never used to be interested in the garden. That was all."

"Good," she said.

THE FROSTS CAME and there was no more gardening. He asked her if he might order a punching bag from the Eaton's catalogue. When it arrived, he strung it up in the enclosed porch. Each day around noon, he'd strip to the waist and pound at that bag till his body glistened with sweat. Sometimes he'd spend another fifteen minutes with a skipping rope. Then he'd shower and join her for lunch, full of good spirits.

One thing especially pleased her. She felt that, more and more, when those pale blue eyes looked at her, she could see love in them. They'd been together for three months and she was happier than she'd ever been in her life.

ONE LATE AFTERNOON in early December, the first snowfall came. They sat by the living-room window watching it slowly erase the last colours of the year.

"It's beautiful," he said over and over again.

"Yes," she said. "Let's stay here, forever."

They were sitting side by side and he was stroking her hair.

That was when she made her announcement. "Rowland," she said, "I'm going to have a baby."

"Are you serious?" he said quietly, looking at her.

"Of course I am," she said.

"Rachel," he said. "That's great!" He kissed her and was quiet for a moment. Then he spoke again, very softly. "Maybe now's the time to straighten things out between us," he said. "Maybe I should tell you who I am?"

She pushed him away. "What are you talking about?" she said. "Do you want to spoil everything? Are you crazy?"

He pleaded with her. "We can't pretend forever," he said.

She was stunned to hear him say such a thing. "Enough!" she said. "That's enough. Don't ever talk about it."

He was silent for so long she was afraid she'd offended him. "Rowland," she said soothingly, leaning against him. "I really do love you. Nothing else matters." She took his hand.

The light was so dim now she could barely see his face. He raised her hand to his lips.

"I love you too, Rachel," he said. "I only hope you're right."

THE BABY WAS BORN and they called him Thomas. They loved him and took him everywhere.

On a Saturday morning in June—the baby was three months old—they went shopping at the market. He was carrying Thomas in his arms, she was carrying the shopping bag. They saw a crowd at the corner and heard a loud voice. They stopped to see what was going on.

On a podium a thin-faced soldier was shouting through a speaking trumpet. He had a Sergeant's stripes on his brown sleeve. Rachel thought he was a very severe-looking man. Behind him was a big poster of an even sterner-looking soldier with a moustache, his finger jabbing at the audience. The message on the poster read: "YOUR COUNTRY NEEDS YOU."

As Rachel watched, the Sergeant beckoned to another brown-uniformed soldier in the crowd. "Up here, Private, on the double," he said.

The soldier climbed the podium stairs awkwardly. He was very young, and when he removed his cap, he looked like a schoolboy, with brown hair plastered back.

"Now, ladies and gentlemen," said the Sergeant. "Keep an eye on this lad if you want to see an example of true patriotism and courage." To the Private, who seemed embarrassed, he said: "Strip."

The young soldier unbuttoned his tunic and handed it to the Sergeant. Then he opened his shirt.

Rachel gasped at the sight.

The soldier's slight body was a mass of livid scars and dark incisions that were barely healed.

"This young man," announced the Sergeant, "was sprayed with shrapnel from a shell, just six months ago on the Western Front. In spite of that, he can't wait to get back to war. Isn't that so, Private?"

"Yes, Sergeant," said the soldier.

"Now for something interesting," said the Sergeant. Out of his pocket he took some shiny little horseshoes and held them up to the crowd. "These are magnets," he said. "Watch this." He held out one of the magnets towards the young soldier's body. Click! He took his hand away, and everyone could see that the magnet was clinging to the flesh of the soldier. He did the same with the rest of the magnets, half a dozen of them. The young soldier winced each time the magnets clicked.

Rachel Vanderlinden, watching, winced along with him. The metal protruding from his body reminded her of a painting of some old martyr.

"See?" the Sergeant said through the megaphone. "This brave young man still has shrapnel inside him. The doctors took a lot of it out, but there's still bits of it floating around inside him like eggshells." He then began roughly pulling the magnets off, ignoring the obvious pain of the young Private. He handed him his tunic. "Dismissed!" he said.

The young soldier buttoned up and stumbled back down the stairs.

The Sergeant spoke urgently into the megaphone: "Now, if a young lad like this wants to get back and serve his country, surely all you able-bodied men should be ashamed to stay home. Come on now, sign up right away!"

WHEN THEY SAT DOWN at breakfast the next morning, he told Rachel he had something on his mind. He said he wanted to enlist.

She wasn't surprised, knowing him now as she did. Yet she was afraid even to think about living without him. For since that moment he'd knocked on her door in Queensville, they'd barely been parted, and their relationship was intense and absorbing.

"Go if you must," she forced herself to say. The words were like some awful, self-inflicted curse.

"Thank you, Rachel," he said. Then, in a coaxing voice: "And maybe now we should be honest. Let me tell you everything, what do you say?"

She wasn't angry with him as she once was. "No," she said wearily. "Not now. When you come back. Tell me everything when you come back."

"But, what if . . . ?" he said.

"Hush," she said. "When you come back. Tell me everything when you come back."

ON A MORNING THREE MONTHS AFTER THAT, baby Thomas still sleeping, she stood at the window, looking into the front yard. She hadn't been able to sleep and had watched the coming of dawn almost as if she alone were re-creating the world. Now the first birds halted the silence. She saw the bright-red slash of a cardinal and the small lightning of finches at the feeders he'd hung in the big spruce tree. He'd said, watching the variety of birds at them, that it was like the Garden of Eden. She imagined him, now, in the trenches somewhere at the Front, missing her as she missed him. His absence was a kind of death to her, alleviated only a little by hope.

She saw an early cyclist turning into the driveway. It was the telegram boy.

Refusing to allow herself to think, she made herself go downstairs to the front door. The boy handed her the brown envelope. She tore it open with extreme care and saw the chilling words:

"REGRET TO INFORM . . ."

"Any reply?" she heard the boy ask.

She shook her head. No reply from the Garden of Eden. She fumbled her way back into the house. She felt as if one-half of her being had been excised. All before her was the abyss.

At that moment, and for a long time thereafter, she was certain that it would be preferable not to live any more.

– 2 –

SPRING, AGAIN, three years later.

A parade was taking place along King Street and Rachel Vanderlinden, free of baby Thomas for the day, sat in the bleachers, along with those other Camberloo women who'd lost family members in the War. They applauded as each of the bands paused before them, playing martial music. After the bands came the veterans themselves, soldiers and sailors. They marched proudly, their hobnailed boots ringing on the pavement. Then came the maimed, who had to be pushed along in wheelchairs. After them came those who could barely walk, wheezing from the mustard gas; others, blinded, their faces still bandaged, leaned on the arms of their comrades; the last group tottered slowly by, some with canes and crutches, others limping badly.

One of these, a thin soldier with a curiously plumpish face, paused a moment to stare at Rachel. Then he hobbled along with the others past the bleachers and along the street.

As the parade went on by, an older woman in a black head-scarf sitting beside Rachel shook her head sadly. "I lost my husband and both my boys," she said. "Maybe they're better off dead. They say, '*Soldiers go straight to Heaven, for they've been in Hell already.*'"

In spite of all her resolutions, Rachel Vanderlinden was deeply touched and couldn't help crying.

The woman put an arm round her. "There, now," she said. "You just go ahead and cry. You'll feel the good of it."

AFTER THE PARADE, Rachel Vanderlinden made her way through the crowds on King Street. She was on her way to see a friend, Jeremiah Webber, a doctor at Camberloo General, where she sometimes volunteered.

They'd arranged to meet at the York Inn, a sprawling build-ing with several bars and a little cabaret theatre upstairs. Rachel went into the lobby. There, behind a table, she saw a man selling carvings. He wore a black hat and black clothes and had a wispy grey beard. Rachel went over to have a look at his carv-ings. They seemed quite traditional: farm scenes, mainly dray horses pulling covered wagons. The man carved while he sat there, wearing a jeweller's eyepiece in his right eye for close work on the bodies of the horses and the sides of wagons. His left eye was all bloodshot.

Rachel picked up one of the pieces to look at the miraculously fine and minuscule work. She held it up close. Then put it down again quickly. For the horses and wagons were ornamented with an endless, interlinked chain of tiny naked men and women performing sexual activities on each other.

"The show begins soon," the carver said, looking up at her. His bloodshot eye was glazed and anguished.

Rachel went across the lobby and climbed the stairs.

The theatre, like every other part of the York, smelled of stale beer, and the ceiling light was like a feeble sun behind a haze of cigarette smoke. The seats, a hundred or so of them, were taken mainly by uniformed veterans accompanied by their wives and girlfriends. Rachel looked around but could see no sign of Jeremiah Webber. She was considering leaving and waiting for him outside when the lights lowered and the crowd quieted down, so she stayed and watched.

The curtain opened on a small stage, bare except for an upright glass cylinder, about six feet tall and a foot in diameter. A wooden stepladder stood beside it.

From the wings of the stage, two performers came on. One was a woman in a long blue robe. Her face was painted so heavily it was hard to know her age or what her real face looked like. Her blond hair was tied up in a bun. Her assistant was a man with a black beard who wore a turban and a white cape.

The assistant walked all round the glass tube and dramatically tapped it with his knuckles to show how solid it was. His face was distorted as he stood behind it and encircled it with his arms. Then he invited one of the audience to come up and check. A young soldier climbed onto the stage to the applause of his friends. He too tapped the tube with his knuckles and was satisfied it was made of some kind of thick glass.

Now the performance was ready to begin.

The woman let her blue robe fall to the floor, silencing everyone for a moment. She was wearing only a pink bodysuit that was so tight-fitting Rachel at first thought she was naked. Some of the men in the audience whistled but were hushed by others. On stage, the assistant gestured to the woman to approach the tube. He took a firm grip on the wooden stepladder, steadying it while she slowly climbed it till she was level with the top of the tube. She placed her hands on either side of the rim and inserted one leg into the tube, then the other.

Rachel, watching intently, suspected what was about to happen but thought it must be quite impossible.

Everything went very quickly. The woman, still holding onto the rim, allowed herself to slide slowly down into the tube. Even by the time she'd reached her thighs, it was hard to tell she had two separate legs. The flesh seemed to have melted together, like candle wax.

The theatre was completely silent.

Now, the upper part of the woman's thighs and buttocks were sliding down. Then, after a brief pause, all of her upper body followed till she reached the shoulders and was propped up only by her elbows on the rim.

Because of the paint on her face, she seemed quite impassive.

All at once, she lifted her arms in the air above her head and began, spontaneously, to slide farther down, till her head, bracketed by her arms, was inside the tube. She slid down the last inches, till her feet touched bottom and only her hands protruded, her fingers waving like the tentacles of some flesh-coloured sea creature.

The entire tube was now a column of pink marble.

Along with the rest of the audience, Rachel applauded. But even while they were applauding, they could see the colour of the woman's arms and legs slowly changing from pink to purple.

Her assistant now grasped the sides of the tube like a roll of carpet and tilted it, leaning it on his shoulder. The shapeless flesh slowly began oozing out of the bottom, filling out the bodysuit as it emerged, till the woman's entire length lay on the stage floor.

The applause continued and became louder as the assistant extended his hand to the woman and helped her to her feet. He held out the blue robe for her and she put it on. The two of them bowed to the audience.

As the applause died down, one of the veterans, who'd been drinking too much, wanted to be involved. "It's just a trick! How do you do it?" he shouted.

A woman near the back of the theatre had an answer. "How do you think you came out of your mother, eh?" she shouted at him.

Another woman joined in. "That's right! The men just stand watching!" she shouted.

Everyone laughed at that and applauded even more loudly as the performers left the stage.

Rachel, at the back of the theatre, was astonished. She wondered how any woman could be so malleable and still be able to breathe.

– 3 –

RACHEL VANDERLINDEN FELT SHE'D WAITED long enough for Webber, who must have been delayed at the hospital. She left the theatre and was going down the stairs when she almost bumped into a soldier carrying a tankard of beer. She stepped aside but he didn't pass her by.

"Mrs. Vanderlinden?" he said, taking off his cap.

"Yes," she said. He was vaguely familiar. He had a plump, shiny face—perhaps a benevolent face—but his green eyes were shrewd. He seemed to be about thirty, though the war had aged these men so much it was hard to tell.

"I saw you at the parade today," he said. "You were pointed out to me."

Ah! She remembered now. This was the soldier who'd stared at her as the parade went past the bleachers.

"Could I talk to you for a few minutes?" he said.

She was apprehensive. But what possible harm could there be in talking to a hero? "Of course," she said.

So the soldier, carrying his half-empty tankard, led her into a quiet part of the inn. He limped noticeably and she saw that his left boot was wrinkled and worn, his right highly polished and unwrinkled. He was breathing heavily as he sat down at a corner table. He sipped at his beer, licked the foam from his lips. Then he stuck out his hand across the table and shook hers. He had a loose, damp grip. "I was in the Highlanders—with Rowland," he said.

She was surprised; she should have been delighted. But instead she was full of dread. What should she expect from this man with his plump face and shrewd eyes? Was he nice or nasty?

He sipped his beer once more, then began talking about his time at the Front, and in particular about three days of September rain. Each of those days, he said, the Highlanders had attempted to advance, in vain, suffered heavy casualties and had stumbled back to their own trenches. They were sprawled everywhere, exhausted from lack of sleep, their uniforms filthy with grey muck. A faint miasma of mustard gas hung in the air, so they had to be ready to pull on their gas masks at any time. Flies as big as barrage-balloons, heavy with blood, buzzed around them. Most of the men were numb, some were shell-shocked. The injured lay around, staring at their awful wounds, their innards exposed to the daylight. Some cowered in corners, whimpering or muttering to themselves; some swatted wildly even when the flies were not near them, while others ignored the real flies that buzzed at their eyes. All of the soldiers were by now used to the stink of the corpses lying around them. Maggots had almost come to seem a development of human life rather than a corruption.

Rachel pictured these horrors.

Then the plump-faced soldier with the shrewd eyes began to talk about a certain man—he looked at her knowingly as he said that—who volunteered to carry a message across a dangerous stretch of no-man's-land to some stranded gunners. He told how the volunteer climbed the ladder in the dusk. How he paused for a moment at the top of the trench to peer ahead, then slithered over the edge and began to crawl forward. How he reached the rolls of barbed wire and got up into a low crouch and began to run. How he hurdled the barbed wire and the scattering of corpses and skirted round the deep shell craters. How he was only fifty yards from the gunners in their dug-out when a flare exploded in the sky overhead and a sniper's shot rang out. How he stumbled and fell. How he lay still for a moment, then began crawling forward. How he had to rise to his feet to cross the final rolls of barbed wire. How a machine gun began to chatter. How he slumped over the barbed wire, his body jerked this way and that as though being worried by a large, invisible dog, till the chattering stopped.

— 4 —

IN THE YORK INN, Rachel Vanderlinden knew what was coming.

"The man who died," said the plump-faced soldier, "was Rowland."

She couldn't think of anything to say.

"We weren't able to get to the body for weeks," he said. "It just lay there among all the others and rotted." The shrewd eyes narrowed and he said: *He died for you.*

That jolted words out of her. "What?" she said. "I don't understand."

"He got into a fight with a man called McGraw. Floyd McGraw. He's the man responsible for Rowland's death. Rowland always treated him like a friend and told him things you only tell a friend." He said this slowly and emphatically.

"What do you mean?" she said.

"You know what I mean," the plump-faced soldier said. "Including the fact that Rowland wasn't his real name." He watched her over the rim of his tankard as he took another drink. "So then, that day, after the advance failed, the two of them got into an argument. They were exhausted and hungry and their minds weren't working properly. McGraw started needling him."

She sat silent, waiting for the blow.

"McGraw said a woman who'd done what you'd done was a whore," he said.

She tried to disguise from those astute eyes how shocked she was at that word.

"He called you a whore," the soldier said again. "That's what they were fighting about. And the officer came along and separated them. He said he wouldn't charge them if one of them would take the message out to the engineers in no-man's-land. McGraw was afraid, but Rowland volunteered."

Rachel Vanderlinden sat stunned, stricken with guilt. She'd survived the past three years by convincing herself that at least he had died for a glorious cause. And now, this.

"I didn't tell you this to make you feel bad," the plump-faced soldier said. "Isn't it a thousand times better for a man to die for the woman he loves than for a cause nobody even understands?" His eyes were burning. "I came to tell you this because I think he might have wanted you to know. He died in a little private war over you, he loved you so much."

She refused to accept that. "He would be alive, but for me," she said, tears welling in her eyes.

The soldier shook his head. "Maybe and maybe not," he said. "Nearly everybody in that trench was killed anyway. And those who survived are worse than dead." He swung his legs out from the table and tapped his right leg, the one with the shiny boot. "Do you know how I got this?" he said bitterly. "They'd order us out into no-man's land at night to go through the pockets of the enemy dead and look for useful information. All I ever found were their letters from home and family photographs. One night I stepped on a mine." Again he tapped the leg with the shiny shoe. "When I got home, my girl didn't want anything to do with me. She loves dancing."

Rachel Vanderlinden was silent.

The soldier now looked at her fiercely. "I hope you've been faithful," he said. "Have you been faithful?"

That word, like a hangman's noose, choked her. "Yes, I have," she managed to say. She believed it was as much for his sake as her own.

He looked at her so sternly she couldn't tell whether he believed her or not.

Just then, a voice called from the doorway of the bar.

"Rachel!"

It was Jeremiah Webber. He signalled to her that he'd be with her in a second.

The plump-faced soldier looked at her with sudden understanding, got to his feet and stumbled away without another word.

Webber ordered beer at the bar then came and sat down. He saw she was upset and thought it was because of his lateness. He promised to keep her amused for the remainder of the day. She told him she suddenly didn't feel well and asked him to take her home.

— 5 —

THAT FALL, ON AN OVERCAST MORNING, Rachel Vanderlinden had gone to City Hall to pay a bill. She was there for a half hour. As she was leaving through the main entrance, she saw a cluster of people, including a policeman, on the sidewalk outside looking up at the clock tower where a flagpole jutted out. She looked up too. A man was hanging from the pole by his arms, looking down. He must have climbed the stairs inside and squirmed out through one of the apertures.

Rachel couldn't bear to watch and hurried away. But she'd only gone twenty yards along the sidewalk when, out of the corner of her eye, she saw the man let go. He plummeted down and struck an ornamental iron fence-post. Even though its tip was quite blunt, the force of his fall caused it to impale him through his chest.

In spite of herself, Rachel stopped to look. The policeman, with the help of two of the men watching, tried to detach the body. The jumper had been killed instantly and there was a lot of blood everywhere, so the men weren't careful. One of his legs seemed to have been broken and flopped around loosely as they lifted him off the post. They laid him on his back on the sidewalk and the policeman tried to straighten the leg out. The entire limb came away in his hand—a wooden contraption with leather straps. Rachel moved a little nearer. Though the head of the dead man was at a strange angle and there was blood from his mouth and nose, she could see it was the soldier who'd told her about the death of the man she loved.

"Does anyone know him?" the policeman said.

"I've seen him around," said one of the men who'd helped.

"Do you know his name?"

"It was Floyd McGraw," the man said. "He was crippled in the War. He's had a rough time since he came back."

Rachel walked away quickly. Floyd McGraw. She'd suspected that was who he was ever since he'd spoken to her in the York. She'd thought of trying to find him, telling him he wasn't to blame either. But she hadn't, and now he'd died, certain there could be no forgiveness. Yet she wasn't excessively sorry for him. In that aspect of her character, she realized, she was perhaps the true daughter of her father, Judge Dafoe.

– 6 –

THE JUDGE'S ANCESTORS WERE DUTCH FARMERS who had domesticated the stubborn northern wilderness. He himself had been too frail for farm work, so he'd been encouraged to stay on at school. He eventually became a lawyer and set up a very successful practice in Queensville, with its wealthy grain merchants and elegant houses along the Lake shore—one of which he lived in. At the age of forty-five, in spite of his chronic bad health and against his doctor's advice, he accepted an appointment to the Provincial Bench. He soon became infamous as the sternest of judges—"Judge Rope" was his nick-name. The long hours he put in took so much out of him, he was warned by his doctor of the risks of a heart attack. Defence lawyers used to say that if Dafoe's heart were to be attacked by anything, it would most likely be by the rat that lived inside it. The Judge was aware of this witticism and enjoyed it.

To the surprise of his colleagues, he decided to marry, at the age of fifty. He chose for his wife Anke Oltmans, the available daughter of an immigrant Dutch merchant. She was a short, robust woman who reminded him of one of those figures in a Rubens painting. She devoted her life to looking after his needs.

Their marriage seemed quite satisfactory to observers and was indeed so to the Judge himself. *A Dutch Wife,* he called her. "You can't go wrong with a Dutch Wife," he liked to say.

Their daughter, Rachel, was born in due course. But after three years, Anke—who seemed so robust—caught measles from the baby, faded rapidly and died.

Thereafter, Judge Dafoe became his daughter's slave. This slight man, whose face was like a skull with only the flimsiest covering of flesh (the first sight of him used to terrify prison-ers in the dock), was the most loving of fathers. It was as if the entire quotient of love he was capable of was heaped together in a single load and bestowed on his daughter. The sight of her would bring a smile—a death's head smile—to his face. And the more indulgent he became towards her, the more aloof and unsociable he became to the rest of the world. "If you get along too well with people," he would tell Rachel as she grew older, "it's a sign of weakness."

ONE NIGHT, WHEN SHE WAS SEVENTEEN and had just completed her formal schooling, the doorbell of the Judge's house rang. He was in his study, so Rachel answered the door.

Under the porch light she saw a young man of middle height with a thin face and hair that was quite long, but tidy. His face was slightly pock-marked, like one of those modern paintings she'd seen in the Art Gallery. Altogether, she thought he looked the way an artist was supposed to look. He even carried a pad of paper. Some pencils stuck out of the top pocket of his coat.

"My name's Rowland Vanderlinden," he said. "The Judge is expecting me." He was a quick, nervous speaker.

"Come in," she said. "I'm his daughter, Rachel."

He seemed surprised to hear that, as she knew many others were surprised that Judge Rope could possibly be anyone's father. She took him up to the study and left him with the Judge. An hour later, she was reading in bed when she heard her father let the visitor out.

AT BREAKFAST THE NEXT MORNING, she asked him about the previous night's visitor.

"Vanderlinden?" her father said. "He's an anthropologist. Writes down every word you say. But at least he was on time for his appointment, and that's unusual." The Judge was renowned for his punctuality. He had a clock even in the bathroom.

"An anthropologist?" She wasn't sure what that was.

"It's one of those newfangled so-called sciences," he said. "They seem to come up with another one each year. He works at the Museum in Toronto and teaches a course at the University."

"Why did you want to see him?"

The Judge shook his head. "I had no desire whatever to see him," he said. "But the Law Society's made it mandatory that we consult with these so-called experts before sentencing."

"Ah," she said. She was aware that in a few days her father would be passing sentence on a serial murderer, Joshua Simmonds, the so-called "Calendar Killer." The case had been made notorious in every newspaper across the country. Rachel, like most of the young women in the province, had followed it with fascination mixed with relief.

– 7 –

THERE WERE TWO REMARKABLE THINGS about Simmonds, the murderer of a number of women throughout Eastern Ontario. The first was that he used a very old-fashioned method—the garotte. The second was that he performed his murders on the first day of each month, selecting only women unfortunate enough to have names associated with the month in question.

Hence the nickname the Calendar Killer.

The initial murder of the sequence, for example, took place in a rooming house in Queensville on the first of April. The victim's name was *April* Smithers, a youthful prostitute. She was discovered on top of her bed with a leather garotte still round her neck. The page of a wall calendar with the date circled in red ink lay beside her. She was fully clothed and had not been otherwise molested.

The Queensville police only began to understand that this was the beginning of a series on the morning of the first of

May. That was when a young woman who worked at her father's farm, two miles out of town, was found murdered in the cowshed. A garotte was still in place, a red-circled calendar page was pinned to her blouse. Again there seemed to be no overt sexual element to the crime.

Such was the pattern of the killings. They went on for several months, the next victims being *June* Lavigne, *Julia* Tompkins and *Augusta* Strathy.

But the end was near.

In late August, James Bromley, a provincial highways inspector and sharp-eyed amateur naturalist, returned from a three-month visit to Australia, where he'd been studying road construction in extreme climatic conditions. While he was abroad, he'd heard nothing about the serial murders in his homeland. Now, he recollected something he'd observed just before leaving for Australia—which happened to be the very week before the killing of Elspeth May. He'd been inspecting surface wear and tear on a rural road near the May farm when he'd spotted an unlikely bird in a bush nearby. He was almost sure it was a blue-spangled oceanic grebe, thousands of miles from its natural aquatic habitat.

The bird flew into some trees and he couldn't resist following it, keeping as quiet as possible so as not to disturb it. He saw it perch on a branch and found himself a hiding place from which to watch it. He had barely settled down when, to his surprise, he saw that another man had been lurking in a nearby clump of trees. This man, unaware of Bromley's presence, was now stealthily heading out towards the road. Bromley himself stayed on for another ten minutes, fascinated by the grebe.

Now, all these months later, having returned from Australia and heard about the serial killings, Bromley thought it might be wise to contact the police, for he had recognized the face of the man he'd seen that morning near the May farm.

A dozen officers immediately went to the Station Hotel in downtown Queensville. They burst open the door to the first-floor room of Joshua Simmonds, a permanent hotel resident. He was a forty-year-old scrivener in the Public Records Bureau—where Bromley had often seen him in the course of reporting to the Department of Roads. In a cupboard in Simmonds's hotel room were several home-made leather garottes and a familiar wall calendar with missing pages.

He was arrested and charged with the murders.

NOW THAT THIS LOATHSOME CREATURE had been caught, the police were anxious to interrogate him. Simmonds seemed just as anxious to confess. He said he'd been planning the murders for a long time. He found the addresses of potential victims in the Public Records Bureau, concentrating on those who lived near his home base. He'd scout them out and even get to know some of them personally in advance of the murders.

On completing the twelve-month cycle, he'd intended to progress to some other interesting patterns, such as days of the week (he'd already found women named Tuesday and Wednesday); trees (Acacia, Olive, Laurel); colours (Amber, Blanche); flowers (Violet, Rose, Anthia, Tulip); and celestial objects (Celia, Stella). As part of his preliminary research, he'd found a "Name Your Baby" book quite invaluable.

He regretted, he said, the fact that he'd killed only women. But as his interrogators could see, he himself was quite a small man, so men would have been too difficult. He had considered children as an option; but he happened to be very fond of children and didn't think he would have the stomach for it.

As for his use of the garotte, he believed it was much more intimate than a weapon such as a knife or a gun. The last thing he wanted was for his victims to feel their deaths were impersonal.

But *why* had he killed the women at all? That was what the police investigators, preoccupied with motive, wanted to know. What was it that drove Simmonds to kill anyone in the first place?

The murderer seemed genuinely surprised at the question. The killings were only meant to be a game, he said, an entertainment to cause a little bit of a distraction for the general public. Nothing grabbed people's attention like a mysterious murder or two. Nothing would convince him that they hadn't enjoyed the whole thing and weren't, in fact, grateful to him for putting on a good show.

The police had to be satisfied with that. When Simmonds eventually went on trial, his lawyer tried to persuade him to plead not guilty on the grounds of insanity. Simmonds was offended at the very idea. He himself took the stand and appealed to the jury's sense of fun. That same day, after less than ten minutes' deliberation, they found him guilty of multiple murders in the first degree.

– 8 –

"WHAT DID YOUR VISITOR HAVE TO SAY about Simmonds?" Rachel asked her father. She sipped her coffee, wanting to hear more about Rowland Vanderlinden, without seeming too curious.

The Judge sighed. "Nothing that should have surprised me," he said. "These intellectuals always seem to find criminals more valuable than ordinary citizens. He went on about what he calls 'a ritualistic aspect' to the murders. He thinks they might come from some deep-rooted impulse Simmonds himself isn't aware of. He said it would be worthwhile keeping such a creature alive—a lot might be learned from talking to him further."

"How odd," said Rachel.

Her father smiled. He was wearing a red-and-white-striped shirt with a red tie. Rachel thought he looked like a peacock with a skull for a head.

"I told him we could talk to Simmonds forever and it would be useless. How can you get rational answers out of a madman? He made a note of that. He made notes on everything."

"Did he himself have an answer?" Rachel said.

"If you can call it an answer," said the Judge. "He said he was opposed to capital punishment, but that if society insists on executing Simmonds, it certainly shouldn't be by hanging."

"Really?" said Rachel.

"Not by hanging, or strangulations or poisonings, or any kind of bloodless method." Her father smiled at the memory. "He said all the great civilizations of the past believed that if a man is to be executed, his blood must flow, or else his spirit won't escape. Then all kinds of social problems would be the result." He shook his head, smiling at her. "Can you imagine hearing such superstitious nonsense from an educated man? Of course, Vanderlinden denies he really believes it literally— just that we ought not to disregard long-held customs too lightly." The Judge put his coffee cup down with a clatter. "I told him this kind of thing might be all very fine down in the jungle somewhere. But not in a modern society. We believe in morality and the protection of our citizens. Hanging's too good for the likes of Simmonds."

Rachel nodded, but she was thinking of how interesting Rowland Vanderlinden looked. And what a brave man he must be to say such things to her father.

ON THE MORNING OF THE SENTENCING, she made up her mind to go to the courthouse in the hope of seeing Rowland. The court was packed so she had trouble finding a seat at the back. She looked around and was disappointed to see no sign of her father's visitor.

A bell rang and a policeman called for silence. Simmonds was brought into the dock by two guards. He was wearing a blue prison uniform, a small, apologetic-looking man with wide eyes and thin hair slicked back.

The clerk called on everyone to rise. Now her father, all in black, came solemnly into the courtroom. He went to the bench, carefully adjusted his robes, sat down and waited for complete silence. He watched the clock till it was exactly on the hour. Then, in the sonorous voice Rachel sometimes heard him practise in his study, he told the prisoner to rise.

Simmonds did so, with the two guards standing on either side, towering over him.

The Judge now picked up a cloth that lay on the bench before him: the black cap. He unfolded it slowly and carefully placed it on his head. He cleared his throat and solemnly pronounced the awful words that reverberated through the crowded courtroom: "By the power . . . hereby sentence you . . . on an appointed day . . . to be taken from this place to a place of execution . . . hanged by the neck until you are dead. May God have mercy on your soul."

Simmonds didn't seem to like the sound of that, for he staggered and leaned on the dock. When he went back to the cells, he had to be helped by the two guards.

THAT NIGHT AT DINNER, the Judge was in a very good humour and sipped the glass of red wine he allowed himself on such occasions.

Rachel, who'd never been to a death-sentencing before, asked him about it. "Isn't it hard, sending men who are younger than you are to a premature death?" she said.

"Not at all," he said. "We all have to die. In fact, these men are luckier than the rest of us—they at least know the exact moment they'll be leaving." He looked very serious.

"Well," Rachel said, "that doesn't sound very lucky to me."

He put his glass down on the table and began to laugh wholeheartedly—a rare phenomenon. He never allowed anyone else to know that he was capable of laughter.

"Simmonds looked so harmless," she said

The Judge smiled at her affectionately. "That's a good lesson for you to learn," he said. "You can't tell a man from a monster just on the basis of looks."

Watching him, Rachel couldn't help wondering how he would look to her if he were not her father but her judge. She imagined him sitting on the bench pronouncing sentence on her. Then those same glittering eyes and thin-lipped smile might make him the most frightening of men. She wondered, too, what Rowland Vanderlinden thought of him: she feared he might have disliked her father and assumed that she would be too much his daughter.

– 9 –

HER FIRST REAL MEETING WITH ROWLAND didn't occur until the following summer. She'd come to Toronto to spend a morning shopping and decided to visit the Museum on the off chance of seeing him. It began raining quite heavily as she went along University Avenue, so she ran the last hundred yards. Inside the lobby of the Museum, she had barely caught her breath when she saw him coming out of an office and heading towards the door, with an umbrella in hand and a notebook protruding from his coat pocket. She looked around her in a general way, as though wondering where to go, making sure she remained in his path. He almost bumped into her, apologized, then looked at her closely. "The Judge's daughter!" he said. "Aren't you Judge Dafoe's daughter?"

She put on a puzzled look.

"I'm Rowland Vanderlinden," he said. "You let me into your house at the time of the Simmonds trial, remember? In

Queensville? I had to talk to the Judge." She remembered that nervous energy in the way he talked and she liked it.

"Oh, of course," she said.

"What are you doing here?" he said.

"I just came in out of the rain," she said.

He laughed. "If it weren't for rain," he said, "museums would have to close down."

She laughed too.

"I was just about to go for lunch," he said. "I usually go by myself and read while I eat. I don't suppose you'd like to join me?"

"Yes," she said, "I would like it."

"Great!" he said. "Let's get out of here."

They went out the door and he unfolded his umbrella. He extended his elbow for her and they went down the stairs in the rain. They walked only a short distance to a little restaurant where they found a table for two. It was a shabby kind of place, one she herself would never have gone into, full of strange food smells. The brown-skinned waiter with shiny black hair knew Rowland and recommended the curry special for lunch.

As they sat there, Rowland Vanderlinden talked, gesticulating with his hands, flicking his long hair back. Those little pock marks gave his face character, Rachel thought. And he had such nice blue eyes, full of life and curiosity.

When the curry came, Rachel ate what she could of it, trying not to show she didn't like it. But he seemed not to notice and talked about this and that, including why he hadn't appeared for the sentencing of Simmonds. "I had to come back here for a meeting of the Board," he said. "I was sorry I couldn't make it. I'd hoped I might see you there."

She was thrilled to hear that, but for tactical reasons she thought she'd better lie. "I didn't go either," she said.

"Then I'm glad I didn't," he said with a smile. "My interest in Simmonds was purely academic, you know. I have a theory that such crimes are often sublimations of ancient, ritualistic impulses."

She just smiled, though she wasn't sure what "sublimations" meant.

"I thought I might find some pretext for visiting Queensville again," he said, "but not long after the trial, I had a chance to go back to Africa for six months. So I took it."

"What did you do there?" she asked. She'd never met anyone who'd led such an exotic life.

"I was studying the customs of the tribes along the Ogowe River," he said.

"That sounds fascinating," she said.

He looked pleased that she was fascinated. "One of the oddest things about people living in the jungle," he said, "is how differently they perceive the world. Because the forests are so thick, they have no real appreciation of distance, especially if they're not near a river. A few dozen yards is about as far as many of them ever see in their entire lifetimes. They just can't imagine greater distances than that." He smiled. "I sometimes think there's a psychological equivalent of that phenomenon in Canada. I mean, some people here are so narrow-minded."

Rachel was flattered by the implication that she wasn't.

THE WAITER HAD TAKEN AWAY the curry plates and brought them a dark sludge for coffee.

"You must be very fond of travelling," she said.

"I am," he said. "I'm not one of those men who can sit around all their lives in the same place, doing the same thing day after day, and then, when they're dying, they say: 'Well that was my fate!'" He shook his head. "That's not for me. I want my life to be an adventure, even though it may not always be fun."

Rachel was sure she agreed with that.

He sipped his coffee and told her he was in the process of writing a scholarly article on his African trip. "You've no idea how hard that is," he said. "I mean, to take incredibly interesting things and put them into language dull enough for an academic journal!"

She knew she was supposed to laugh at that and she did.

"What exactly are you writing about?" she said.

"Fetishism," he said.

She confessed she didn't know what that was.

"Most people don't," he said. "A fetish is some object— usually inanimate, but not aways—that a spirit lives in." He smiled. "In other words, it's the kind of thing your father would consider to be absolute nonsense."

They both laughed.

"Please tell me about the article you're writing," she said.

"Only if we have another coffee," he said. She had a feeling he was enjoying her company and the idea thrilled her.

When the coffee had been poured, he began to talk, and she listened carefully. She wanted to be intelligent for him.

– 10 –

"NEAR THE END OF MY LAST MONTH in Africa," said
Rowland Vanderlinden, "I went to Ndara, the main village of
the Boma tribe. You won't know about them, but one of the
Boma customs had been reported widely amongst anthropologists: if a young Boma woman was infertile, her husband was
expected to start sleeping with her mother. Then, if the mother
produced a child, it was given to the daughter to rear as though
it were her own. As a result, family relations amongst the Boma
could be immensely complex.

"But I was more interested in another aspect of Boma life:
I'd heard the tribe's fetishistic practices were most unusual, so
I thought I'd see for myself.

"I'd never been to Ndara and didn't realize the trip would be
so difficult. I had to go by the Ogowe River, for the jungle was
thick and there was no possibility of going overland. I travelled
in a dug-out canoe with three coastal tribesmen. Two of them
rowed. The third was an old man who'd been to Ndara before.
His name was Efua.

"Not that going by river was all that safe either. The tribes
along the Ogowe weren't friendly and were liable to attack
strangers. Also, it was the rainy season, so the river was swollen
and dangerous with rapids and whirlpools.

"Anthropologists discover things in the oddest ways. We'd
only been on the river a few hours when I learned one lesson
I'll never forget.

"I was sitting at the stern of the boat and by noon I was
starting to get hungry. Efua was dozing in the bow and the

paddlers didn't seem to have any intention of stopping for lunch. So I reached into the food sack and took out a banana. I peeled it and was just about to take a bite when one of the paddlers swung his oar and knocked the banana out of my hand. The dug-out almost toppled over. Efua wakened up and was horrified at me.

"I'd no idea what I'd done wrong. Efua and the paddlers talked for a while, and when they'd finished, he looked at me and shook his head in disgust. He said I was so ignorant I was a menace. He'd just convinced the two paddlers not to maroon me ashore and let me take my chances with the jungle and the hostile tribes.

"I kept asking what I'd done. He said if it hadn't been for the quick action of the paddler I'd have taken a bite out of that banana. Didn't people with skins the colour of dung-snails (that was what they called white people) have any sense at all? Didn't I know that eating any kind of food while in a boat on water was absolutely taboo? Even the youngest children knew how stupid that was.

"Of course, I asked him why there was such a taboo. He told me to shut up with my 'why's. The reason for taboos was not a subject for discussion. Taboos were taboos and that was that. Even to wonder about them was another taboo.

"Anyway, shortly after that we went ashore and ate. Then we went back on the river and paddled for several more miles up a tributary. In the late afternoon we reached Ndara.

"It really was big—a village of about five thousand people. We had to pay our respects right away to the Boma Chief. His compound was in the middle of the village near a huge fig tree.

Efua warned me now to walk carefully as we passed it. It was, apparently, the major fetish of the Boma. Every leaf, every little twig that fell off was taken home and treasured by the tribe.

"I met the Chief and gave him a Swiss Army knife, which he was very pleased with. He said I could stay as long as I liked.

"Now, as things turned out, I was only able to stay a few days. But even in that brief time, I saw a curious example of just how important fetishes were to the Boma.

"What happened was this. On our second night, I went with Efua to watch a purification ceremony in the clearing at the back of the Chief's compound. A big, muscular man was tied to a stake in the middle of the square and a Shaman was chanting and sprinkling some kind of powder on him. The ropes looked very flimsy but the captive made no attempt to break them.

"Just after we arrived, the Chief and all the elders of the tribe came out of the main compound. The Chief himself was carrying an ornate club with a big knob on the end of it. I didn't like the look of that.

"Without a word, he went up to the man at the stake and smashed the club onto his head, breaking his skull open. Then each of the elders took turns with the club, until the man's head was nothing but a bloody stump.

"After that, some of the younger tribesmen untied the body. They carried it out of the village and down to the river and threw it in. Within a few minutes, the crocodiles were at it, ripping it to pieces.

"Efua told me that what we had just witnessed was the killing of a man who had desecrated the fetish. Apparently, he'd been one of the most successful hunters among the Boma, but he'd had a run of bad luck in the past few months. In his compound, he kept a branch of the big fig tree in a leather bag tied to the beam of his hut, and he'd sacrificed to it over and over again—chickens, fruit, the very best betel nuts—with no result.

"Now it wasn't that he expected the gods always to act on his behalf. He knew very well how arbitrary they could be. But he expected at least some consideration for his devotion to the fetish.

"Instead, things just got worse and worse. Not only was his hunting unsuccessful, but three of his children died of some mysterious kind of poisoning. Then, their mother, his favourite wife, was so distraught she drowned herself in the river.

"It seems he was able to put up with everything else, but not that.

"He went directly to his hut and cut down his fetish from the central beam where it had pride of place and brought it to the very square we'd just been in. A lot of the Boma were there, watching him. He took the fetish out of its leather bag and spat on it. Then he lit a fire and threw both the bag and the fetish on it. He waited till they were nothing but ashes.

"After that, the tribal council knew they had to get rid of him: they couldn't risk the fetish turning against the whole tribe. The Shaman demanded that the offender be turned loose in the jungle after dark to be tormented to death by the night-demons. But the Chief was more humane and opted for the more traditional method of clubbing him to death. He argued the man deserved that consideration because he'd done his awful act publicly, for them all to see. If he'd done it privately, they might never have known and the tribe would have been doomed.

"So it was that punishment we'd witnessed. I was looking forward to finding out more about the fetish, but the next day, I came down with a little bout of malaria. I'd have sweated it out and stayed a few more days to do some research. But Efua told me one of the canoemen, after too much palm beer, had let it slip that I'd attempted to eat a banana on the boat. The Boma Shaman deduced that my fever was some kind of punishment by the river spirits and that the entire tribe might suffer for allowing me to stay in their village. He wanted all five of us to have our heads crushed—quite amicably of course—to placate the river spirits. It was time for us to leave, so even though I was quite feverish, we did."

– 11 –

ROWLAND VANDERLINDEN SIPPED WATER from his glass.

Rachel watched him, fascinated. She'd never met anyone who'd been through such things. Here most of us were, she was thinking, preoccupied with nothing but pedestrian ideas—while men like Rowland Vanderlinden were unravelling the mysteries of the universe. She was deeply flattered that he should confide in someone as unsophisticated as she was. She hoped more and more it might be his way of wooing her.

"Of course, the fetish matter was interesting," said Rowland. "But what impressed me most was that it was because of his favourite wife's suicide that he destroyed it. He obviously loved her so much, nothing else mattered to him. Isn't it astounding what a man will do for the woman he loves?"

"Yes, it really is," Rachel said. She was thinking, though she barely knew him, that it would be wonderful to have someone like Rowland die for love of her. But she put that idea out of her head. "I'm so glad you got away. I mean, I don't like the idea of fetishes. They sound awful and primitive."

"Do you mind if I call you Rachel?" he said, smiling.

"Of course not," she said.

"It's such a pleasure to see you again," he said. "I'm so glad you agreed to come for lunch. I've thought about you often since that night in Queensville. I'm sure your father said something unflattering about me. He has quite a reputation for not liking experts."

"Well, he didn't say he didn't like you," she said.

He laughed at that. "What exactly did he say?"

"Oh, that he doesn't think intellectuals really understand what the law's for," she said.

"I'm not surprised to hear that," Rowland Vanderlinden said. He frowned and tried to sound like her father: "'You intellectuals can't see the difference between right and wrong. It's always shades of grey. You'd never find anyone guilty of anything.'" Rowland laughed. "He's from the old school, all right."

Rachel laughed too, pleased that he didn't seem to mind her father too much.

While they waited for more coffee, he told her a little about his own family. Like the Judge, his ancestors had come from Holland long ago—to escape religious persecution. They'd settled in the north country and farmed the land. Rowland's father had become a schoolteacher and made sure his son received a good education.

"Isn't it odd we both have famous names?" Rowland said. "I mean, Dafoe's almost like Daniel *Defoe*—you know, the man who wrote *Robinson Crusoe*."

"Yes," Rachel said. "But I've never heard of anyone called Vanderlinden."

"Not many people know the name," said Rowland. "You remember John Locke? He called himself Vanderlinden when he was an exile in Holland. He may actually have borrowed the name from my ancestors."

Rachel admitted she'd no idea who John Locke was, either.

"The philosopher," Rowland said. "You know: the *Essay Concerning Human Understanding* and all that stuff about the random association of ideas?" He saw she knew nothing about it and smiled. His fingers touched her fingers on the table to reassure her. "Oh, don't worry, Rachel. It's not important. The important things in life aren't found in philosophy books."

She was so thrilled at his touch she could hardly breathe.

"My mother had Dutch ancestors too," he said. His voice became so soft she was suddenly aware of the clatter of restaurant noises. "My father always told me that if I ever got married, I couldn't do better than to get myself *a Dutch Wife*."

Rachel was startled. "A Dutch Wife!" she said. "That's what my father always called my mother. He used to say, 'You can't go wrong with a Dutch Wife.'"

They both laughed and looked at each other with delight.

– 12 –

SIX MONTHS AFTER THAT CONVERSATION, Rachel Dafoe and Rowland Vanderlinden were married in a civil ceremony at the Queensville Registry Office. Her father hadn't been very keen, either on the speed with which she married "the first man she'd met"; or on her choice of such an unconventional groom (Rowland's engagement gift to her was a shrunken head from South America, which had pride of place on the Dafoe living-room mantelpiece till it somehow managed to fall into the fire when only the Judge was at home).

For his daughter's sake, he tried to get along with Rowland, though he feared such a marriage couldn't possibly endure. It was clear to him that Rowland was obsessed with his studies in remote parts of the world and showed no signs of giving them up for the domestic life. Indeed, he'd just been awarded a Lifetime Endowment from the National Association of Anthropologists.

From the Judge's standpoint, Rowland didn't seem to understand that stability was necessary for a marriage. "He doesn't have his heart in it," he remarked to one of his clerks.

But Judge Dafoe didn't have to tolerate his son-in-law for long. A year after the marriage, his own unreliable heart let him down for the last time. He died, as he would have wanted to, at the bench. It was in the Spring Sessions, and he'd just passed a life sentence on a woman who'd tried, unsuccessfully, to poison her husband and her three children. Suddenly he leaned back in his chair and stopped talking. His eyes were still open, so it took the court officials a while to realize he was dead; his head had always looked so much like a skull.

He was buried, as he'd requested, in Camberloo, his second residence, where he'd intended to retire.

Her father's death stunned Rachel. She'd lost someone quite irreplaceable—a human being who loved her no matter what she did. She was well aware already that the kind of love that existed in her marriage to Rowland Vanderlinden was of a much less durable sort.

"Easily built, easily destroyed," the Judge used to say ominously.

In the year following his death, it was apparent to her that her relationship with Rowland Vanderlinden was indeed beginning to crumble.

Rowland now spent most of each week at the Museum, writing papers on various anthropological matters, staying overnights in his apartment in the city. On weekends, when he was home with her in Queensville, he would write up his notes. After that, he was like a dog circling around its basket, sniffing here and there, not finding a satisfactory place to rest. He would talk to Rachel occasionally about his work, but he was impatient and always made her feel stupid. As though her own ideas were little fish that ought to be thrown back into the Lake till they grew up.

Even making love was only a temporary distraction for him; his mind seemed to be elsewhere.

When he was sent on a field trip to Egypt on behalf of the Museum, Rachel persuaded him to allow her to go with him— the first time she'd ever left Canada. Aside from the sea voyage and a few days in a hotel in Cairo, the rest of the experience turned out to be most unpleasant for her: living in a tent in the desert sands, with no privacy, yet unable to communicate with the hordes of Egyptian workers; on top of that, there were the stifling heat, biting flies and onslaughts of mosquitoes. She had nothing to do. Rowland, on the other hand, was in his element: passionate about stone slabs with incomprehensible writing and buried papyri; and obviously popular with the locals.

They'd been there only a month when she became violently ill, probably from the water. An Egyptian physician recommended Rowland take her home. Reluctantly, for his project was unfinished, he packed up and brought her back to Canada.

After a week in Queensville, she could see he was restless again. "But I'm sure he still loves me," she'd say to herself. "And I'm sure I still really love him." She willed herself to believe that, for she was afraid she might easily come to hate him.

BY THE SECOND ANNIVERSARY of her father's death, Rachel couldn't put up with the situation any longer. She imagined the Judge telling her what she already knew: "You've made a blunder." Had he been there, he'd have dealt with the problem on her behalf. But he wasn't, so she steeled herself to face it alone.

One Saturday night, she and Rowland were sitting at the back of the house. He was writing in his notebook, and she was watching the sun go down on the Lake.

She felt now was the time to speak. "You've changed," she said to Rowland, as though she were reciting the opening lines of some traditional play.

"What do you mean?" he said, putting down his notebook but giving her no help.

"You're no longer the man I married," she said, surprised at how spontaneously she used the well-worn phrase.

He looked at her in the failing light and gave an unexpected answer. "Ah, but I am," he said. "I am."

Her heart sank, for she knew he was right.

They were silent for a while.

"I can't go on like this," she said, sticking to her lines regardless. "I'm not the kind of Dutch Wife you needed."

He didn't seem shocked. "I have an idea," he said in the growing darkness. "The British Museum's just received a load of artifacts from a new dig. They'd like me to go over and help with the cataloguing. Maybe I should go. That would give us a chance to think about our situation."

"How long do you think you'd be gone?" she said.

"Four or five weeks, perhaps," he said. The horizon of the Lake had almost completely disappeared now. "We could settle things when I came back. One way or another."

TWO DAYS LATER, he was packed for England. Before going out the front door for the last time, he took her hand. "No matter what happens," he said, "remember this: if you ever need me, you only have to send for me." Then he picked up his bag and left.

FOR TWO MONTHS, she neither sent for him nor heard anything from him. Then a telegram came saying he'd be catching the train from Halifax and would be home the next day.

Thus it came about that she was sitting in the kitchen, waiting for him, her mind made up to settle things once and for all. She heard the ringing of the doorbell. She opened the door. A fair-haired man with a rugged face and pale blue eyes, a man who looked nothing like Rowland Vanderlinden, was standing there, saying: "I'm your husband."

And she let him in.

– 13 –

IN HIS BED IN CAMBERLOO HOSPITAL, Thomas Vanderlinden stopped talking. He reached over for the oxygen mask, put it to his face and breathed deeply. He closed his eyes and his head sank back in the pillows.

I was a bit worried, for he suddenly looked so tired. "Are you all right?" I said.

"I'll be fine," he said between breaths. "Don't go yet." Whatever his illness was, his battle with it had weakened him, and now he had to beat a tactical retreat.

In the silence that followed, I thought I heard voices in the corridor, but it was only the murmur of some piece of equipment in the nurses' station.

Thomas put down his mask. "So, that was the story my mother told me," he said. "It was all news to me." He glanced towards the bedside cabinet at her photograph as a young woman looking out with that self-sufficient expression. "She always liked her own way," he said. "I suppose I shouldn't have been surprised."

He closed his eyes again and took a few more breaths from the mask.

Of course, I was itching to ask some questions. Principally, *why* his mother had let in a complete stranger claiming to be her husband. And, even after they'd become lovers, why she wouldn't let the man tell her who he really was. But I could see Thomas was exhausted. "I should go," I said.

He put his thin hand on my arm.

"Will you be able to come and see me tomorrow?" he said.

"Of course I will," I said.

"Good," he said. "I've a lot more to tell you—if you're interested."

"Don't worry," I said. "I'm interested."

He nodded and lay back with his eyes closed again, the mask to his face. He looked as though his soul was gradually seeping out of his body.

– 14 –

THAT NIGHT, I ATE A LATE DINNER, then poured myself a second glass of wine and phoned my wife on the West Coast. She was about to travel north for a trial and would be out of touch with me for a while. I didn't look forward to that, for we enjoyed talking to each other. When she was at home with me, we always used to enjoy our after-dinner conversations over a glass of wine.

One of our recurrent topics was the nature of love and the various theories about it. The idea that it might only be an illusion, a romanticization of animalistic impulses, we didn't even consider. We both favoured the notion that, in its perfection, love was the uniting of the only two souls in the world destined for each other (we liked to think that was our own state).

Just for the sake of argument, I'd once posited the counter-theory: namely, that love is divided into a million pieces and can be reassembled only by making love to as many people as possible in one's life. Oddly enough, we'd agreed that, though that theory might sound a little self-serving, from certain points of view it might also be a form of idealism.

Frequently, we'd come to the conclusion that while love might not be an illusion, attempts to define love might well be.

"Someone could be in love," my wife had once wisely said, "without even having a word for it. And someone else could have all the right words yet never have experienced the feeling."

Anyway, in the course of this particular phone conversation, I told her all about Thomas Vanderlinden's mother and the man who appeared at her door and how she took him in and lived with him for two years without ever knowing who he really was. "Can you imagine?" I said. "Their entire relationship was founded on mystery. I must say, I was surprised Rachel put up with that. I always thought that, for women especially, real love depends on openness and complete honesty. Isn't that so?"

Four thousand miles away, my wife laughed. I loved her laugh, just as I loved talking to her about love, because we loved each other.

"Men always think they know what women feel," she said.

I was still considering that when she said something that surprised me even more. "Rachel must have believed it was boredom, lack of mystery that ruined her marriage," she said.

"So she felt she'd be better off living with someone who was essentially a stranger. It certainly seems to have worked for her. She spent two happy years with that man who appeared at her door. Then she spent the rest of her life remembering him as her great love."

"But what about honesty?" I said. "Doesn't true love mean you're able to unveil your soul to the person you love and he or she will love you even more for that?"

"Maybe it's the other way round," she said. "Maybe you have to love someone first, before you really know all that much about them. Then, no matter what revelations may come, the love's too strong to be destroyed by them." She paused for a moment. "Certainly a mother's love's like that, isn't it? How do you explain a mother's love?" It was one of those questions asked to call attention to the impossibility of an answer.

At the end of our phone conversation, I told her how much I loved her and I promised I'd let her know how the Vanderlinden story worked out. Then I went into the library and sat in front of the fire with my wine. Corrie came in too and jumped on my knee, making little cat-noises as she often did, trying to simulate conversation. So we chatted back and forth for a while till I'd finished my wine and stumbled up to bed.

– 15 –

THE NEXT DAY, I drove to the hospital around one o'clock. The sun was shining brightly and the few clouds were like cotton balls that had been squashed. When I got to Thomas's room, I was delighted to see he'd had another of his little resurrections—as though overnight his soul had trickled back into his body.

"It's good of you to come!" he said as I sat down with my coffee. "But you look tired."

I realized he was right. I suppose other people can know more about us than we do about ourselves, for they can see our unconscious body language.

"I guess I had too much wine last night," I said. "On top of that, I had a weird dream I can't get out of my head."

"Tell me about it," he said. That was one of the reasons I liked him—that he didn't mind hearing about my dreams.

So I did tell him about it: I was walking along the street towards the house when I noticed for the first time that some of the ancient maple trees that lined the sidewalk had faces carved into them—as if those massive totem poles on the West Coast had taken root again and were sprouting branches. I was stunned to discover that one of the faces was my own father's. He'd died more than twenty years ago when I was on my travels, far away. His face was just at head height and it was so gnarled it was as much tree as human—soon it would be indistinguishable from the trunk itself.

"Interesting," Thomas said when I'd finished. "I don't suppose you've read Gilberto's *Nox Perpetua?*"

I made my usual admission of ignorance.

"It was one of the popular books on dreams in the mid-sixteenth century," he said. "Gilberto contends that you don't choose your dreams; your dreams choose you."

I said I didn't like the sound of that.

"The main proposition of the book," Thomas said, "is that the world isn't nearly as rational as we like to think. For Gilberto, night-time proves the point. When darkness falls, sleep comes, bringing with it madness and terror."

I didn't like the idea of that either. "But surely, back in those old days," I said, "there were so many awful things in daily life it would have been easy to believe the world was insane."

Thomas Vanderlinden shook his head and for a moment looked at me the way he must have looked at especially dull undergraduates. "Well, that's a matter of opinion, of course," he said. "But arguably it would have been a lot easier to make a case for the world's sanity then than now."

I was awaiting the inevitable lecture.

But he spared me and instead started to talk about his mother again. "You surely must have been wondering why she let the stranger in, in the first place," he said, "and why she would never let him tell her who he really was."

"Indeed I have," I said.

"I asked her those very questions, of course," said Thomas. "She said the only man who could answer them properly was her husband—the real Rowland Vanderlinden—and she wanted me to find him! I was astonished, for I'd just assumed he must be dead. So I told her it would be pointless: the kind of man he was, he was almost certainly dead and buried at the other end of the world somewhere. And, even if he was alive, why would he want to see her after all these years? And why would he know anything about the man who knocked on her door?" Little crow's-feet of irony appeared at the edge of Thomas's eyes. "But I was wasting my time. You've no idea how frustrating it could be arguing with my mother when she'd made up her mind about something. She was a very stubborn woman. She just kept saying: '*Track him down! Bring him to me!*'"

He reached over and, from the drawer in the little bedside table, took out another photograph, this time without a frame. He handed it to me.

"She gave me this. She thought it might be some help to me," he said, "though it had been taken a long time ago."

It was one of those old sepia photographs with the edges fading. A man in tropical gear—vest full of little pockets, white pith helmet—was standing in front of some pyramids. In fact, the photograph made him look as tall as the pyramids, yet, at the same time, so small and flat I could hold him in my hands. He was thin-faced and serious-looking, with the beginnings of a beard. There were tents nearby that looked as though they belonged to an archaeological expedition.

"That was the first time," said Thomas, "I'd ever seen the real Rowland Vanderlinden. I was on leave from the University that year. I had time at my disposal. So, with that photograph, I began my search."

PART TWO

ROWLAND VANDERLINDEN

For who hasn't been struck, while struggling to recall some fragment of the past, by the sudden impression of sifting through ash; and then by the slowly dawning realization that who we are is composed of what, perhaps only what, we can never reclaim from that rubble?

—SHEROD SANTOS

– 1 –

THE EVENING THOMAS'S MOTHER ordered him to find Rowland Vanderlinden and bring him to her, Thomas asked for guidance from Doctor Webber after she had gone to bed. Webber, retired from the practice of medicine now, had moved into the house to keep an eye on her while she was ill.

Thomas and the Doctor sipped brandy and smoked thick cigars, sitting in wide armchairs, the leather of them soft with age, before the library fire—it was a cool night for early September. The heavy brocade curtains were drawn against the night.

This room was the repository of most of the books Thomas had read as a young man. If there was such a thing as the geology of a mind, his was formed here. Rachel herself had never been much of a reader, so few additions had been made to the library since he'd left home. He liked to think he could still have found his way around these shelves blindfolded—that he could have picked out many of the books by feel. Some were old friends he was comfortable with. Others were trophies, hard won. Others represented defeats or unfinished struggles.

Doctor Webber, the moist cigar smoke trickling out of his dark nostrils, was watching him. Thomas was accustomed to those green eyes that had a certain flatness about them, as if they lacked one of the dimensions. He seemed to Thomas an ancient man, though he was in fact only a few years older than Rachel. He was the essence of thinness—thin legs made thinner by pinstriped pants, thin veined hands, thin bony face, thin long nose.

Except for his lips, filtering the cigar smoke. They were thick and red and moist—the lips of the man Thomas had once heard say to his mother: "The only reason I'd like to have my innocence again would be to enjoy losing it once more." She had laughed.

The Doctor was yet another descendant of those Puritan farmers who, generations ago, fled some religious persecution in the South and lumbered northwards in covered wagons. Clothed in black, they'd arrived in this vast, forested country and had instinctively begun to eradicate the mortal enemies of farmers—the forests themselves. They had succeeded in that task, prospered and become the first burghers of the towns they'd built.

From such unlikely stock, Doctor Webber had arisen. He had become acquainted with Rachel when she was a volunteer at the hospital during the War years. Thomas hadn't particularly liked his mother's thin, special friend. Then, one day, when he wasn't doing as well as he ought at school, he overheard her ask Webber for advice on how to deal with him.

"Let him be. He's a fine boy. You should be proud of him," Webber told her.

After that, Thomas was ashamed he'd ever disliked the Doctor and forgave him whatever there was to forgive. Especially this: Rachel often invited Webber home to dinner after a hard day at his surgery or the hospital. And sometimes at night he was still sitting with her when Thomas went to bed.

On such a night, when Thomas was twelve, he awoke after midnight and couldn't get back to sleep. He went down to the kitchen for some milk. As he passed his mother's room, he noticed the door was ajar, and at the bottom of the stairs, he saw the kitchen light was already on. Half asleep, he opened the door, expecting to see her. Instead, he saw Doctor Webber, who'd been a dinner guest. The Doctor was standing by the open refrigerator, completely naked, his thin body startlingly hairy. He looked at Thomas awkwardly and Thomas didn't say anything but quickly went back up to his bedroom. Soon, he heard the Doctor come back upstairs. In a few minutes, there was more creaking on the stairs, and the front door opened and closed.

It was a week or so after that Thomas heard Webber speak in his defence. Hence, the forgiveness. Now Webber could stay overnight without any subterfuge. At no time, however, did Thomas see him kiss or touch his mother, the way an ordinary lover might. Most often, after their shared dinner, the Doctor went back to his own house in the central part of Camberloo, near the hospital. This odd relationship had continued even into their old age.

IT WAS TO WEBBER, then, the faithful lover of his mother, that Thomas turned for advice. He was just about to say, "She wants me to find someone," when the Doctor, as he often did, anticipated him.

"So, she wants you to find Rowland?" he said. "I gathered she was going to ask you."

"Did you know him?" said Thomas, not quite convinced the Doctor hadn't read his mind.

"Only very slightly," said Webber. "I met him occasionally when I worked for the Coroner. We'd occasionally consult him. That was a long time ago. Before I knew your mother."

"Should I do as she says?" Thomas said. "Should I try to find him?"

"I don't see why not," the Doctor said. He sipped his brandy and licked those lips that seemed to defy old age. "Anyway, you know what she's like when she's made up her mind." He said this fondly, the way he always did when he talked about Rachel. "Give it a try—just to please her. Maybe it'll be hopeless. Rowland always seemed to have been drawn towards the most unhealthy parts of the world. I wouldn't be surprised if he died long ago."

"All right," Thomas said. "I'll see what I can do. But I don't know where to begin."

"I know a man," the Doctor said. "If anyone can find him, he can."

– 2 –

ON A MORNING A FEW WEEKS LATER, Thomas received a phone call from a woman with a smiling voice. She said she was the secretary of Mr. Jeggard, of the Jeggard Agency, and that he wondered whether Thomas could come to his Toronto office the next day.

So it came about that on an October day, when the leaves on all the trees along the highway were dying in their most dramatic colours, Thomas Vanderlinden drove to Toronto. He parked outside Jeggard's offices on York Street, just north of the Strathmore Hotel. The sign, JEGGARD INVESTIGATIVE AGENCY—3RD FLOOR, was discreetly inscribed on a brass plate beside the entrance of the elegant, angular building. Thomas's footsteps echoed on the stone staircase on which the Fall sun beat down through skylights, making the air stuffy.

He reached the third floor and pressed the buzzer beside the glass door. From a speaker beside it, that same attractive voice he had heard on the phone asked him to identify himself. Then the door automatically opened. From her desk, Jeggard's secretary, the woman with the voice, greeted him. She was a scrawny woman with wire glasses and sparse hair. Thomas tried not to notice the huge goitre that protruded from the right side of her neck, like a third breast. He did, however, see a man wearing a bowler hat sitting in the corner of the waiting room, reading a magazine.

The secretary said Jeggard would see Thomas right away. She opened a frosted glass door for him and shut it softly behind him.

The man at the desk, working with some papers, pushed them aside, stood up and put out his hand. He was tall, tough-looking, with cropped grey hair and seamed face.

They sat down and Jeggard talked. But apart from the occasional direct glance at Thomas, he talked as though he were addressing someone sitting a few feet to the left of his visitor.

"We've come up with something in our search," he said, "more by good luck than anything else." He smiled confidently to the invisible third person, then glanced at Thomas. "That's often how things turn up in this business: when you're not really searching you get the best results."

One of his agents in San Francisco, working on a shipping insurance matter, had been interviewing the Captain of a freighter just back from an extended voyage. This agent had the poster of Rowland Vanderlinden on his wall—it was based on the photograph Thomas had supplied.

The Captain of the freighter had told Jeggard's agent that the face was somehow familiar. Questions were asked, conclusions were reached.

"I arranged for the Captain to come here," said Jeggard. "You ought to hear for yourself what he has to say." He pressed a button on the intercom on his desk. "Bring him in," he said.

The office door opened again and this time the secretary ushered in the man Thomas had seen in the waiting area. He was about sixty, ruddy-faced, wearing a dark-blue business suit that seemed a little tight. He was still wearing the bowler hat. He ambled slowly into the office and took his hat off. He had only a lick of hair on his freckled skull.

"This is Captain Jay Jonson," said Jeggard, not looking at either of them.

Jonson nodded to Thomas and sat down. He took a long time to settle in his chair, pulling up the knees of his pants, carefully crossing and recrossing his legs, placing his bowler hat on the edge of Jeggard's desk. He was clearly a very methodical man.

"Now, Captain," said Jeggard, "tell us what you know about the man in the poster."

"Well." Captain Jonson sighed, collected his thoughts, joined his hands and cleared his throat. "I recognized the face all right. Though when I met him, he was a lot older. But I knew it was him. I ran into him more than a year ago." He nodded. "Yes, just over a year ago."

The Captain was obviously not a man to be rushed. In a slow, thorough manner, he told Jeggard and Thomas about the meeting. He said his ship, the *Medea,* had unloaded a cargo of farm machinery and spare parts in Sydney, Australia. On the voyage back to San Francisco, they'd called in at the Motamua Archipelago, hoping to pick up a load of copra.

"Yes," said Jeggard, trying to hurry him.

"Company policy, you see," Jonson went on. "The owners don't think much of a skipper who brings home a ship with an empty hold."

"Yes, yes," said Jeggard.

Captain Jonson couldn't be hurried. He said that at Vatua, the main island of the archipelago, he couldn't find any copra. But a shipping agent there recommended he should try Manu, a few hours away to the north. So he upped anchor and went there. Unfortunately, as the *Medea* was coming through the narrow entrance in the reef round Manu, the right propeller struck an outcrop of coral, bending the shaft. She would have to lay up for repairs. Captain Jonson beached the ship at high tide so that the engineer could get to work on the shaft.

As Jonson talked in his slow way about the incident, Jeggard had begun drumming a pencil on his desk impatiently. Now he could stand it no longer. "To the point, please," he said. He was looking directly at Thomas though he was speaking to Jonson.

The Captain smiled. He didn't seem offended, nor did he seem like a man who'd ever be rushed. He sighed and thought for a while. "The point?" he said. "Well, I suppose the point is that while we were stranded in Manu, I stayed at the Equator

Hotel." He told them that though the place was called a hotel—and it was the only hotel on the island—it was really less a hotel than a collection of thatched huts along the lagoon. Since there was nothing for his crew to do while the ship was beached, they'd been given shore leave. None of them stayed at the hotel: they were off elsewhere, drinking and womanizing. The Captain was glad of that, for the walls of the hotel were of bamboo and it would have been too easy to hear what was going on in the adjacent huts. At least he'd have his rest.

The Captain smiled at Thomas: "The hotel had the only real restaurant on Manu." As was the usual thing in the islands, the meals on the hotel's menu consisted mainly of canned meat. Yet shoals of fish swam undisturbed in the lagoon. "I had to pay extra to get the cook to catch some fresh fish for my meals." He said this to Jeggard, who immediately looked away, so he told Thomas: "The islanders with any money generally prefer cans of corned beef to the fresh natural foods they used to eat before. The missionaries tell them their own food's uncivilized."

Jeggard was shifting restlessly in his chair. "Please, Captain," he said earnestly, looking at the wall behind Thomas, "Mr. Vanderlinden and I are busy men."

The Captain sighed patiently, uncrossed his legs and recrossed them, again carefully plucking the rather tight trousers away from his thighs. "After a week," he said, "the engineer got the shaft straightened out and told me we'd be able to leave on the next afternoon's high tide. So that was to be my final night in the hotel. And that was when I met the man in your poster."

AT SUNDOWN, AS USUAL, he went into the small hut with the raised floor that served as a restaurant. On this occasion, there was another diner—an elderly white man. They chatted and drank gin slings as they waited for the fish to be cooked.

The elderly man was quite talkative. He said he'd lived in Manu for many years and that he came down from the Highlands only three or four times a year when the mail boat arrived, bringing with it accumulated copies of the *The Pacific Times*. He'd always stay at the Equator Hotel for one week. He'd sort the newspapers into chronological order and read them from start to finish. He had the sensation of being in a different dimension of time from the rest of the world. He was frequently tempted to jump ahead in his reading, to see what had developed in some impending crisis. But he never gave in to the temptation—even when the threat of global warfare was in the news.

Why was he in the hotel now? He'd heard that a ship had come into the lagoon and assumed it was the mail boat, a little early. He'd made his journey down and discovered, of course, that it was the *Medea*. He didn't mind the mistake too much. He always enjoyed chance meetings with travellers. He was from Canada originally and wondered if the Captain had ever been there on his voyages. Captain Jonson said no.

They ate dinner then went out to the verandah overlooking the lagoon. They sat there for hours, drinking two bottles of palm wine, swatting away mosquitoes and fruit bats and talking about world affairs. Captain Jonson was not the kind of man to pry into another's private life, so all he ever found out about this stranger was that he lived in the mountains and studied tribal customs.

Around two in the morning, they parted and went to their huts.

The Captain didn't get up till lunch the next day. The owner of the Equator told him that his dinner companion had checked out not long after sunrise.

"THAT'S ABOUT ALL THERE IS TO IT," said Captain Jonson. "It was over a year ago. There was no reason for me to remember the details."

Jeggard frowned at that. "I think we can safely say you've given us more than enough detail," he said to the wall. "Now what about his name? Do you remember that? Did he give you his name?"

"It was so long ago," said the Captain. "I only heard it once. It might have been Rowland Something-or-Other. You know, like the name on your poster."

"How old do you think he was?" said Jeggard.

"The climate down there ages people a lot, so it's hard to be sure," said Captain Jonson. "He must have been at least in his seventies." He took the poster from Jeggard's desk and looked at it again. "That's him, all right," he said.

Jeggard was satisfied. He stood up to indicate that Jonson was no longer required, but Jonson remained seated. So Jeggard rang a bell on his desk. "My wife will see you out," he said, looking at the wall beside Jonson.

His secretary came in, her goitre quivering. So she was his wife, Thomas thought. Perhaps, with Jeggard's oblique way of looking at people, he scarcely noticed her blemish at all.

The Captain slowly got up, smoothed his tight trousers and

picked up his bowler hat. "I hope I've been of some help," he said to Thomas. Then he ambled out of the office, as though balancing himself on a swaying deck.

Jeggard, after the door closed, said that if Thomas was in agreement, he would act on the Captain's information. Radio messages would be sent, and, if necessary, letters would be written, embassies contacted—everything possible to verify that it was indeed Rowland Vanderlinden the Captain had met.

"Please go ahead," said Thomas.

"I'll contact our man down there right away." Jeggard confided to the wall near Thomas: "We have agents in many parts of the world."

Their business was over.

"Please convey my best wishes to Doctor Webber," Jeggard said as they parted.

"I shall," said Thomas.

"He's sent me many medical insurance cases over the years," Jeggard said. "He asked me to make a special effort in this instance." As they shook hands, Jeggard's eyes squinted briefly at Thomas. "When we have confirmation, we'll contact you," he said.

– 3 –

THOMAS VANDERLINDEN ARRIVED back in Camberloo four hours later. He had just opened his apartment door when the phone rang.

It was Jeggard's wife. "It's confirmed," she said. Her attractive voice was now a little contaminated by Thomas's memory of the goitre. "Mr. Jeggard just received a telegraph from the Motamuas. Rowland Vanderlinden is alive and well and his habitation is known. Should we send our agent to talk to him?"

"I'll check with my mother first. I'll call you back later," Thomas said.

"Mr. Jeggard says he'll await your orders," said Jeggard's wife.

THOMAS WENT STRAIGHT TO Rachel's house.

She was sitting alone by the fireplace in the library. Her long grey hair had been braided into a pigtail that hung over her shoulder. Thomas kissed her on the cheek. Her green eyes, behind her silver-framed glasses, were deeply recessed in her skull, giving her the look of some sharp-eyed creature peering from the depths of its cave.

"So?" she said. "What do you have to tell me?"

"They've found Rowland. He's in one of the most remote places you could imagine—down on an island in the Pacific. He's been there for many years, it seems," said Thomas.

Her eyes became little points. "All right," she said. "Go and get him. Bring him here. I want to see him."

"But Jeggard already has a man down there," Thomas said. "He can take Rowland any message you wish."

"Of course not," she said. "You go. He won't pay attention to anyone else. If you go, he'll come back with you."

"Come back with me?" said Thomas. "Why don't you just send a letter and ask him what you want to know? Surely there's no need for him to come all this way just to talk to you. He's an old man."

"No," she said. "I've things I want to ask him, face to face. If he needs persuading, you can persuade him."

Thomas tried again. "But what if he can't come?" he said. "What if he isn't able to travel? After all, he's old and it's so far away." He felt this was surely reasonable.

But she just shook her head. "Go to him," she said. "He once told me that if ever I needed him, he'd come. Remind him of that if you have to. Ask him to come back with you. Tell him I need him now."

That was that. There was no more to be said.

Thomas, accordingly, consulted once more with Jeggard, made travel arrangements and packed his bag. Two days later he set out for one of the most distant corners of the world.

– 4 –

THOMAS VANDERLINDEN, who'd always been an enthusiastic mental traveller, was not at all keen on real travelling. *"People's lives would be much simpler if they never left their own houses"*: that was what one of his favourite authors had written, and Thomas agreed with him. Yet here he was, on a journey to the other side of the earth, in spite of everything.

To begin with, it wasn't too bad. The train west was comfortable enough for a few days, in spite of the smell of stale smoke in his little compartment. The Great Lakes were pleasing to view. The prairies were indeed flat. The mountains, when they appeared, were impressive enough to begin with, but after a while monotonous as bookcase after bookcase full of the same flashy book. They actually made Thomas nostalgic for the prairies, made him feel perhaps there might have been some deeper significance to all that flatness if he'd only had the mental toughness to penetrate it.

None too soon, the train steamed into Vancouver. The oppressive bulk of the mountains made the city seem to Thomas like a precarious heap of rubble ready to slide into the deep. The rain was constant, the people scuttling between buildings like beetles with carapaces of umbrellas.

He had to stay there three days, but he didn't go out much. He spent most of each day in the damp bedroom of his small hotel by the docks, sitting by the window. The frame was warped, the white paint peeling. He alternated reading with watching the rusty freighters anchored out in the harbour, small boats coming from them like animals being born. Each night, the rain seemed to get heavier. The sound of it lashing against the window made his sleep uneasy. The old grandfather clock in the hotel lobby would strike midnight as though from another world.

The rain stopped on the third morning, just after he boarded the ship to Hawaii. He was apprehensive about the journey, never having travelled by ship before and having been warned it was the season of storms. But for the entire crossing, the weather remained benevolent: the sun shone all day, the stars dazzled at night, the steamer was as stable as the train had been.

But pleasantness, he knew, never lasts.

The ship arrived at Honolulu and he looked forward to a few days of finding his land legs again. He discovered he had no time to spare: he must go immediately to another dock. He went there and boarded the *Innisfree,* the monthly schooner to the Motamua Archipelago. Her Captain, anxious-looking and Irish, had been waiting for his arrival. Thomas had been on board only an hour when the sails were raised and she was underway.

In the tiniest of cabins, lying in a narrow bunk with a board siding that was clearly meant to prevent the occupant from tumbling out, he soon felt ill at ease. It was like being in the belly of some unhappy monster, the timbers groaned so noisily. The schooner was already so responsive to winds and waves, he didn't want to think about how it would do in a storm.

These things were going through his mind as the vessel passed into deep waters. The regular ocean swell brought on his first bout of seasickness.

THOMAS VANDERLINDEN KEPT TO HIMSELF as much as the size of the *Innisfree* would permit. Aside from the Captain and a half-dozen crew who made up the various watches, there were four passengers. Thomas presumed they were typical of the kinds of people who made such journeys.

He got to know the Berkleys first. They were a missionary and his wife from Saskatchewan and they sat on deck much of the day. They were returning to the Motamuas after a sick leave. Mr. Berkley was a tall thin man with protruding cheek-bones and big ears. He was in his forties, though at times he looked twenty years older.

His wife was small and plump with short brown hair, a sweaty face and narrow eyes. She wore a waistless blue dress—her "frock," as she called it. She explained to Thomas that "the

Reverend" (as she referred to her husband, even in his presence) had just spent a month in hospital being treated for a tropical disorder she kept calling, over and over again, "dengue." She said the climate of the Motamuas was responsible. "It's killing both of us," she said.

"What exactly is dengue?" Thomas said.

"Oh, you haven't heard of it? A disease from mosquitoes," she said. "They've never seen as bad a case as the Reverend's." She looked at her husband with pride.

Mr. Berkley, who'd been quietly eating, glared at her as though he hated her or was in pain, or both. It would have been hard to tell the difference on that thin face.

"We didn't catch your name," Mrs. Berkley said to Thomas.

"Vanderlinden," he said. "Thomas Vanderlinden."

Both looked at him with sudden interest.

"Vanderlinden?" said Mr. Berkley. The distaste in the way he said the word was heightened by the severity of his face. "We know a Vanderlinden. He lives in the Highlands of Manu. Are you a relative of his?"

"In a way," said Thomas.

"Is that why you're going there? To visit him?" said his wife.

"Yes," said Thomas. "It's a family matter." He didn't like this inquisition.

Mr. Berkley's face was stern and evangelical. "I regret to say your relative's the type who makes our work harder," he said. "He makes no effort to disabuse the islanders of their superstitions. Indeed, he encourages them."

Thomas made no comment. Rowland apparently hadn't changed much from the way his mother described him.

"You mentioned a family matter," said Mrs. Berkley. "What's that about?" She asked this bluntly, as though she were entitled to know.

"It's private business," Thomas said, just as bluntly. They were offended. He hoped they would leave him alone.

IN FACT, HE WOULD HAVE PREFERRED to have been alone for the entire voyage. But that was all but impossible on such a small boat as the *Innisfree*. In due course, the other two passengers, Schneider and Cameron, tried to make friends with him too. They were short-haired young men, clean-shaven, and they wore brand-new tropical shirts and pants. They were Foreign Service operatives on their way to their first offshore postings.

But they were disappointed about that. Cameron said his colleagues in the Home Office called the Motamuas "the smelly underarm of the planet." In fact, they were disappointed in everything, from the size of the schooner ("a toy boat," said Schneider, the dark-haired one) to the fact that the only woman aboard was a plump, middle-aged missionary ("Lord, save us from temptation," said Cameron of the ginger hair, looking up to the skies).

They were soon disappointed, too, by Thomas's obvious reluctance to socialize with them. Eventually they allied themselves with the Berkleys. One very calm day, as Thomas was about to enter the dining salon, he couldn't help hearing his fellow passengers' voices above the usual creaking of the timbers.

"He's a relative of the most degenerate man on the islands," Mr. Berkley was saying. "He's going there to visit him."

"Really!" said Cameron.

"He didn't tell us anything," said Schneider. "We could barely get a word out of him."

Mrs. Berkley summed it all up. "That's the type he is," she said. "He won't tell anyone his business."

Thomas came into the salon and they changed the subject. But he guessed, from the smirk on Schneider's face, that if they were aware he might have overheard them, they didn't really care.

FOR THE NEXT TWO WEEKS, each day on the *Innisfree* was an uneventful replica of the day before, except for an occasional visit by wandering dolphins or sharks. The latter made Thomas conscious of how flimsy the schooner's hull was.

Captain Bonney, who'd renamed the schooner after his home in Ireland, seemed to spend much of each day inspecting rigging or helping the crew with caulking seams—an endless task, it appeared. He made his private library—mainly books abandoned by previous travellers—available to the passengers, though only Thomas seemed to take advantage of it. The Reverend read only his Bible, with Mrs. Berkley sitting beside him, vicariously sharing the experience. Schneider and Cameron played chess and dominoes, and, if they read anything, it was their Foreign Office manuals.

Thomas had acquainted himself with the library the first day he felt well enough. It consisted of one side of Bonney's cabin, made up entirely of shelves full of books half rotten with damp. The books were in no particular order. Some were technical seafaring books, probably Bonney's own. Many of the others were cheap mysteries and romances. At the end of the top shelf, four of the most mildewed volumes looked as though they'd never been opened. They were called: *Inspecting the Faults; The Paladine Hotel; The Wysterium; First Blast of the Cornet*. Thomas glanced through a few pages and saw why they were unread—they were appalling rubbish.

Fortunately, he came across a trio of books that were good as well as in readable condition—old friends he could now revisit at leisure: Burton's *Anatomy of Melancholy;* Browne's *Religio Medici;* and Hobbes's *Leviathan*. He was glad that someone, in some past voyage, had had such excellent taste.

That visit to the library made the prospect of the entire journey bearable for Thomas. And indeed, during those endless days as he sat on deck reading, he'd often quite forget he was on a frail sailing ship in the middle of the Pacific Ocean. From time to time, he'd realize afresh just why he loved reading so much: it seemed to make the material world, even his own physical self, superfluous. Yes, it was indeed like thought, thinking itself.

ON ONE MEMORABLE DAY, a week out, he sat alone in the prow of the schooner, reading. He'd enjoyed his lunch, in spite of the company, and was feeling drowsy, what with the warm wind and the *swi-i-i-sssh* of the bow wave as the ship cut through the sea of deepest blue. The book he was reading was *Leviathan*. He had come to the passage containing Hobbes's famous admonition about *"the life of man, solitary, poor, nasty, brutish, and short,"* and was marvelling that such an unpleasant idea could be expressed so delightfully and memorably.

Just then, off the starboard bow, he heard a thunderous splash and saw an amazing sight. Not more than a hundred yards from the *Innisfree,* the Leviathan itself—a great black sperm whale—was leaping into the air and plunging back into the deep with a flourish. It jumped three times in all, making the air even saltier. After the third jump, the whale didn't reappear and the surface of the sea was unruffled except for the occasional whitecap. Thomas stared for the longest time. Nothing. He wondered if anyone else on the schooner had shared his experience, for there was no one else on deck except the steersman behind the bulging mainsail, and he seemed to have noticed nothing odd. The whale had come and gone, as though its appearance had been for Thomas's illumination alone.

FROM THE MOMENT THEY'D LEFT Honolulu, Captain Bonney had warned that the *Innisfree* would almost certainly run into at least one major storm on the voyage and that was why it was necessary to keep everything shipshape—hence the constant caulking and rigging inspections. Thomas was apprehensive, for it seemed to him that the one tiny lifeboat couldn't possibly hold all the passengers and the crew.

He needn't have worried. For though on some days the skies indeed looked ominous, the seas were swollen and the wind howled in the rigging, the *Innisfree* did not encounter anything more than occasional rough patches.

On the afternoon of the fourteenth day of the voyage, on the southern horizon, a smudge appeared, which became in turn a high column of clouds. An even darker smudge gradually took shape under the clouds: Vatua, the main island of the Motamuas. By daybreak, the *Innisfree* was only a few miles offshore, and everyone was on deck, looking at the mountains skirted by dense green forests and black, volcanic sands.

Thomas was standing near Captain Bonney, who for a moment at least was not occupied caulking the seams. He had taken off his seaman's cap. His fine ginger hair was thinning and his skull shone through, freckled by the sun. Thomas thanked him for the use of the library.

"Sure now, some of the books were left there by your namesake," said the Captain.

"My namesake?" Thomas was surprised.

"Aye," said the Captain. "Mr. Vanderlinden. He's made voyages with me a few times over the years. Always a pleasant man. Will you be seeing him?"

"Yes," said Thomas.

"Then give him my regards," said Captain Bonney.

THE SCHOONER CHARGED THROUGH the entrance of the reef into the calm waters of a lagoon. Several other sailing ships lay at anchor, and outrigger canoes slid over the surface like water spiders. The *Innisfree* tied up at a wooden dock, where a number of men in sarongs waited to unload the cargo. Thomas, standing on the hot deck with his bag, had never before seen so unappetizing a place. The corrugated iron roofs of the bamboo buildings by the dock were rusted and askew. The palm trees that had seemed quite exotic from the distance were, without exception, yellowing and raddled with some vegetable disease. The heat, now that the *Innisfree* was stationary, was so intense he could feel the sweat running down his body inside his clothing. He envied the islanders— their sarongs looked cool and right in this hot place.

He stepped down carefully onto the Vatua dock. He'd forgotten how the stability of land after the constant sway of the ship would cause him to stagger, and he had to steady himself on a mooring post. A deep breath made him aware of the smell of rotting fish. He felt the first bites of the mosquitoes that hung over everything like miniature cumulus clouds. He looked back at the *Innisfree*, but no one had paid any heed to his departure. Captain Bonney and the crew were busy organizing the removal of the wooden covers from the cargo hold. His fellow passengers had gone below decks.

"Mr. Vanderlinden?" An islander in a sarong and a sailor's hat was coming along the dock towards him.

"Yes."

"You come," said the islander. "I take you to Manu ferry." He picked up Thomas's bag and led him off the dock and along the beach.

Thomas stumbled as he followed, his feet now further confused by the fluidity of the sand. A hundred yards along the beach, they came to a big outrigger canoe with a slack, triangular sail. The canoe was half in, half out of the shallow water, and several islanders with children and chickens in cages were already aboard

His guide threw the bag into the back of the canoe and helped Thomas in after it. He and another of the islanders then pushed the canoe out into deeper water, jumped aboard and began to trim the sail.

For about an hour, the canoe sailed southwards, hugging the coastline of Vatua. Then it cut seawards and dashed through a very narrow opening in the reef at a speed that made Thomas cringe.

– 5 –

FOR THE NEXT THREE HOURS, the canoe sailed across open ocean towards the island of Manu. Thomas sat on an uncomfortable bamboo strut across the stern. There were four men, three women and three children aboard, all with brown skin and jet-black hair. Though they often glanced towards him, they talked only to each other in a soft, alien language that reminded him how far away he was from his own familiar world. But he dozed off and on in the heat, and time passed quickly. Soon the canoe neared another island with its own set of jagged mountains and fringe of black sand. After another frightening plunge through a gap in the reef, the canoe spilled into a lagoon so calm and clear that shoals of fish with yellow and blue and red stripes, and willowy fins and tails, were startlingly visible beneath the hull.

The canoe was met on the beach by a noisy crowd of islanders, who made a great fuss of the other passengers. A ramshackle village faced onto the beach. Thomas stepped ashore last, awkward and stiff.

In the crowd was a man who wasn't an islander. He came towards Thomas. He was of middle height, looked about thirty, with long, untidy black hair tied back in a pigtail. A cigarette dangled from his lips. His shirt and trousers were yellowish-white, stained with sweat. His face was sallow and lined and he needed a shave. "Thomas Vanderlinden?" The stranger put out his hand. "Alastair Macphee, at your service." He had kindly brown eyes with shadows, perhaps of sickness, under them.

Thomas knew the name. In Toronto, Jeggard had told him this man would take him to his quarry.

"We'll be staying here overnight," Macphee said, lifting Thomas's bag. "We start for the Highlands in the morning."

Thomas followed him along the beach towards the village. They had to make their way through a large crowd of islanders, who were watching some activity in the shallow water about twenty feet out from the shore.

"It's a marriage ceremony," said Macphee. "Let's wait till they finish. It's not polite to pass by."

Thomas watched with interest. A young woman with long black hair and a colourful wrap was standing in the water before a line-up of men of various shapes and ages, all wearing white loincloths. She went to the youngest-looking man in the line and embraced him.

"He's the groom," said Macphee.

She disengaged herself from him and began to wade along the line of men, stopping in front of each of them with her mouth wide open. Each man in turn leaned forward as though to kiss her, but instead spat into her mouth. She made a great show of swallowing the spit.

After she'd reached the end of the line, she went back to the groom and embraced him again. Then the wedding party came out of the sea and joined the spectators on the beach amidst laughter and hugging.

"That didn't seem very hygienic," Thomas said as Macphee began walking towards the village again.

"It's actually just sea water they spit into her mouth," Macphee said. "Most of these people depend on the sea, that's why they stand in it to be married. The bride actually marries all those men, even though only one of them's her husband for the moment." He lit a cigarette. "A lot of men here are drowned, or killed by sharks, or lost at sea. So all the groom's male relatives marry the bride—as back-ups. If her husband dies at sea, one of the others is obliged to take her as his wife." He said all this between long draws on his cigarette.

"How peculiar," said Thomas.

"After you've lived here a while," said Macphee, "it makes a lot of sense."

They left the beach and walked along a sandy street of rickety bamboo houses with tin roofs. Near the end was a larger structure. It had a sun-bleached sign in flaking red paint—Equator Hotel—over its entrance.

"Here we are," said Macphee, holding the door open for him.

Inside, a heavy islander sat behind a desk. He had bulging eyes and the loose, fleshy face of a toad, and he greeted Macphee familiarly. "So, your guest arrived," he said.

"Yes. We'll both be staying tonight," Macphee said. "We're off tomorrow."

"I'll give him the room next to yours," the hotel-keeper said. He got up from his desk. He wore only a sarong, and as he stood up, he began fiddling with what looked like a matchstick that was somehow attached to his swollen belly. He fiddled with it, Thomas noticed, even as he waddled ahead. Behind the main building was a row of thatched huts. He opened the door of one of them and left, saying dinner would be served in an hour.

Thomas went into his hut and put down his bag. The bedroom hut contained nothing but an iron bed with a mosquito net hanging over it like a tattered cloud, a bamboo chair and a hook for hanging clothes.

A separate hut was used for communal showering and toilet. Thomas immediately showered. He looked at himself in the rusted mirror and saw that his own chin was as stubbly and his shirt as dirty as Macphee's. As he shaved, he was tormented by mosquitoes and a variety of little wasps that seemed to have no trouble penetrating the bamboo walls of the shower hut.

When he eventually got to the dining room—another porous hut with a few bamboo tables and chairs—Macphee was already waiting. They drank lukewarm beer straight from the bottles till the dinner was served by the owner. It consisted of canned tuna and canned potatoes on dented tin plates.

After they'd been served, Thomas asked Macphee about the matchstick attached to the owner's belly.

"You don't want to hear about that before dinner," said Macphee.

Thomas didn't pursue the matter. The meal was as unappetizing as the food on the *Innisfree,* but he was hungry after his journey.

Macphee ate only a few mouthfuls then drank another bottle of the warm beer. "It's the only liquid I trust here," he said. He then lit a cigarette and told Thomas a little about himself.

He was an Australian with legal training. He'd wanted a more adventurous life than a lawyer's office, so for the last ten years he'd acted as an agent for various shipping insurance companies and investigative agencies such as Jeggard's. Over the years, he'd visited every island, no matter how remote, that was on the shipping routes. He exhaled and gestured around the dining room. "Now this," he said, "may not look like much to you. But believe me, it's heaven compared to some of the places I've been." The words were wreathed in clouds of smoke, as though a dragon were speaking. "And you'd be surprised at the number of foreigners who end up in these out-of-the-way corners of the world," he said. "I get to hear about them in my travels. I meet a lot of them too. Like Rowland."

"So, you know him?" said Thomas.

"Quite well," said Macphee. "He comes down to the town regular as clockwork to meet the mail boat. And I've been up to visit him at his place once. He knows more about the people of these islands than anyone I've ever met. I sent a message up to him when Jeggard got in touch with me. He knows why you're coming to see him. He'll be expecting us."

"Then he's not here, in town?" Thomas said. He'd hoped to get this over with quickly. "Does he live near?"

"Oh no. I wish he did," said Macphee. "He lives quite a way off."

"But we'll see him tomorrow?"

"No chance," said Macphee. "His place is up in the Highlands and it takes two days to get there. As I say, I've been up there once and I wouldn't go again if Jeggard wasn't paying me to."

"Why not?" said Thomas.

"Well, it's a rough trip," said Macphee. "The terrain's not easy. But on top of that, some of the natives can be unfriendly."

THEY LEFT THE DINING HUT and went out onto a verandah over the lagoon, where some of the islanders were fishing by lanterns—it was very dark now.

The owner brought more beer and lit a candle on the table. Thomas noticed once again how he fiddled with the matchstick on his belly. After he'd left, he asked Macphee about it once more.

"Okay, I can tell you now without spoiling your appetite," Macphee said. "It's a Guinea Worm."

Thomas had never heard of it.

"It's a worm you can get from drinking unpurified water," said Macphee. "That's why I prefer alcohol. The worms can grow to three or four feet. Sometimes they stick their heads out. The islanders try to pull them out by winding them round a twig and pulling a little bit each day. It usually doesn't work."

He saw the look of horror on Thomas's face.

"Now you understand why I didn't want to tell you before you ate," he said. "Be careful with the water here. Same with fruit and vegetables—never eat anything you can't peel. Water and food are your enemies." He drew on his cigarette. "I only smoke these things to keep the mosquitoes off!" He laughed a smoky laugh.

Thomas was still thinking of the worms. "They sound awful," he said.

"They say the female worms are the worst," Macphee said. "They're the hardest to get rid of. Down here, if a man has a dreadful wife, they call her a Guinea Worm." He smiled. "In that kind of situation, they say the Worm's taken charge and it's the husband who can only stick his head out once in a while."

As Thomas was thinking about that, Macphee launched into a monologue on the various health hazards—leprosy among them—he'd faced in the course of his work. He also spoke of the perils of voyages in leaky boats in typhoons and what he called "the unfriendly customs" of some of the people he was forced to deal with.

"Are you married?" Thomas asked, wondering what kind of woman could put up with such a life. "Do you have a wife?"

"A wife?" Macphee exhaled cigarette smoke in a fit of coughing. "Not on your life," he spluttered and laughed. "Not unless you can call a *Dutch Wife* a wife."

A Dutch Wife!—that expression again. Thomas's mother had used it. The Judge, her father, had used it. Rowland had used it. But by it, Macphee seemed to have something else in mind.

"What do you mean?" Thomas said.

"You don't know what a Dutch Wife is?" said Macphee. "It's quite a common thing here. It's a pillow you put between your legs at night—a thigh pillow."

Thomas was puzzled. "Why would anyone do that?" he said.

"To stop the heat rashes," said Macphee. "If you live in this climate long enough, you've got to have something between your legs at night, or you're sure to get rashes and infections."

"Ah," said Thomas, understanding at last that Macphee was

using the expression in a different way. "But why's it called a Dutch Wife?"

"You've got me there," said Macphee. "But there used to be some Dutch colonies in the islands. Maybe that's how the name came about. Doesn't sound very flattering to Dutch women, anyway, does it?"

They finished their beers, then Macphee stood up. "Time for us to hit the sack," he said. His speech was a little slurred at last. "It's going to be a hard day tomorrow. Do you have a pair of boots and some old clothes for roughing it?"

"Yes, I do," said Thomas. He got up too and he too staggered a little, partly because he was drunk and partly because his body was lagging behind his mind in realizing it was no longer on a ship at sea.

When he got to bed, he lay there marvelling at the fact he was in a bamboo hut on a minor island in a minor archipelago of islands half a world away from home. He could hear the night sounds of strange animals, as well as Macphee snoring through the bamboo walls of the next hut. He was exhausted but feared he was in for a restless night under the tattered mosquito net. He kept thinking of the Guinea Worm and how horrific it must be to be inhabited by one. But his last conscious thought was of the sweat trickling between his legs and of how nice it might be to have a Dutch Wife to comfort him.

– 6 –

THOMAS VANDERLINDEN AWOKE AT DAWN and, through the window aperture in the bamboo wall, watched the sun spread its wings slowly like some huge bird of paradise. A thousand other tropical birds squawked their greeting to it. He got up and dressed. Macphee was already awake, so they went to the dining hut for some fruit and a foul kind of coffee. Then they walked together to the beach. Macphee carried a knapsack heavy with clanking bottles.

Near the dock, four islanders with stringy muscles were waiting for them beside two dugout canoes. They shook hands with surprisingly limp handshakes for such strong-looking men. Macphee got into one canoe, Thomas into the other, and they set off.

At first, they travelled along the coast only a hundred yards out from the beaches of black sand, which were fenced in by the inevitable palm trees, all of them stricken with some kind of tree-jaundice. The wind was refreshing and kept the mosquitoes away but left a residue of salt on the lips. Thomas dozed much of the time, comforted by the rhythmic splash of the paddles. Around noon, the rowers called to each other then headed towards the beach. They took a basket of fruit out of the leading canoe and they all sat on the sand to eat.

Thomas was impressed again by the muscles of the rowers. "They look so strong," he said to Macphee. "But why are their handshakes so limp?"

"Partly, it's just politeness," said Macphee. "But also they try to conceal their strength. Especially from potential enemies."

THE CANOES CONTINUED DOWN THE COAST. After a while, they rounded a headland into what seemed at first like a bay

but was actually the estuary of a river. The water was a brown-
ish colour. Up this river they began to travel.

"What's this river called?" Thomas said to Macphee, whose
canoe was alongside.

Macphee, who'd been half dozing with a cigarette between
his lips, threw what remained of it into the water. It sizzled
for an instant before being snatched into the jaws of a long
yellow fish.

"It's a funny thing," Macphee said. "They don't have
specific names for rivers, or mountains, or any of those
things. They just don't seem to go in for it. For example,
they just call this 'the-river-in-the-bay-that-leads-to-the-
mountains.'"

Now that they were out of the sea-breeze, the air was like a
huge sauna full of mosquitoes escorting squadrons of little
wasps. The canoes made their way through a great swamp
overhung with black, labyrinthine trees whose long roots
snaked round the paddles. The air stank, and even the water
seemed to release a sulphurous smell every time the paddles
disturbed it. At times, the bottom was so shallow they all had
to climb overboard and push the canoes through the putres-
cence. Thomas was thankful for Macphee's cigarettes to burn
off the swollen leeches.

About four o'clock on that nightmarish day, the journey by
water was over. They pulled the canoes ashore and covered
them with branches, then they walked till they reached a
damp clearing where Macphee called a halt for the day. After
they made camp, the rowers gathered dead, damp vegetation
and made a circle of it around the area. They lit it and it

began to smoulder, like a very acrid form of incense, causing general coughing.

Thomas asked if this was another one of their rituals to ward off spirits.

"That's a good one!" Macphee said, laughing. "No, they do this to keep the mosquitoes down. Otherwise, they'd drive us crazy!" He blew a great cloud of cigarette smoke into the air as though to assist in the task.

The islanders now made a soup of breadfruit and bamboo shoots boiled together in a tin filled with murky water. One spoonful of it was enough to make Thomas gag. Macphee offered him whisky from one of the bottles he carried. Sweaty and uncomfortable as he was, Thomas was glad of a few swigs to kill the awful taste left by the soup.

At six o'clock, darkness dropped like a stone. The only light came from the campfire and the red glow of the circle of smouldering vegetation around the travellers. They all lay down to sleep on bamboo mats as the campfire died. Thomas, on his back, could see an astonishing array of stars, flickering and alive, as though he were looking down on a great city at night. He was exhausted and wanted to sleep, but the angry whine of mosquitoes around his head kept him awake. Whenever the whining momentarily stopped, he knew they were pumping their fever into him. He would slap at them and try to protect his face by covering it with his arm, till he feared he was suffocating himself.

The night passed slowly. Thomas felt the ground beneath him slowly breaking his bones. But he must have dozed, for suddenly, it was dawn, the sun peering down at him through its bloodshot eye. The mosquitoes had gone and the air was cool. Now he could have slept soundly, but the islanders were awake and had lit the fire to reheat that awful soup. Soon it was time to go.

THEY WERE WALKING NOW into increasingly thick jungle. The ground was beginning to rise and Thomas had to lean forward slightly as he walked, breathing hard, unused to such exertion. He could see Macphee panting along ahead of him, an aureole of cigarette smoke around his head to keep off the insects. As the day became hotter, the climbing was just one more torment in a sweaty hell that was home to a million leeches and mosquitoes and wasps.

After what seemed like miles of steady climbing, Thomas's legs were so tired he thought he couldn't go on. He was just about to tell Macphee this when all at once the whole party stopped. The thick jungle was very silent and the islanders were peering nervously around them into the gloom. The lead paddler said something to Macphee and pointed up into a tree ahead of them. There, hanging by its feet from a leafless bough, Thomas could see a dead bird with a chain of glossy bright shells around its bedraggled neck.

The paddler spoke nervously to Macphee for a while. They seemed to reach some agreement.

"That's it," Macphee told Thomas. "They won't go any farther. They'll wait for us here till we get back." He pointed at the bird. "That's a Hupu warning."

"What does that mean?" said Thomas.

"The Hupu—they're a mountain tribe," said Macphee. "They have a reputation for not being too friendly to these coastal islanders. I don't blame them for not wanting to go on." He lit a cigarette and exhaled slowly.

— 7 —

MACPHEE AND THOMAS WENT ON ALONE. They were making their clumsy passage up through a thicket of ferns as big as trees when the silence around them was shattered by loud croaking noises, as though they'd disturbed a den of giant bullfrogs. There was also a distinct jingling, as though of bells.

"Stand absolutely still!" said Macphee.

The ferns on either side of them parted and through the gaps came a dozen of the most ferocious-looking men Thomas had ever seen. Their bloodshot eyes were circled with red paint, their faces striped with white. What made them look even more frightening were the long wooden beaks attached to their noses, from which came the croaking noises. They were quite naked and carried sheaves of thin spears.

Thomas could see what had caused that jingling sound. Some of the warriors had bells, like small cattle bells, dangling from rings attached to the pouches of their genitals.

The croaking became deafening. A warrior stretched out his hand and touched the sleeve of Thomas's shirt. Thomas winced and wanted to run away.

"Don't do anything to annoy them," Macphee said.

The warriors examined the travellers closely, then began ushering them out of the grove of giant ferns till they came to a beaten path through the jungle. They were urged along this for about a mile and finally arrived at an extensive clearing.

Another large crowd of beaked warriors, similarly painted, appeared, all croaking noisily. They escorted Thomas and Macphee through a gate in a high fence into a village of thatched huts. Hundreds of naked women and children, beakless but painted the same ferocious way as the warriors, greeted them. The air was full of one giant *C-R-O-A-K*.

Thomas was terrified, wishing he'd never come on this awful journey.

The croaking stopped. Thomas thought his ears had been damaged, for at first he could hear nothing. But after a few seconds, from the direction of a large hut whose doorway was framed by dozens of skulls—some of them were human—he could make out the twittering of birds. Through this doorway, a old man emerged. His face was painted like the others but he had no beak, nor was he naked. Instead, he wore a long multicoloured cloak that seemed to vibrate as he moved. He looked at the travellers for a moment, then raised his arms and let out a loud squawk.

Suddenly, in some miraculous way, hundreds of fragments of the cloak rose into the air. Thomas realized with astonishment that they were actually small birds, and that the cloak was made of netting upon which they'd been perched. They fluttered around the man's head, screeching and cheeping.

He made another squawking sound and the little birds descended again and settled noisily on the strings of his cloak. He was like a nesting tree on legs. Now he came towards the strangers with mad, red eyes.

At that point, Macphee put his hand on Thomas's shoulder. "Don't worry!" he shouted above the clamour of the birds. He opened his knapsack and pulled out a bottle of whisky. He held it out towards the bird man, who smiled horribly and took the bottle from him. He then pointed at Thomas and called out something to the crowd. Everyone laughed loudly— hearty, delighted laughter. The warriors began to untie their beaks, and they and the women and children seemed to relax.

"They were laughing at how scared you looked," Macphee told Thomas. He too was looking at ease now. The bird man again said something to him, and they talked for a while and laughed. Then the bird man, clutching his bottle, went back into his hut.

"He's the Shaman," Macphee told Thomas. "He was asking me how effective the paint-job was. He says it's a new design and they even frightened each other with it. I told him it was quite scary. And he wanted to know how the dead bird in the tree worked. I told him it frightened the men from the coast out of their wits. He liked that."

Thomas naturally felt quite foolish. "So it's all a game?" he said. "You mean it's like Hallowe'en?"

"Well, there's one big difference," said Macphee. "If we hadn't really looked scared, they'd have been insulted. Then they might just have decided to kill us anyway."

THAT NIGHT A SPECIAL FEAST of roast wild boar and pineapple was held for the visitors. They squatted around a big fire in the village square along with the rest of the tribe.

"The main course might easily have been us," Macphee said as they began eating.

Thomas wasn't sure he meant that seriously, for the Hupu were so friendly. They'd promised to give a display of their skill when the feast was over, to make up for having frightened him. Thomas, accordingly, ate well and drank several coconut shells of palm wine.

After the feast, everyone moved to another part of the village and hunkered down in the moonlight on an area of well-beaten earth before a hut with a woven curtain. As they sat waiting, there was a general buzz of excited conversation, of anticipation. To Thomas, it was like a night at the theatre in some great city—except that this was a remote island in a primal jungle with the mosquitoes beginning their nightly rampage. The theatre lighting consisted of a few smouldering torches, a huge moon and a dazzling array of stars. The audience, of course, was unlike any he'd ever seen in a theatre: an assembly of naked men, women and children, their faces still painted horribly.

The Shaman arrived last. His cloak was laden with his birds, silent now, settled down for the night. He gave a signal and the woven curtain was pulled back.

Thomas, his head dizzied by the palm wine, concentrated on the scene before him.

He had expected a performance but saw instead, on a bamboo platform, an exhibit of a dozen figures carved with amazing skill. They seemed to represent a battle scene from some tribal war. Some were balanced on one leg, or were arched over backwards in the act of falling. Others were shrinking from the blow of an axe or an enemy spear. Others were half leaping in the air as if they were striking the foe.

Thomas couldn't help admiring the extraordinary skill of the carvers who had managed to instill into these inanimate figures such an impression of energy and vitality—he thought it must be comparable to the great sculptures made by the masters of the Renaissance period.

Then the figures moved. He couldn't believe his eyes at first. It was as though he were standing in an art gallery, admiring some statue, and saw it move. What he had thought were carvings were actually living Hupu warriors.

For the next half hour these warriors on the stage went through an astonishing variety of postures, many of them so difficult that Thomas couldn't imagine how the human body could maintain them for any length of time. The audience watched with obvious appreciation of the skill involved, pointing and whispering comments to each other.

At last the Shaman gave a final signal and the warriors on the stage immediately relaxed, breathing deeply, massaging their strained muscles. The audience shouted its approval, the Shaman's little birds awoke and shrieked and the curtain was drawn.

THOMAS GOT TO HIS FEET NOW, with everyone else. He was stiff from squatting on the ground, and that made him admire all the more the ability of the Hupu performers. According to Macphee, they practised the art from childhood, the way children elsewhere practised baseball or football.

Now, one of the Hupu warriors led the two visitors out of the village and along a pathway through the jungle. A hut was visible in the moonlight a hundred yards away. The warrior signalled them to go on but he himself went back to the village.

As Thomas and Macphee approached the hut, they were assaulted by an awful smell, like a million rotting fish.

"It's from there," said Macphee, pointing to a large tree beside the hut. "They call it a Stink Tree. The smell's from its fruit."

Thomas, bloated from the food and the palm wine, felt like vomiting. At first he thought the fruit of the Stink Tree had to be the black, pendulous objects in its boughs. But some of them began to flutter as the travellers came near.

"Bats," said Macphee. "They're safe hanging there. The smell keeps snakes away." Then he pointed to some kernels that looked like white nuts on the path. "Those are the fruit—try not to step on them." He toed one of them gently and from it, amid the general smell, arose the stench of something long dead.

Thomas gagged. "I can't stay here!" he said.

"You'll get used to it," said Macphee. "Anyway, it's the best place to be at night in the jungle. Even the mosquitoes don't like it. The smell seems to get into your blood and they'll leave you alone for a full day after this."

"But why can't we stay in the village?" Thomas said.

"It's another taboo, in case hostile spirits are hiding in us," he said. "Rowland would probably say it's quite practical and protects them from diseases brought up from the coast."

The hut itself was quite clean inside. They stretched out on the dirt floor and Macphee lit a cigarette. The smell of the smoke was very faint.

Thomas couldn't help noticing the absence of the usual mosquito whine around his head. As he lay there, he had to admit he was even becoming a little used to that astounding stink. In fact, under it he thought he could detect a certain sweetness. By the time he fell asleep, he was breathing it in without reserve.

THEY LEFT THE HUT EARLY the next morning. It was raining, as it seemed always to be in the mornings. They were half protected from the rain by the canopy of leaves. No one was awake in the Hupu village, only some dogs barked. As they continued on their way, Thomas Vanderlinden was very thirsty and wanted to drink from a brown torrent that skirted the path.

"Don't," said Macphee, and he held out a bottle of liquor from his bag. "Have some of this."

"But it's water I need," said Thomas, tempted by the stream in spite of its off-putting colour.

Macphee shook his head. "The palm wine's making you silly," he said. "Believe me, a hangover's better than a Guinea Worm any day of the week."

That awful image was the best argument possible, so Thomas put up with his thirst.

AFTER ABOUT AN HOUR'S WALKING, the terrain gradually became flatter. As Macphee had promised, the mosquitoes seemed to have no interest in them at all after their night under the Stink Tree, and that was a relief. Then they came across a coconut grove. Macphee showed Thomas how to split the nuts for their milk.

By late afternoon the jungle had thinned out, and eventually they emerged from it entirely into an area that seemed once to have been cultivated, though the fields were now overgrown with tall, wild grasses. The rain, now they were in the open, was quite heavy again.

"We won't have to put up with it for long," said Macphee.

Soon they were walking on a beaten track in the red dirt, and after a while, a pathway of crushed stone. They followed it and rounded the corner of a low hill. A hundred yards away Thomas saw a building that looked quite modern.

"There it is," said Macphee. "Rowland's place. It used to be a Medical Centre."

It was a wooden bungalow with a shingled roof, and it was surrounded by an elegant verandah in the colonial style. Some dogs barked. Three people were sitting on the verandah awaiting the arrival of the visitors.

– 8 –

THOMAS VANDERLINDEN, approaching the bungalow, was very curious about the man he was about to meet. But he made himself walk slowly, lagging a little behind Macphee.

Two scrawny brown dogs leapt down and ran across a stretch of bristly lawn to meet them, barking but wagging their tails in an unthreatening way. They sniffed at each of the visitors, then led them up the three steps of the verandah to the house, where a man and two women were sitting in high-backed rattan chairs. The man, who'd been reading, put his book on the floor and got up to meet the visitors. He gently helped down a black cat that had been curled on his shouders.

Thomas recognized the Rowland Vanderlinden he'd seen in the old photograph. His short beard and longish hair were grey now, but his thin face, though the lines were deeper, hadn't really changed that much. His eyes were blue and over-bright, perhaps with fever. He wore a white shirt and pants and sandals. The cat was rubbing itself against his legs, looking the visitors over with eyes that were also of an un-cat-like blue.

Rowland Vanderlinden held out his hand first to Macphee. "It's good to see you again," he said. He had quite a deep voice, but it quavered a little. His face was slightly pock-marked and some of his front teeth were black.

"You too," said Macphee. He introduced Thomas. "This is the man who's come all this way to find you."

"So," said Rowland, holding out his hand, "you're Rachel's son." His eyes narrowed, as though he was trying to find her in Thomas. His hand was dry and cool. "How is your mother?" He asked this in a very quiet voice, as though the matter was strictly between the two of them.

"She's fine," said Thomas.

"That's good," said Rowland. "You can tell me all about her later." He then gestured towards the older of the two women, who were still sitting. "This is my Consort," he said, empasizing that odd word. She was a heavily built islander dressed in a plain green wrap. Her eyes had pouches under them and her long black hair was streaked with grey. "And this is our daughter," he said, nodding towards the younger woman, who was heavy like her mother, with glossy black hair. She wore a blue wrap adorned with flowers. Rowland said something to them in their own language.

The women's eyes gleamed for a moment as they inspected Thomas.

He noted that each of them wore a white orchid over the left ear, and how, just between their breasts, the fringe of a tattoo—the petals of a red flower—protruded from their wraps. But he was mainly interested in Rowland, thinking how incredible it was that this man, whom he'd never heard of till a few weeks ago, had once been his mother's husband. He tried, in vain, to imagine them together all those years ago.

The black cat now jumped lightly up from the floor onto Rowland's shoulders. It stretched forward, peering with those deep blue eyes into Thomas's face for a long moment, assessing him. Rowland stayed still while it made its inspection. The two women watched till the cat suddenly lost interest and jumped down once more onto the floor. Rowland made some comment and the women nodded their heads. He turned to Thomas. "Cats are taken very seriously here," he said. "You seem to have passed the test."

On the floor, the cat began to gnaw at its belly looking for some flea or parasite.

THOMAS VANDERLINDEN AND MACPHEE were still standing awkwardly on the verandah. Now the Consort and her daughter got out of their chairs. Rowland handed the book he'd been reading to the Consort. The two women walked slowly to the slatted door and went into the house. The dogs and the blue-eyed black cat trotted after them.

"The women will cook something," Rowland said. "You must both be hungry."

Thomas said he'd been feeling a little nauseated all day.

"Ah yes, nausea," said Rowland. "It's endemic here. In time, we get so used to it we don't notice."

Macphee nodded and lit a cigarette.

"I hope," Rowland said to Thomas, "you don't think it was impolite of me not to introduce my Consort or my daughter by their names."

Thomas had noticed that.

"Up here in the Highlands," said Rowland, "they reveal their names only to someone they've known a long time. They're always afraid a stranger might use it in various spells and curses."

Thomas expected him to make some joke about that, but he didn't.

"Now, to matters of more immediate interest," said Rowland. "I'll show you to your rooms. You can wash up, then we'll have a drink before dinner." He led Thomas and Macphee round the corner of the verandah to the back of the house, where there were several slatted doors in a row. He opened the first of them for Thomas. "I hope you find this comfortable enough," he said.

It was a very small room with a bed and mosquito netting, a table with a chipped basin and big jug of water. A rusted mirror hung over a small chest of drawers with a white towel lying on top. A green robe hung from a hook on the wall with a pair of sandals on a cane chair underneath.

"You can take off your damp things and hang them up to dry," Rowland said. "The robe will be more comfortable." Then he took Macphee to a room farther along.

Thomas stripped and washed himself carefully, sponging away the rot that had attached itself to him on the journey. He put on the green robe and the sandals and did indeed feel better.

MACPHEE, ALSO IN ROBE AND SANDALS, was already sitting with Rowland on the verandah when Thomas joined them. It was getting dark and a lantern hung from a pole. The girl plodded in with a tray of glasses and a carafe of a yellowish liquid and placed them on a little table. Thomas was aware of her hooded, dark eyes lingering on him for a moment, then she went back into the house.

Rowland poured three glasses of the liquid. "It's gin in a mix of fruit juices," he said.

Thomas put it to his lips and sipped. It was very refreshing and he drank deeply.

The girl came in again, this time with a small plate. On it was a fish about the size of a minnow, with a red speckled belly. It seemed a very tiny fish to share among three people.

"A *paru!*" Macphee said. "I haven't seen one for years."

"We don't often have one," Rowland said. "The local Shaman heard I was having visitors today and sent this one as a gift."

"Is it all right if I go first?" said Macphee. He picked up the fish by the tail, licked its belly twice and put it back on the plate. "Lovely," he said.

Rowland held the plate out to Thomas.

"No thanks," Thomas said.

Macphee shook his head. "Oh, the ignorance of strangers!" he said. "If you said no to a *paru* in some places up here, it would be regarded as such bad manners they'd feel obliged to cut your head—or something—off."

"We don't exact such severe penalties here," Rowland said, smiling.

Thomas was a little embarrassed. "Did I make a blunder?" he said.

"You could call it that," said Rowland. "You see, this house is in the territory of the Tarapa people. Tarapa actually means fish-lickers. This little fish is quite rare and can be found only in the high mountain streams. The speckled part of the belly has a narcotic effect. The Tarapa spend weeks fishing for them and sometimes don't catch any at all. When I first came up here, I quickly discovered it would be impossible to understand the Tarapa fully without sampling the *paru*." He picked the fish up and licked its belly twice. "If nothing else," he said, "for some reason it's very good for hangovers."

"I can bear witness to that," said Macphee.

Thomas was already feeling a little giddy from the alcohol on an empty stomach. "In that case," he said, "I'll at least give it a try." He took the *paru* by the tail and touched it with the tip of his tongue. It had a rough texture and the slightest flavour of liquorice. He licked it again more vigorously, twice.

After that, the *paru* was passed around and licked several times till the flavour was almost gone.

The girl came in again, put down another jug of gin and left. Rowland filled the glasses.

This time, when Thomas picked up his glass, he took particular note of the beads of sweat on his hand. He also became acutely aware of the rain pounding on the tin roof.

Its intricate rhythms were like a drumbeat meant especially for him. He tried to figure out its message, pausing with his glass halfway to his lips.

As he held his glass there, a mosquito landed on his wrist. It sucked his blood, all the while watching him with multiple eyes as big as lumps of coral. He was aware, as he never had been, that it was a living being, a creature of flesh and blood, one of a kind, like himself. He allowed it to drink its fill and fly heavily away.

Now a terrifying thing happened. On the floor near his feet, a long-snouted black rodent, bigger than any dog he'd ever seen, was slithering towards him, its glistening eyes concentrated on him. He tried to jump out of his chair and get away from it, but he was stuck as if in some invisible quicksand. He tried to shout out but could only make a grunt.

He heard the voice of Rowland, deep, echoing, from a thousand miles away.

"It's all right. It's just a little *arat*," he said. "It's quite harmless. It helps keep the vermin down." The huge creature passed Thomas by. It began nibbling at Macphee, its horrifying fangs flashing in the lantern light. "It's looking for lice," Rowland's distant voice boomed. "The main thing is not to move, or it'll bite."

Now the *arat* came back towards Thomas. He felt the brush of its whiskers. He braced himself for the pain but felt only a tickling sensation as it browsed at his ankles. He giggled and the creature began to shrink. Then it scuttled away, suddenly a small black animal, out into the rain.

Thomas would have told his companions what he'd just seen but his mouth wouldn't work. He was aware they were talking though he couldn't concentrate on the totality of what they were saying: each individual word seemed so loaded with implication, he became bogged down. After a while, however, he was able once again to follow their conversation and the words no longer seemed so significant. They talked about an old chief they'd both known who had died; about the pros and cons of a plan for widening the passage through the reef; about the need for employment for the young islanders; about the inevitable decay of the traditional ways.

Neither Rowland nor Macphee seemed to have noticed anything odd in Thomas's behaviour, and he was glad of that.

The young woman came out and said something to Rowland.

"Time for dinner," he said.

They all went into the house. The walls and floor of the inner hallway were adorned with a variety of conch shells and with grotesquely shaped pieces of wood. Some of them looked quite surreal: cats with antlers, dogs with swordfish jaws, birds with human faces and tragic eyes. They followed Rowland through an open doorway into a dining room, lit by a hurricane lamp. Most of the room was taken up by a table made of a dark wood, with three place settings. Masks painted in lurid colours adorned the walls; but there were also three bookcases full of books, each bound in the same brown cover, like the one he'd seen Rowland reading on the verandah.

From his seat, Thomas reached over and selected one of the books and flicked through it. The pages were quite mildewed but were entirely filled with a spidery, energetic handwriting that seemed quite recent.

"My notebooks," Rowland said. "I'm an inveterate note-taker."

"Oh, I'm sorry," said Thomas, putting it back.

"Nothing to be sorry about," said Rowland, smiling. "This evening will eventually appear in my notes."

"That won't make for exciting reading," said Macphee.

Rowland laughed. "Perhaps not," he said. "But living up here, I've seen things most anthropologists only dream of. I hope to publish my notes eventually. One of the major problems in my business is that when the researcher dies, his work dies with him."

The girl came in carrying a wooden platter on which were pieces of cooked meat and vegetables. She placed it before Rowland and left.

"Roast turkey," he said.

The meat smelled wonderful. Thomas filled his plate and, after the first bite, knew he'd never again taste anything so delicious. The room was quiet, with only the sound of eating and occasional comments on the food from Macphee or Rowland.

When they finished the meat and vegetables, the girl brought in a dish of some kind of plantain for dessert. Rowland warned Thomas he might find it a little hot. The first bite seemed, in fact, sickly sweet. Then, suddenly, his mouth was on fire. Rowland and Macphee laughed as he downed a whole glass of gin in an attempt to douse the flame.

– 9 –

THEY WENT BACK OUT onto the verandah. The night was black, the rain was heavy, and there was even a slight chill in the air.

"In the Highlands, we have cool nights for a month at this time of year," Rowland said. He gave his visitors blankets that looked as though they were made of rabbit fur to drape around themselves.

Thomas felt he'd been too quiet for too long. "When I was on the schooner from Hawaii," he said to Rowland, "I met some people who knew you. Berkley was their name."

Rowland nodded, but it was Macphee who spoke. "What a pair!" he said. "They can't wait to change these islanders into carbon copies of themselves. Can you imagine a worse fate?"

"I'm afraid it'll happen soon enough," said Rowland. "The Berkleys are like most of the foreigners who come to these places. They think they have nothing to learn. Because the people can't read, they regard them as illiterates. As though it wasn't the illiterates who invented the Bible—and all literature for that matter. Of course, the Berkleys regard people like me as heathen lovers, in more than one sense." His black teeth glinted in the light of the hurricane lamp.

"Wouldn't it be nice to send the Berkleys to the Lumbas for a while?" said Macphee. "That would straighten them out." He laughed and lit his cigarette.

Rowland explained to Thomas: "The Lumba people live on some islands a thousand miles south of here. They're notorious for trepanning. They drill a little hole in the skull right over the frontal lobe. They believe it releases the noxious gases that make some people unpleasant."

Thomas was trying to absorb that when Macphee spoke again. "On the subject of noxious gases, we ran into the Hupu on the way up. We had to sleep in the hut by the Stink Tree."

"Ah, the Hupu," said Rowland. "They're quite something."

"Tell Thomas about the marriage bells," Macphee said to Rowland, who obviously didn't need much encouragement to keep talking about these matters.

"That's a custom peculiar only to the Hupu so far as I know," said Rowland. "All newly wed warriors, for the first six months of their marriage, have to wear little bells attached to the scrotum. When a man approaches his wife for intercourse, the sound of the bell is believed to have the power to chase evil spirits away. And when they're in the act, the bell's tinkling sound is supposed to please the fertility gods so much, they'll visit the couple with a child." He laughed. "But one old Shaman told me the real reason for the bells is very practical. At night, it reassures the girl's parents that the husband's doing his duty. And on the other hand, the jingling's a deterrent to infidelity."

They were laughing over that when the girl padded in with more of the yellow gin-and-fruit-juice mix.

As she left, Macphee nodded towards her. "The Tarapa are supposed to be a weird lot, aren't they?" he said to Rowland.

"Yes, you might say that. My Consort and my daughter are both Tarapa," he told Thomas. "It's one of the most fascinating of the mountain clans, full of little sects and secret societies. In fact, everything indicates the Tarapa have been here for thousands of years." He was very much the scholar now, absorbed in his subject. "A rule of thumb in anthropology is this: the more ancient the people, the more impenetrable their customs." The rain battered heavily on the roof as they sipped their gin. "I've lived here now for many years and I have a Tarapa woman and child. I've found out quite a good deal. But

there's a lot they either won't or can't tell me about their tradi-
tions. I hope some day they'll let me in on their secrets. That
would be quite a coup for an anthropologist."

"Macphee said this house was formerly a Medical Centre,"
said Thomas. "So there used to be a doctor here?"

"Indeed there was—a Medical Officer," said Rowland. "Most
tribes welcome the benefits of modern medicine. But not the
Tarapa. The Medical Officer was a Frenchman called Dupont.
He loved it up here and you couldn't imagine a more sympa-
thetic man. But he could make no headway at all with the
Tarapa. You see, they believe in reincarnation. For them, all
illnesses must be endured, otherwise they'll come back in an
even worse form in the next existence." Rowland shook his
head. "Poor old Dupont. You can imagine that way of thinking
was quite a challenge to him. I asked him why he didn't tell
them that things like quinine were gifts from the gods. He
might have had some success then. But he was a rational man,
a scientist, and he wouldn't have considered telling what he
considered to be outright lies. In his own way, he was as stubborn as the Tarapa. He practises at Venuva Atoll now."

– 10 –

THE RAIN WAS STILL DRUMMING steadily and the jug of gin
was empty again.

"I'll go get us some more," Rowland said and went into the
house.

Macphee yawned and got up from his chair. "I'll turn in
now," he said to Thomas. "I'm sure you two have lots of things

to talk about." He leaned closer and said softly: "Make sure you lock your door tonight." Then he left.

Thomas wondered what he meant, but for the most part, he thought about Rowland Vanderlinden, whom he'd come all this way to find. At times throughout the evening, Rowland had seemed like a younger man, prematurely aged by the climate here. At others, he'd seemed an old man who'd miraculously retained the enthusiasm and mental energy of his youth. No matter; Thomas couldn't help admiring him as a scholar and an idealist who'd devoted his life to this remote place.

Rowland returned with more gin. "So, Macphee's had enough?" he said. "That should be a warning to us. Let's just have one last glass to celebrate the occasion." He filled Thomas's glass and they toasted each other and drank. Rowland inspected him again. "You do look very like your mother," he said.

Thomas had heard that before. He'd often looked in the mirror, searching in vain for the resemblance that was so clear to others.

Rowland now began, in a most friendly way, to interrogate him. Was he married? What did he do for a living? Did he have any brothers or sisters? Then he asked more about Rachel. He was shocked to hear she'd been ill, and even more surprised that she'd been living in Camberloo all those years. "I'd always envisaged her in Queensville in the house by the Lake," he said, shaking his head at this new image of her. Then his eyes narrowed—he was all attention. "Does she have . . . someone?"

"Yes, she does," said Thomas. "They've been friends for years—since I was a boy. He's a physician, retired now. His name's Jeremiah Webber. He says he knew you. You were helping the Coroner and he was an assistant."

"Webber?" Rowland said. "Yes, I think I remember him. And you say she's known him since you were a boy? So he's not your father?"

"No," said Thomas. "My father died when I was a baby. He was killed in the War. That's why she wants to see you. She seems to think you can tell her about him."

Rowland seemed puzzled.

"He just showed up one day using your name," said Thomas.

Rowland sat quite still, saying nothing. So Thomas briefly told him Rachel's story about that day, so long ago, when the stranger had knocked at her door.

Rowland heard him out. "Ah!" was all he said when Thomas had finished. Then a particularly heavy downpour caused a loud drumming on the roof. It was well after midnight now, and mosquitoes, sheltering from the rain, were whining around them.

"So, does it make sense to you?" said Thomas when the drumming eased up. "Do you know who he was?"

Rowland slowly nodded his head.

"Yes," he said. "Indeed I do."

"Then you'll come back with me and talk to her?" said Thomas. "She said to remind you you'd once promised her you'd come if she needed you." Then he said something he hadn't even allowed himself to think. "I don't know how much longer she has to live. It would mean a lot to her."

Rowland didn't hesitate. "Of course I'll come. I haven't forgotten my promise. I'm looking forward to seeing her again.

Even though we separated, we were never nasty to each other. We just couldn't live together." The black teeth glinted. "As a matter of fact, I've been planning a book on my research among the Tarapa. I'll take some of my notebooks along and see what the University Press thinks. But you must understand—you have to make Rachel understand—I won't be able to stay long. This is where I belong."

Thomas was delighted it had been so easy. "When should we start?" he said.

"Tomorrow morning," said Rowland. "There's no point in lingering." He got up out of his chair. "Well, we'd better call it a night. I must go now and tell my family I'll be gone for a while. I can't say I'm looking forward to that." He picked up the *paru* and licked it and passed it to Thomas. "Have a last lick— it'll help counter the effects of the gin."

Thomas took the fish and ran his tongue along the spotted part twice, like Rowland. It clung to his tongue, though it had no taste any more. He got to his feet unsteadily.

"By the way," Rowland said, "make sure you shake your boots out in the morning before you put them on—there are scorpions and poisonous spiders and various other insects that like to climb into them at night."

Thomas thanked him for that information. And he wondered, for the thousandth time, why anyone would want to live in such a place.

Rowland again seemed to read his mind. "To an outsider," he said, "it may seem like chaos here. But under it all, you have a sense there's really some kind of order that's so complicated you can't quite pin it down. Maybe if you could just find that order, it wouldn't matter where you lived." His face looked very weary. "At times, I've thought it might have been nicer just to have stayed at home, studying the slowness of change—you know: watching the pattern fade on the sofa in the living room and all of that. It seems to satisfy most people. But it wasn't the life for me."

Rowland looked his age now and Thomas wondered about him. How capable would he be of making the strenuous journey down through the jungle to the coast? Then sailing halfway across the world? And then making the return trip? He was thinking that as Rowland said goodnight and went inside. Thomas got to his feet and had to hold on to the arms of the chair to stop falling. He walked as steadily as he could, the rain pounding an accompaniment, round the corner of the verandah to his room.

– 11 –

THE ROOM WAS LIT BY A CANDLE that made little hissing noises as it incinerated wandering mosquitoes and moths. On the table beside the candle was a red orchid in a green vase. Thomas's attention was again drawn to the drumming of the rain on the roof. It had undergone another remarkable change in pitch and rhythm and seemed no longer a random production of nature but something artificial and full of meaning. He was both astonished and too fatigued to think about it. He slipped off his sandals. The night was cool, so he kept the robe on. He blew out the candle and got into bed, pulling the mosquito net around him. The few mosquitoes that had managed to come in with him whined around his head. He swatted at them tiredly and, in the midst of that activity, fell asleep.

Not long after, he heard the door creak. The rain must have stopped, for the moon had come out and was lighting up the entire room. He would have turned towards the door but felt as though a heavy boulder lay upon him, pinning him down.

Two shapes approached his bed, one on either side. He tried to speak but could manage only a whimper. The mosquito net was lifted and in the moonlight he could clearly see two women—he was sure they had to be the Consort and the daughter. But he couldn't be certain which was which. They wore lurid wooden masks, like those he'd seen on the wall of the dining room. Their heavy bodies were completely unclothed and shone with oil. Each of them was tattooed from the neck down to the navel in the shape of an intricate red orchid. In the very heart of the flower crouched a great insect, its tattooed eyes yellow in the moonlight.

One of the women leaned over him and opened his robe. The other held out a little box, opened the lid and shook something from it onto his belly—something light and cold that felt like a dead leaf. The leaf began to move. It scrabbled softly along his body onto his chest towards his face. With a grunt of effort, he was able to raise his head a few inches to look.

A huge scorpion, its tail raised to strike, stood on his chest. He braced himself, ready for the stab of pain. But suddenly, the scorpion wheeled around and began to move down his body in the other direction, over his belly, and down, down. He sobbed, and tensed his body, awaiting the excruciating sting.

At that very moment, the woman with the box lowered it on the scorpion and scooped it away from him. He could have wept with relief, with joy. Now the other woman climbed heavily onto the bed. She straddled herself over him and looked down at him. Through the holes in the mask, he could see dark, oily eyes. Whether it was mother or daughter, he didn't care. A wave of euphoria swept through him as she enclosed him in her soft, moist warmth. She rocked back and forth, back and forth. He was unable to restrain himself. He let out a great howl of pleasure.

MACPHEE CAME THROUGH THE DOOR, pulling on his robe. "Are you all right?" he said. "What's the matter?"

Thomas, who found he could move now, pulled his own robe together and raised the mosquito net. The little room was clearly illuminated by the moonlight, and there were no women.

"I . . . I'm sorry," he said. "I thought someone was here . . . Look," he said. On the floor lay a broken vase with the red orchid spilled out of it.

"It must have been the cat," said Macphee. "I thought I saw it running out of here. Your door was wide open. I told you to lock it. Bolt it now after me."

He left, and Thomas slid in the bolt and went back to bed. He lay for a long time trying to re-create that strange dream— if dream it was. But it was like looking at the outline of something through frosted glass, and the effort wore him out. He fell into a deep sleep.

At first light, the crowing of a cock awoke him. He felt quite refreshed, in spite of the gin the night before. He got out of bed and looked around the room carefully but could find no sign of intruders—only a regiment of ants swarming over the red orchid on the floor. He picked it up between thumb and finger, went out onto the verandah and dropped the orchid and its tiny predators into the long, wet grass.

– 12 –

THOMAS VANDERLINDEN DRESSED and walked round the verandah to the front door. Macphee was already sitting there, looking well rested, his long hair slicked back. He was smoking one of his first cigarettes of the day and was contented. "We're to have breakfast out here," he said.

Thomas sat down and waited. After a while, the girl came padding out of the house carrying a tray of food and coffee. Her hair was freshly oiled and she was wearing a bright yellow wrap with the tattoo protruding. Thomas, sure now he knew what that tattoo was, looked at her for any hint that he hadn't been dreaming the night before. But she seemed quite at ease, her dark eyes betraying nothing. She put the tray down on the little table, poured cups of thick coffee with a steady hand and left. If she was innocent, Thomas thought, might it have been the Consort who straddled him? In those masks, in the moonlight, it had been impossible to tell which was the younger of the two women. Of course, it might have been strangers, interlopers. Or it might all have been a dream.

He ate some fried plantains from a platter on the tray and was sitting back sipping his coffee when Rowland joined them. In the morning light, his face was wrinkled from too much sun and yellowish from whatever fevers he had contracted over a lifetime in such a climate. Like his visitors, he was now dressed for travelling, wearing brown walking boots that were well worn. He seemed anxious and didn't talk much over his coffee.

When he'd finished, he got up and took a deep breath. "Well, I'd better get this over with," he said, and went inside.

THOMAS AND MACPHEE WERE WAITING, ready to depart. Rowland had been gone for ten minutes. There was a loud noise from inside the house and he came through the door, carrying a duffle bag. The two women followed him, howling. Indeed, now that they were outside, their howling was raised a notch into a scream. Thomas had to brace himself against it, as if against a strong wind at sea.

"Don't worry," Rowland shouted. "It's a custom!" He seemed quite proud of the noise they were making.

Thomas could see that the women's eyes were quite dry and that they were watchful.

The three men set off down the path, the noise pursuing them.

"It doesn't mean they'll miss me that much," Rowland told Thomas. "They just want to give the spirits a sample of the kind of racket they'll make if I don't come back."

As soon as they entered the outer fringe of bush, the screaming stopped. Then the jungle birds, which had been silent, began to make their sounds. They were tentative at first, as though after a storm, then confident, then so raucous all human cries would have been obliterated.

– 13 –

AFTER THE RELATIVE COOL of the Highlands, the journey back down to where the two canoes were waiting seemed to Thomas like a slow immersion in a sauna—a sauna into which a million biting insects had been released with no desire for any food except human flesh and blood. Rowland worried about the notebooks in his bag—he refused to wade through deep water in case he might ruin them. "I've lost all my notebooks once before," he said. "I don't want that ever to happen again." He seemed impervious to the insects, however, and didn't slow their descent in any other way.

He even saved them time by taking a route that skirted round Hupu territory. "They'd expect me to stay with them for a while," he said. "They've no conception of what it means to be in a hurry."

The canoes and the four paddlers were ready at the appointed spot. They spent the night there before the final part of the journey down to the coast.

BEFORE LEAVING ON THAT LAST MORNING, they ate some bread Rowland had brought, toasted over the campfire.

Macphee had already breakfasted on gin, and that loosened his tongue. "I forgot to mention to you, Rowland," he said, "Thomas thought he had some visitors in his room at your place. Why don't you tell him about it, Thomas?"

Thomas was reluctant, but described the visitation briefly. "Maybe it was only a dream," he said when he'd finished. "But I don't usually remember my dreams, and this one seemed so real. Maybe it was the fish-licking brought it on."

"I warned him to lock his door," said Macphee.

"You can't lock your door against dreams," said Rowland. "And if it was a dream, Thomas, it was very curious. Among the Tarapa women, there's a cult called the Cult of the Scorpion, and it so happens that their major fertility symbol is a scorpion with its stinger raised."

"Are your Consort and your daughter members of the cult?" Macphee asked.

Thomas was uncomfortable with such bluntness, but Rowland seemed quite happy to answer. "They might well be," he said. "They have the scorpion tattoo, but so do many other women who aren't in the cult. As I told you, the Tarapa love their secrets. So even if my family are members, they certainly wouldn't tell me. But, you know, Thomas, among the Highland tribes, when sex is involved in a ritual, it's usually for a benevolent purpose. A kind of a blessing. It could have been anyone— if your door wasn't locked, visitors could have come in and taken advantage of you!" He laughed at that. "Anyway, no real harm was done, was it? The whole thing sounds quite enjoyable, aside from the scorpion part." He seemed amused by the entire matter.

Macphee blew a smoke ring towards Thomas. "Well, that depends," he said. "If anyone dropped a scorpion on me during sex, I'd lose all interest. How about you, Thomas?"

Thomas just shrugged.

"If I remember rightly," Macphee said to Rowland, "two government officials were tied up and scorpions let loose on them by some tribe up in the Highlands years ago. Isn't that so?"

"All I can say is I've lived there for twenty years," said Rowland, "and no one's ever tried to terrorize me."

"As if you'd even notice," said Macphee. He turned to Thomas. "What's terrifying to most people is fascinating to Rowland." He was a little drunk, but he meant this as a compliment. And Rowland took it as such.

– 14 –

THE JOURNEY TO THE COAST was uneventful. They got back to the Equator Hotel in the late afternoon and stayed overnight. The next morning, Macphee and Rowland and Thomas went down to the beach where the big outrigger canoe for Vatua lay alongside a jetty. Macphee would be remaining on Manu a while longer. He'd been retained by Lloyd's to make inquiries about a freighter that had run onto a reef a few miles to the north and sunk, all hands lost.

At the jetty, he shook hands with Thomas. The familiar smell of alcohol and tobacco that emanated from him now made Thomas a little sentimental, but he confined himself to formalities. "Thank you for all your help," he said.

Macphee, accustomed to a life of transient friendships, was matter-of-fact. "It's my job," he said. "But if you're ever down this way again, look me up and we'll have a drink." He said this as though he actually believed it was possible Thomas might come back in the foreseeable future. Perhaps that was his way of dealing with these final partings.

Macphee then shook Rowland's hand. "Radio me the date of your return and I'll meet you here," he said.

Thomas and Rowland walked along the jetty and climbed into the big outrigger canoe. A dozen islanders were already aboard, and it was clear from their anxious whisperings and the way they looked at Rowland that they wished he were not coming with them.

The outrigger cast off before a brisk offshore breeze and skimmed quickly towards the gap in the reef. As it surfed through and out into the swells of the ocean, Thomas looked back to the shore. Through the palm trees, he caught a glimpse of Macphee walking along the path in the direction of the Equator Hotel, no doubt looking forward to a liquid lunch.

But Macphee was soon gone from his mind. The wind was strong, the sky was gloomy, the canoe was tossed about in the menacing waves. The crew and the passengers—even the children—looked fearfully towards Rowland, who sat with a strained smile on his face.

After a while, Thomas couldn't stand it. "What's wrong with them?" he said.

"They know I'm from the Highlands," Rowland said. "They blame me for the rough weather." He reassured Thomas: "Don't worry about it. We're safe. They're afraid it might bring them even worse luck if they threw me overboard."

THEY ARRIVED AT VATUA in time for the schooner. It wasn't the *Innisfree*, as they'd hoped. Rowland had looked forward to renewing his acquaintance with Captain Bonney, but he hadn't yet returned from a voyage south.

Nor was the trip a pleasant one. This Captain was an aloof Englishman who had nothing to do with the passengers, of whom there were only two: Thomas and Rowland. In addition, the ship was slowed at first by adverse winds, and then it was becalmed in the doldrums—nothing but oily seas, creaking timbers and boredom. Both passengers tried to keep themselves busy. Thomas read and Rowland wrote for hours each day in his notebook. Sometimes he'd read those other bound notebooks he'd brought in his duffle bag—the ones he intended to show to the publisher. As he read them, he'd frown, smile, sigh, purse his lips or roll his eyes. "It's like living my experiences over again," he said when he saw Thomas watching. "But without most of the bodily discomforts."

THEY WERE BOTH DELIGHTED when, in due course, they docked at Honolulu. During the one-day stopover, Thomas cabled Jeggard to inform him of their progress. Then they caught the steamship for Vancouver, looking forward, at last, to a restful trip.

But this voyage too was disappointing: the ship experienced the worst kind of Pacific winter weather—high winds and huge seas. Wet tablecloths had to be used in the dining rooms to stop the plates from sliding off the tables during meals. Most of the passengers—and even some of the crew—were seasick. No one was unhappy when the ship reached the sheltered waters of the Gulf Islands and docked at Vancouver on a chilly December morning. Thomas bought winter clothing for each of them, and the next day they caught the train for the journey eastward.

– 15 –

DURING THAT FIVE-DAY JOURNEY, as the train wormed its way ever deeper into the continent, Rowland Vanderlinden marvelled at the beauty—in spite of the now frequent snow—of the Canadian landscape that slid past the window of the double-bunked compartment.

"Why did you leave, if you like it so much?" said Thomas.

"That's one of the great paradoxes for the traveller," Rowland said. "If you leave, you wish you'd stayed; if you stay, you wish you'd left."

Thomas didn't dispute this. During their long ocean voyages they'd got along very well together. Rowland had worked daily on his notebooks but had often encouraged Thomas to tell him about his study of obscure matters of the sixteenth and seventeenth centuries. He'd been the ideal, inquisitive listener.

Now, during these five days, Rowland began to talk more and more about himself in the years before he finally settled in Manu. Thomas suspected he was rehearsing what he intended to tell Rachel about his life since they had parted so long ago.

Once or twice, he hinted grimly at something quite devastating he'd gone through at one point.

Thomas pressed him to talk about that, too, but Rowland seemed genuinely distressed. He said not yet, that he was afraid talking about it would cause him to relive it. "A little later, perhaps," he said.

Otherwise, he seemed to enjoy telling Thomas about "the early days," as he called them. Often, the view from the window reminded him of some incident. For example, on a morning when the train was traversing a mountain pass through the Rockies, dwarfed by the granite walls, he turned to Thomas, his eyes milky blue as though he were remembering a dream. "These mountains," he said, "are just like the approaches to the Hai'ia Mashina Range. It stretches for six hundred miles south of the Great Plain of Tibet. When I left Canada for the last time, I managed to get a berth on a freighter bound for Calcutta. I wasn't really sure where I was going from there. The only other passengers on the ship were some mountain climbers who were headed for the Hai'ia Mashina range. They said I was welcome to join them. I wasn't a climber but, like many anthropologists at that time, I did have a great interest in comparative religions. I knew that no outsider had ever visited the great monastery of Masalketse, which was renowned for its esoteric practices. It just happened to be in the Mashina Range, in one of the most forbidding landscapes in the world."

Thomas, as he did throughout the rail journey, settled in the corner of the compartment and listened, half looking out at those granite heights, wondering why Rowland always seemed drawn to places most people avoided.

ROWLAND ACCOMPANIED THE EXPEDITION till it trekked near the monastery, which looked like a huge, dark fortress on a snowy plateau. He wished good luck to his climbing friends and he himself went to the monastery gate.

The Porter, who spoke broken English, was not very welcoming but agreed to consult the Abbot. When he returned to the gate, he told Rowland that the monks were just about to begin the Spring fast, which lasted one lunar month. If

Rowland would join the fast and successfully endure it, the Abbot would regard this as a sign that he be allowed to stay on for a time and observe their singular monastic practices.

Rowland agreed to give it a try. He'd been in many rough situations in his work and hoped he'd be able to cope. He was assigned a stone cell with a blanket and no heating, in the sub-zero temperatures. The only food permitted was goat's milk once a day.

He got through the first night with some difficulty, for it was very cold. The second day was tougher. His cheeks were so cold that the saliva in his mouth was turning to ice. All the hairs in his nose became little stalactites. He eyes felt like ice cubes—they clicked when they moved. On the third day, after drinking the goat's milk, he became violently sick and overnight he developed a fever. Whether because of the fever or the cold, his teeth chattered so hard together that three of his incisors splintered.

The Abbot, a wizened little man with bright eyes, came to see him in his cell. With the help of the Porter, he congratulated Rowland on having achieved so quickly a near-death condition—a rare privilege, and just the thing, apparently, for entering a state of deep meditation.

At least, that was what it sounded like to Rowland, who in any case had had enough of his monastic experience. He managed to make the Abbot understand that he really didn't want that enviable near-death state. He'd rather have a full belly and a warm fire, thank you.

Accordingly, bread and roast lamb were brought and a brazier of red-hot coals was placed in the cell. Because of his broken teeth, he had an awful job eating. But after two days of recuperation, he was well enough to be escorted to a nearby village. Feeling a little embarrassed, he wanted to send his apologies to the Abbot for being so frivolous and weak-willed. But according to the Porter, the Abbot had told the monks that Rowland was actually a divine messenger: "This stranger," he'd said, "was sent to teach us that enlightenment is not possible in each incarnation. Learn from him."

ROWLAND, ON THE EASTWARD TRAIN, smiled at Thomas. "At least, those may have been the Abbot's words," he said. "The Porter's English wasn't that good. I fear it's often been the case in anthropology that what we took to be gems of traditional wisdom turned out to be simple mistranslations. The great lesson I learned in the monastery—which of course I ought to have already known—is just how easy it is to idealize another culture from a distance. Once you're a participant, it's quite a different matter."

The train rumbled through a long tunnel and the compartment lights flickered. When it re-emerged, Rowland lifted his upper lip and showed Thomas his three black teeth. "See?" he said. "They're my permanent souvenirs of that time in the monastery. Years later an Abyssinian dentist made them out of black ivory to replace the incisors. But that's another story."

TWELVE HOURS LATER, as the train was descending into the foothills of the Rockies, the terrain reminded Rowland of another of his earlier experiences. "The landscape was just like this," he told Thomas. "The Maharajah of Bakhstan's Summer

Palace was built among the foothills. I worked there for a very short time—at the library. The previous librarian had died suddenly. Shall I tell you about that? It has a certain interest, if I may say so."

"Please do," said Thomas.

THE LIBRARY ITSELF WAS QUITE PALATIAL and was renowned for its collection of ancient manuscripts. As was quite common in old libraries, some of the parchments that dealt with occult matters had been treated with an acidic residue that could corrode unprotected skin and blind naked eyes. So Rowland had to wear glasses and gloves whenever he handled them.

He also acted as curator of a little museum in which the Maharajah's ancestors had gathered the usual oddities: a stuffed, three-headed cobra, a hill tribesman's hand with seven fingers (including two juxtaposed thumbs) and so on.

The centrepiece of the collection, however, was a ten-foot-high, one-thousand-year-old pyramid built from the preserved heads of the Maharajah's male ancestors. Their expressions were exactly as they looked at the moment of death, and the family likeness (especially the huge ears) over a millennium was remarkable.

But from Rowland's standpoint as an anthropologist, what made the job most valuable was the proximity of the library to the territory of a remarkable tribe in the foothills—the Kori. According to all reports, they had, over the course of time, reversed the normal behaviour of the sexes. Among the Kori, it was the women who were the swaggering, hard-drinking warriors. The Kori men, on the other hand, cleaned house, cooked and reared the children. Observers said the men were not happy with their lot. Their major complaint (when they were washing linens down at the riverbank with the other house-men) was that only when their wives were drunk did they show any affection.

Rowland had never heard of anything so odd and was looking forward to doing some definitive research on the Kori.

But before he could, a problem arose.

The problem took the shape of the Maharahnee of Bakhstan, who had personally interviewed Rowland for the library position. She had studied at Oxford and wrote poetry in the traditional Bakhstan forms. She was an enticing woman with a throaty voice and heavy, dark eyelids. One day, not long after Rowland's arrival, in the midst of a discussion about new acquisitions, she told him—as though it were part of the job description she'd forgotten to mention at the interview—that she would expect him, like the preceding librarian, to be her lover. She was quite beautiful, and Rowland was not averse to that prospect. Till she added, as an afterthought, that in a palace with five hundred servants, their love affair would inevitably be discovered. Her husband, the Maharajah, in turn, would be duty bound to have Rowland decapitated.

From the way she said this, Rowland could see that, to the Maharanee, it should be an honour for any man to sacrifice himself in this way. He thought it better to inform her immediately that he'd forgo the honour.

The Maharanee's heavy eyes now bulged with anger. Didn't he understand, she said, that it was impossible to refuse? That she herself would be obliged to inform the Maharajah of the insult? That her husband would certainly have him beheaded for refusing his wife? Hadn't anyone told him that this had been the fate of the previous occupant of his job? She'd give him just twenty-four hours to come to his senses.

Rowland didn't need twenty-four hours. That night, in the darkness, he slipped out of the palace, carrying only his notebooks in a backpack, and braved swamps, jungles and the ubiquitous spoor of the Maharajah's guard-tigers to escape to the relative safety of a neighbouring state.

IN THE TRAIN, Rowland shook his head at the memory and smiled at Thomas. "Not the kind of predicament you'd expect a librarian to get into!" he said.

Thomas might have said he wasn't all that surprised when the librarian was Rowland Vanderlinden. But instead he just smiled back.

THE TRAIN LEFT THE ROCKIES far behind. It steamed across the flatlands of the western provinces like an ocean liner, its bow throwing up a great wave of snow. On an afternoon of low clouds, Rowland, sitting by the window, sipping a cup of coffee, put down his notebook.

"I've just been reading over my notes on my visit to the Institute for the Lost," he said. "I went there not long after I left India. I must say, the Institute was a very interesting place. I wonder if it's still in existence."

"The Institute for the Lost?" Thomas said. "I don't think I've ever heard of it."

"It was located on a island off the Great Barrier Reef," said Rowland. "I went there to interview the founder. Doctor Yerdeli was her name—Hungarian, I think. She was one of the most famous psychologists of that time. She'd come up with the idea of manufacturing pasts for those who suffered from some irreversible amnesia."

"Please tell me about her," said Thomas.

"With pleasure," said Rowland.

DOCTOR YERDELI WAS A TINY, DYNAMIC WOMAN with an odd kind of stutter in her speech. She'd had such great success in her therapy that she'd begun to expand her scope. Now she offered the service not just to amnesiacs but to *all* who were dissatisfied with their personal histories. For a modest sum, she and her team of experts would invent a new, guaranteed original past, tailored to each client's needs.

Rowland, like many of his peers, was skeptical. As Doctor Yerdeli showed him around the Institute, he said that, as an anthropologist, he believed in the *natural evolution* over time of individual histories and cultures. He wondered how she could justify such artificial interventions.

She said it all began with the infamous case of the Mackenzie family: two brothers and two sisters. When they were very young, their father—a doctor—had murdered their mother, cut off parts of her body and implanted them in the abdomens of the four children. They survived the awful surgery. He was hanged in due course.

By the luckiest of chances, Doctor Yerdeli, who was working in Outer Borneo at the time, came across one of the children—

the younger brother, Amos. He was in a jungle hospital, dying and convinced he was slowly being transformed into some kind of tropical plant.

Doctor Yerdeli was convinced that his delusion was the inevitable result of his past trauma. She was certain, if she'd had the opportunity, that she could have invented a plausible, alternative childhood for him to believe in and he would have survived quite happily.

It was too late for Amos Mackenzie, but that meeting had inspired her to found her Institute.

Rowland spent one entire day with her, meeting her staff and clients, listening to her views, discussing, debating.

At the end of the day, she invited him to stay on at the Institute. He was flattered by her offer but turned it down, saying he didn't have the kind of training that would be of any use to her.

Doctor Yerdeli raised an eyebrow when he said that, and Rowland realized that he'd completely misunderstood. It was as a patient, not a colleague, that she wanted him to stay. He was quite shaken and was glad when the boat for the mainland arrived and took him away from the Institute.

ROWLAND VANDERLINDEN LOOKED OUT the compartment window. The snow was now falling so thickly that the world outside was blotted out. Only the noise of the wheels on the rails indicated that the train was still hurtling eastwards along the track.

Rowland looked at Thomas. "I wonder if she was right, not only about me, but about all of us," he said. "I mean, that we're all constantly trying to adjust our pasts to account for what we've become, and that often our narratives aren't satisfactory—we don't have the imagination to do them properly. Maybe if we allowed someone highly skilled to invent them for us, we'd have a better chance of being happy."

"I'm sure I've read about the Mackenzies somewhere," Thomas said. "I assumed it was just a silly piece of fiction."

Rowland frowned. "Well, Doctor Yerdeli certainly told me the story as if it were the truth," he said. "And I assumed she wasn't the kind of woman who was capable of lying."

ON A MORNING when the snow was brilliant under a killing blue sky, the train, fringed with icicles, made its way across Manitoba. The landscape was so flat that no matter how loud the engine's whistle, it couldn't find an echo. Thomas had been enjoying a book he'd picked up in Vancouver: *Purchas His Pilgrimage,* a seventeenth-century travel book. Rowland was bent over one of his notebooks. After a while Thomas noticed that he'd put it down and was staring out the window. But his eyes were looking inward, at something visible only to himself.

At that moment, the Porter came in with a tray and poured them each a cup of coffee. Rowland sipped, then talked. "At one point in those days," he said, "I decided to spend some time in South America, so I got on a ship in Cape Town, bound for Rio. We'd been at sea for only a few days when everyone noticed a bad smell coming from the drinking water."

Thomas closed his book and listened.

THE CAPTAIN HAD TO MAKE A DETOUR to the Island of St. Jude to replenish the water. The island was volcanic in nature, with a single mountain in the middle, like a handle on a lid. It had once been a thriving penal colony, then had become a settlement. But during a catastrophic storm, the settlement and the entire population had been completely erased by a great tidal wave.

The island was of great interest to Rowland Vanderlinden, because in its heyday a number of important sociological and anthropological studies had been written about it. The Captain gave him permission to go ashore with the watering party.

The ship anchored a half mile offshore under a heavy sky.

When the boats landed on the rocky shore, Rowland, along with the rest of the crew, was assailed by mosquitoes and stinging flies. As far as the eye could see there was nothing but a sleek, black, rocky plain running to the mountain. The very soil that had once been used to plant gardens on the island had been imported from abroad. The tidal wave had swept away both the soil and all the plants that grew in it, leaving the rock bare once more. Only on the higher slopes of the mountain was a little greenery still visible.

The watering party went past the area where the settlement had once stood. All that remained were a number of huge blocks of stone lying around, like parts of a game abandoned by gigantic children. These stones had been the foundations of the settlement's battlements. Other small, geometrically shaped excavations in the bare rock were postholes indicating the location of houses and assorted structures.

The watering party now arrived at an excision the size of a football field and six feet deep. This had been the settlement's cemetery, also filled with imported soil. The great tidal wave had scoured it clean.

For months after the disaster, ships had come across floating coffins, hundreds of miles from the island, with bones still inside some of them.

This massive indentation was now deep with rain-water. From it the crew began filling their barrels.

They had no sooner started than the sky, which had been very overcast, became even blacker, and flashes of lightning were seen around the top of the mountain. The crew were superstitious, so it didn't take much urging for them to finish their work quickly. They trundled the barrels back to shore and loaded them into the boats in a swelling sea. As they rowed back to the *Cumner*, the only living inhabitants of St. Jude—those mosquitoes and stinging flies—escorted them all the way.

"I'LL NEVER FORGET THAT EXPERIENCE," said Rowland. "St. Jude was a symbol, if ever there was one, of just how flimsy is our grip on this earth."

Thomas was silent. The prairies outside were flat and brilliant, stretching forever.

"It was an awful place," said Rowland. "It was hard to believe anyone had lived there."

This, from an expert in awful places, Thomas thought.

– 16 –

ROWLAND HAD ALLUDED, SEVERAL TIMES on their journey, to one devastating matter he'd never before spoken about.

Now, apparently, the moment had arrived. The train had passed along the shore of Lake Superior and was heading south through interminable spruce forests cloaked in snow. It was dusk, and Rowland's thin face seemed even thinner than usual in the harsh overhead light of the compartment.

"I'd been doing some work along the Pacific Coast of South America at the time," he said. "How often I wish I'd never gone there." He took a deep breath and composed himself.

Thomas sensed what was coming. He made himself comfortable, but alert—the perfect listener, ready for anything.

ROWLAND HAD WORKED at a variety of jobs—anything that intensified his knowledge of the Andean culture. One of the things he'd most enjoyed was assisting archaeological teams to explore Inca ruins in remote, high mountain valleys. He was on such an expedition when, on the very day of his thirty-fifth birthday, he came down with yet another bout of malaria. This time it was complicated by a pulmonary oedema brought on by the altitude—the ruins were in a hidden valley at ten thousand feet. The team's medical doctor told him he might soon die if he didn't get back down to Quibo, the regional capital, and rest up.

So, unexpectedly, Rowland found himself in Quibo, confined to a hospital bed for a week. When his breathing and blood pressure became normal, he left the hospital and checked into a cheap hotel in the Old Quarter. He had time on his hands and took the opportunity to explore the city. Three worlds collided in its architecture: the labyrinthine walls of the Incas, the colonial palaces of the sixteenth-century invaders, the tawdry barrios of the oppressed. Rowland found the mixture intoxicating.

During his convalescence, the position of Assistant Curator at the Quibo Museum of Andean Culture came open. He applied and was interviewed by the Head Curator, John Forrestal, an American who seemed to be in his sixties—a gangly man with greyish-ginger hair and a tall man's stoop. The interview went well; they were comfortable with each other.

Forrestal told Rowland that the previous Assistant Curator had left for a better-paying civil service job. "But you," he said, "seem to me the kind of man who has other interests in life than acquiring wealth."

Rowland understood this to be both a compliment and an oblique hint that the salary wouldn't be very high. "Thank you," he said.

Forrestal stood up. "Welcome aboard," he said. Through his office window, the brilliant Quiboan sunshine glinted on the fine ginger hair on the back of the hand he stretched out.

FORRESTAL HAD SPENT THE LAST TWENTY YEARS trying to preserve ancient Quiboan artifacts. He was more dedicated than were many native Quiboans. Some of the Museum's Board members actually had a hand in the pillaging of ancient graves and archaeological sites for the international black market.

Forrestal (who was really twenty years younger than Rowland had thought) had the ability to tolerate such unpleasant realities. "We do what we can," he said, "which isn't always what we'd prefer."

He was a curious mixture of a man. One Saturday morning, he invited Rowland to coffee and rolls before work at a little café near the Museum. Afterwards, as they were walking to work, he carefully avoided stepping on the dew worms on the sidewalk, and even helped some of them into the shade. Yet, that very afternoon, he took Rowland to the bullfights, where he seemed quite impervious to the suffering of the bulls.

Rowland could hardly bear to watch the sickening violence.

Forrestal assured him that was because he was seeing the spectacle wrongly, that a bullfight was actually the performance of an ancient sacrificial ritual. "The bull represents a tragic hero," he said, "and the Matador stands for the arbitrariness of Fate. He'll sever its spinal cord so that its death will be relatively painless."

Rowland tried hard to look at it that way. But no matter how hard he tried, all he could see was an elaborately costumed butcher, hacking at the bull's neck with a sword, having great difficulty finding its spinal cord; and a staggering, terrified animal, spouting blood from a hundred wounds.

That was the last time Rowland went to the bullfights.

HE CAME TO KNOW HILDA, Forrestal's wife, quite well. The Curator was very proud of her charitable work and her selflessness: she was a trained nurse who laboured daily in the barrios. She was painfully thin, having caught from her patients more than her share of fevers and diseases.

Rowland was often a guest at their home, an old stone house on the mountainside, the walls adorned with woven Quiboan blankets full of ancient hieroglyphs, the rough furniture made by a local carpenter from the now rare Quiboan mahogany tree. Only a photograph of a ship with the Statue of Liberty in the background and a bookcase with the *Encyclopedia Britannica* and a variety of books in English indicated that the Forrestals might have come from another place.

ON ONE OF THOSE NIGHTS when Rowland was invited to supper, he arrived before Forrestal came home from the Museum. Hilda greeted him and poured him a drink. They sat together in the living room. It was the first time he'd been alone with her.

"You must find your work with the poor very satisfying," he said. He was astonished at her response.

She began to weep.

Alarmed, he asked her what was wrong.

"Why do men always have to drag their wives to these awful places?" she sobbed. "Why can't they find things to do in their own countries? Why must they come to these godforsaken parts of the world?"

She wept helplessly for a while, then calmed down. "I'm so sorry," she said. "It's just that I'm worn-out. I'm afraid I'm going to die in this place. I'd give anything to go back to the States. That's where we belong. I want to be able to speak my own language and breathe clean air again."

"Have you told John?" Rowland said at last. "What does he say?"

"I haven't told him," she said. "You know him well enough. He'd never forgive me."

Rowland feared she might be right.

HE WAS SORRY TO HEAR that the Forrestal marriage wasn't all it seemed to be, for he was very fond of them. But he was even fonder of their fair-haired daughter, Elena, who'd been born in Quibo twenty years before. Fondness, in fact, was no longer the word for what Rowland felt about her.

When he'd first started to work in the Museum, she'd been out on a field trip: the Museum employed her to track down and examine sites of archaeological interest. Three months later, she'd returned and been introduced to Rowland. He liked her immediately. She had an office in the Museum and they often talked. She was a mixture of both her parents—an idealist, but practical, too.

One thing led to another. Before he knew it, Rowland had fallen in love with her and—miracle of miracles—she loved him back. It was as though she'd been specifically trained with him in mind, their interests in archaeology and anthropology were so complementary: they both loved to unearth that which was concealed. Even their discussions of their work were a form of love-making.

As for their physical relationship, at times, when they were twined together, Rowland felt they had become one unified being, as when different types of trees are grafted together to become a new species. Elena believed their growing sense of physical dependence on each other was the outward expression of a deep spiritual affinity.

The Forrestal parents approved of the relationship. It was assumed the lovers would marry, in the course of time.

ROWLAND, OF COURSE, HAD A PROBLEM. He hadn't told Elena that he was already married. He'd tried to several times, but she was so convinced their love was predestined and unique that he was afraid his revelation might taint the experience for her. Their love story, for her, was something marvellous: a mysterious stranger (Rowland) from a distant land (Canada) is driven by destiny across the seas to an exotic place (Quibo) and meets a soul-mate (Elena); they fall in love at first sight (almost); they marry and live happily ever after.

Rowland enjoyed that story. Yet he wondered if the true story might not have been a good one too: after an unhappy marriage, a restless traveller (Rowland) washes up by pure chance in a distant country in a strange city (Quibo) and finds, at last (isn't that a miracle too?), a woman of similar temperament and interests (Elena); they marry (after his divorce, of course) and live happily ever after.

Or something of the sort.

Rowland knew he'd eventually have to tell that story to Elena, but not right then, when she was so happy. So he kept putting off the moment he'd have to reveal his earlier mistake.

ELENA ASKED HIM to accompany her, along with a team of six Quiboan workers, on an expedition to explore some deep caves under Mount Arribo. Her father believed that an ancient people might have used those caves for their rituals and that some artifacts might be hidden there.

A week's hike through forests and foothills brought the party to Mount Arribo. It was part of the great Cordillera which, though massive in dimension, was a newcomer in geological time. The sight of the high ranges put Rowland in a melancholy mood. "Every time I see these mountains, Elena," he said, "I realize just how transient human beings are."

"That's why, Rowland," she said, smiling, "we must never waste whatever time we have."

He loved her even more for that.

THEY SET UP CAMP at the entrance to the caves and began their work. For the first two days, they didn't venture in too far in their search for relics of the ancient people. They found nothing but a few wall hieroglyphs that had already been observed by previous expeditions. Disappointed, they came back out and spent the nights in tents outside the entrance.

On the third day, Rowland suggested that this going in and coming back to the camp was wasting too much time. Why didn't they advance as deeply as they could into the cave and stay down there overnight? In this way, the next day they'd be starting from an advanced point.

Elena thought that was a good idea, but three of the Quiboan crew refused to stay overnight in the cave even though they were offered extra pay. Elena wasn't surprised. The Quiboans were superstitious, and it was hard enough persuading them to go into the caves even in the daytime hours. But Sanchez, the foreman, and two other crew members reluctantly agreed to the plan out of loyalty to Elena.

So, the party of five set out into the cave after breakfast. By two in the afternoon, they'd reached the point where they would normally have turned back. This time, they were able to keep going, and by four o'clock they came to a vast cavern. To their delight, they saw, on a flat wall beside a pool of water, a painting of several intertwined snakes with some hieroglyphs underneath. In the light of the torches, the colours were as bright as if the painter had finished his work just that very day.

Elena decided this was a good place to stop for the night. So they made camp in that cavern.

It was an eerie experience, sitting there listening to the echo of water drip-dripping from stalactites into the pool, watching the snakes on the wall painting come to life in the flickering torchlight. Once in a while, they heard a long, sad groan from deeper in the cavern. Rowland and the Quiboans were alarmed, but Elena assured them it was only the wind that had found its way through some fissure in the mountain above.

The night passed slowly. The Quiboans were uneasy and slept with their machetes handy. Rowland held Elena's hand under their blankets. For the first time in weeks, they couldn't make love, because of the lack of privacy.

NEXT MORNING, after some biscuits and water, the party descended deeper into the mountain. The air was becoming warmer so far underground and they no longer needed sweaters over their shirts. Sometimes the passages were so narrow that they had to douse the torches and crawl along, relying on candles in their helmets for illumination. At other times, the ceilings of the galleries were so high that the light of the torches wasn't strong enough to reach them. Rowland noticed, too, that the air was becoming less pure and breathing required a conscious effort.

Around noon, they came to a short, narrow tube at waist height that gave onto another large cavern. The tube was smooth, like the neck of a bottle, and Rowland said he felt just like a cork sliding through it, it was such a tight fit. On the other side, they relit their torches and saw how yellow the flames were in the thin air. Elena wasn't sure they'd be able to go much farther, but they did manage to progress through a number of slightly wider tubes for another hour. They had just come into an especially large chamber when Sanchez, who was in the lead, called out and pointed at the wall ahead. On it were a set of ornate hieroglyphs that weren't painted but chiselled into the surface.

Elena was excited. She explained to Rowland that these chiselled hieroglyphs usually meant a major burial site wasn't too far ahead. Searching for it, however, would have to wait for another time and a better-equipped expedition. She would just make some rubbings of the hieroglyphs for study at the Museum, then they'd head back to the surface.

That was when they all felt a slight *bump*—as though the cavern had been lifted an inch and dropped. It didn't amount to much, and Elena wanted to go ahead with the rubbings. But Sanchez, who'd been her ally so far, said no. His men were disturbed by that noise they'd just heard and would like to get back to the surface. Reluctantly, Elena agreed.

THE RETURN JOURNEY was slightly uphill and so a little more awkward, especially in some of the narrow tunnels where there was little purchase. Whoever was in the lead would laboriously scramble through, then help pull the others.

Everything went well till they arrived at that brief, waist-high tube they'd traversed earlier. Rowland, who'd found it the tightest fit on the way down, was in the lead. Again he had trouble slithering through till Sanchez grabbed his legs and gave him a hard push. Rowland popped out on the other side. He called to Elena to follow. She entered the tube and stretched out her arms towards him. He took her hands and pulled. She was coming through quite easily, her head and shoulders already protruding on his side, when there was another, much louder bump from the mountain above.

Rowland kept pulling on Elena's arms, but she stayed where she was.

"I'm stuck," she cried.

At first, neither he nor she could quite believe it. He pulled, she squirmed, the Quiboans in the chamber behind her pushed. It was useless. The tunnel had somehow constricted and encircled her waist, like a tight ring round a finger.

"I can feel something on my back," she said. "It's heavy. It feels like a rock." She was gasping.

Rowland tried pulling harder. He called to the men on the other side to push as hard as they could. When that didn't work, he tried pushing her back towards them while they pulled. That didn't help. Rowland tried not to panic, but the Quiboans on the other side were becoming desperate. The air in the chamber had been bad enough, but now it was becoming foul. Elena was blocking off whatever fresh air there had been.

Her breathing was now very harsh. She could no longer raise her head to look at Rowland. One last desperate session of pushing and pulling took place, then she begged him to stop. She said she was being slowly crushed by the weight on her back. After that, she became silent and wouldn't respond to his questions. She was unconscious; her pulse was feeble.

ROWLAND VANDERLINDEN CONSIDERED his awful dilemma. Elena was doomed and was slowly killing three other people. Sanchez, his voice weak, appealed to him to do something.

But what was he to do? He waited and he waited. Elena's head was sunk between her dangling arms. Again he felt her pulse: it still beat faintly. Sanchez's voice, faint too, still called out to him for help. But if Elena was going to die, Rowland didn't care if the others died. They were not the ones he loved.

He waited and he waited. In spite of himself, he knew he must do what she would she have wanted him to do. He remembered the bullfights. He slid his knife from its sheath. He remembered the way the Matadors had tried to kill the bulls.

In this case, too, it took many attempts before he succeeded.

THAT WAS ONLY THE BEGINNING of the nightmare. Rowland, at his end of the passage, worked with his knife; Sanchez, at the other, worked with his machete. When the tube was cleared, they could see that the cylindrical stone that had pinned her had been released through a hole in the roof. It was covered in bloody hieroglyphs. They found a way of propping it up while the Quiboans squeezed through the passage. Rowland would have stayed where he was, but Sanchez, himself all bloody, took his arm and coaxed him along with them back towards the surface.

They walked all day long till they reached the outside of the mountain. The other Quiboans greeted them like men who'd risen from the grave, for they'd heard rumbling from the mountain and feared their workmates were entombed. And, indeed, the survivors had been outside only an hour when the mountain shuddered and an infinite number of rocks rolled down and covered the entrance to the tunnel.

HILDA FORRESTAL COULDN'T FORGIVE her husband. She packed her bags and went back to her own country. Forrestal, his stoop even more pronounced, remained. Rowland, haunted by guilt and by nightmares, left Quibo and moved to the coast.

The night before he left, Sanchez, the foreman, came to his apartment. He wanted to assure Rowland that he and the two other men in the party would always be grateful to him. Elena herself would have made the choice he made.

Rowland was too miserable to accept this consolation. In fact, he now wished he hadn't acted. At least he'd have been spared his awful remorse, even if the Quiboans had suffocated. Or if they'd to cut Elena to pieces of their own accord, he'd have been able to accept it. But to have done what he did, to have initiated it, to have participated in it—that was unbearable.

Before Sanchez left, he told Rowland that he and his men were finished with this kind of work: it was clearly unwise to disturb the graves of the ancients. As he stood by the door, hesitant, ready to leave, he spoke again. "I came to tell you this," he said, his dark eyes glistening. "The Señorita Elena . . . she had a baby inside her."

Then he quickly left.

FOR A MONTH, Rowland Vanderlinden was a resident in a seedy hotel near the docks at San Pedro. He felt as though he'd fallen into himself—a brief, devastating fall from which there could be no recovery. He had great difficulty sleeping and drank too much tequila to make himself senseless.

On one very muggy Saturday night he sat at one of the curb-side tables of a café in an alleyway near his hotel. At the other tables, some sailors with their girls were drinking and talking. Rowland sipped his tequila and listened to his heart beat. After a while, it wasn't his heart he heard but the sound of drums from an approaching party of street entertainers. They stopped only a few yards away from his table.

Two of the group were drummers; they wore unpainted wooden masks with curved beaks and recessed eyes. The other two were wrapped in long, hooded black cloaks and stood perfectly still. The drums beat faster and faster. Rowland, in spite of his sadness, watched, along with the others in the café.

Now the hands of the drummers were a blur, the sound a continuous, deafening roar. They stopped. The two cloaked figures stepped forward, slowly unwound their cloaks and allowed them to fall to the ground. Rowland shrank back, knocking over his glass. For instead of the human beings he'd expected to see, the flickering street light showed two lizards, their skins green and blue, moist and warty.

Rowland's mind, slow-witted from a diet of tequila, became conscious of hand claps and admiring calls from the other patrons of the café. He began to realize that the two figures were actually women, their bodies painted brilliantly. According to the way the street light caught them, at one moment they were gorgeous, exotic, seductive. At another they were repulsive, cold, alien.

The drumming began again; the brief show was over. The lizard-women put on their cloaks and came among the watchers, holding out wicker baskets. Rowland dropped some coins into a basket, careful to avoid the glistening, colourful hand.

"It's not paint," said a sailor at the next table. "They're tattooed." His voice was slurred. The mascaraed eyes of the woman with him glittered. "They're from one of those islands near Vatua. The women there are all tattooed like lizards," the sailor said.

The entertainers finished their collection and, with drums still beating, moved down the street, looking for another place to perform.

"Vatua?" Rowland said. He'd heard the name before, he couldn't quite remember where. "Where's Vatua?"

"It's one of the islands in the Motamuas," said the sailor. "The men believe their women can turn into real lizards whenever they feel like it." He smiled at the woman with the mascaraed eyes. "Imagine waking up with a big reptile beside you."

She didn't smile back.

LATER THAT NIGHT in his hotel, Rowland lay in bed listening to the thumps and yells and laughter that penetrated the flimsy walls of his room from other rooms along the spongy corridor. Through a tequila haze, he wondered if the mention of that name, Vatua, which he was certain he'd heard before, might not be a message directed especially to him. He was reaching for any idea that might keep his head above the dark water of despair. He desperately wanted to believe that though, on the surface, life seemed to be as arbitrary as a poker game, it was actually a highly complicated jigsaw puzzle, and that, with persistence, he might discover how everything was connected. Consoled by this thought and by the tequila, he fell into the deepest sleep he'd had since Elena's death. When he awoke, late the next morning, he went down to the docks and booked passage on a ship sailing west, to the islands.

In this way, over a number of years, Rowland Vanderlinden found himself in the Motamua Archipelago, and in course of time arrived in Vatua. From there, he'd eventually settled in the Highlands of Manu, married the Consort and become a father. He'd devoted his life since then to the study of the Tarawa people, hoping, in the end, to produce a definitive account of that enigmatic culture.

– 17 –

IN CAMBERLOO HOSPITAL, Thomas Vanderlinden became silent.

I waited for more. The low hum of the big machine outside the door, which had been like the bass accompanying his voice and every so often coming to the fore, was also silent now. I could see in Thomas's eyes that he was still with Rowland on the train from Vancouver all those years ago. Then he looked at me.

"After he told me about the death of Elena, he was quite drained," Thomas said. "I didn't say anything. I just kept thinking how incredible his life had been and how I didn't envy him in the slightest. His experiences were fascinating to listen to, but who would have wanted to undergo them?"

"Wasn't it awful?" I said. "I mean, what happened to Elena."

"Yes," said Thomas. "He told me later that not a single day had gone past throughout the rest of his life that he didn't remember it. And when he did, his heart would break all over again. He hoped their love had some meaning. He was afraid that if he ever conceded that it could be so arbitrarily wiped out—and that he'd had a hand in it—he'd go mad. Even some mysterious purpose that might always be incomprehensible to human beings was preferable . . . anything at all was preferable to believing that their love and her death were without any point at all."

"How sad," I said.

He shook his head. "He never got over it. Just as my mother never got over the great love of her life." He reached for his oxygen mask and breathed for a while. Then he gave me a little smile. "You've been extraordinarily patient with me. What you want to know is, what happened when we got to Camberloo and he met up with my mother again, after all those years."

Of course, I denied that. "Not at all," I said. "It's been very interesting."

Thomas didn't believe me. "I'm taking so long to bring them together, you must feel I don't want them ever to meet," he said. "I'm not playing games for the sake of suspense. It's just that in life, as well as in books, certain important preliminaries have to be got through before the characters meet. So bear with me. I'm just about to come to their meeting. That's a promise."

At that very moment, a nurse appeared at the door. "It's time for your visitor to go now," she said to Thomas.

"See?" he said to me with a sigh. "Here's another preliminary."

"I'll be back tomorrow," I said.

PART THREE

THE PLAGUE

For Beauty's nothing
but the beginning of Terror
—Rainer Maria Rilke

– 1 –

NEXT MORNING, I sat in the garden, trying to work on *The Kilted Cowpoke*. But I was half thinking about Thomas Vanderlinden and some of the wide-ranging conversations we'd have over the hedge. Just a week before, he'd appeared at the gap with a little smile on his face.

"If you don't know what you're looking for, how will you know what you've found?" he'd said to me.

I'd thought he was talking about my difficulties with my novel, but he wasn't.

"That was Matthew of Paris's question," he said. "His book, *Mundus Mirabilis*, was published in the early sixteenth century when much of the world was a mystery. Sailors still thought the earth was flat and were afraid that if their ships were blown out to sea they'd sail over the edge. Matthew was one of a group of scholars called the Anti-Geographers—they were founded just after the New World was discovered. They said if they had their way, all further exploration would be declared anathema. If voyagers did stumble accidentally on a new land, they'd be forbidden under pain of death to reveal its existence to anyone else."

"That's crazy," I said. Thomas barely noticed I'd spoken.

"Matthew's reasons," he said, "were unusual for a man of his time. They weren't the typical theological objections—you know, the way orthodox astronomers used to argue that there couldn't be any new planets since the harmony of God's universe was already perfect, and that sort of thing. No, Matthew's was an entirely human point of view. He was afraid any new parts of the earth we discovered would be as disappointing as the rest. So he believed it was much better not to look for these places, but to leave them up to our imaginations. He even encouraged those who did travel to distant parts of the known world to invent things about them that would make them more interesting than they actually were." He looked at me with those astute blue eyes. "Maybe Matthew was right. Maybe we've been expending our efforts in all the wrong places. We've explored every nook and cranny of this earth. But as for the understanding of why we are the way we are—as for what's in here," he tapped his head, "there's been virtually no progress whatsoever. In fact, there's probably been a regression. The people driving at one hundred miles an hour, or flying overhead at thirty thousand feet, or living in apartments with all modern conveniences—do these people actually know any more about who they are than the average European four hundred years ago?"

"But back then, didn't they believe some supernatural being was behind everything?" I said.

"Yes, indeed, most of them did," he said. "And it's quite understandable when you consider that survival was very precarious in those days. To drink the water was to invite E. coli; to eat a meal was to risk botulism; to breathe the air in a town like London was to expose yourself to innumerable contagions; to lie down in your own flea-ridden bed was to flirt with bubonic plague. In fact, when you think of it, to wake up alive in the morning in that era was a miracle. Yes, if ever there was a time when people needed to believe in God, or in Something that would give their lives meaning, you would have thought that was just such a time." He nodded his head, pausing for emphasis. "But in spite of all those incentives to belief, there were some people who just couldn't convince themselves. They thought the world was so awful that no god worthy of their respect could have made it. Have you ever come across Robertus Magister's book, *De Periculis Invitis?*"

Naturally, I hadn't.

"It's still well worth reading," he said. "Early in the first chapter he says: '*To ask "Who am I?" is to take a step towards the unavoidable answer "I am nothing."*' Now doesn't that sound very modern? Later on, he says: '*We can no longer remain enchanted by our dreams; nor can we further sustain our souls on the illusions of the ancients; our sole comfort in this present age is the prospect of oblivion.*'" Thomas knew the words by heart and recited them with relish.

"Sounds quite depressing," I said. "I think I'll skip it."

That was another of those rare times I heard him laugh.

"You're missing the point," he said. "It's the novelty of the ideas that matters. How incredible that someone should be saying such things long before our own enlightened times." His laugh was so unexpectedly pleasant I was quite proud of myself for bringing it out of him, even though it was at my expense.

"But where do you stand?" I said. "Do you agree with this man, Robertus?"

His blue eyes gleamed.

"I'm a doubter," he said. "If there is a God, and if he ever comes looking for an honest man, he'll have to choose from among the doubters."

– 2 –

I ARRIVED AT THE HOSPITAL around one o'clock, coffee in hand. Thomas was waiting for me, full of vigour, as if it was the anticipation of telling me his story that had injected new life into him, and not the hypodermic needle.

I sat down. "Well?" I said. I wanted him to get to the point, as he'd promised: the eventual meeting of Rowland and Rachel Vanderlinden after all those years apart.

Thomas pretended to look puzzled. "Well what?" he said.

I enjoyed this little bit of playfulness from him. It seemed to crop up unexpectedly from time to time.

"Oh, now I remember," he said. "You mean what happened when Rowland arrived in Camberloo and met Rachel again? Very well, let me think." He composed himself for a moment; I sipped my coffee. He began to talk.

THE TRAIN CARRYING THOMAS and Rowland Vanderlinden arrived at Union Station in Toronto at ten o'clock on a chilly December morning. Mr. Jeggard, in a heavy winter coat with a fur collar, met them in the Great Hall.

"Welcome back," he said, shaking Thomas's hand but looking, as usual, somewhere past his shoulder. "I'm glad everything went as planned."

Thomas introduced him to Rowland.

"So you're the man who tracked me down?" Rowland said. "Well done!" He glanced slyly at Thomas to let him know how delighted he was at the idea that a man who couldn't look you in the eye should excel in the business of finding people.

Jeggard raised his hands to fend off any praise for himself. "It's teamwork," he said, looking around for their luggage, wanting to be on his way. It wasn't in his nature to indulge in superfluous conversation. "I have a taxi waiting to take you both to Camberloo," he said. "It's already paid for." He led them through the heavy doors of the station out into the chilly morning.

Rowland, who had seemed to Thomas more and more ener-getic the farther they travelled from Vatua, gasped at this sudden exposure to the cold air. His already yellowish skin looked transparent and he shivered in spite of the woollen coat Thomas had bought him in Vancouver. He stopped a moment, looking around to check that he really was back. He breathed through clenched teeth. "I'd forgotten how cold it can be," he said to Thomas. "I can feel the little hairs in my nose freeze up."

Thomas too felt bludgeoned by the sub-zero weather.

They followed Jeggard down the stairs of the station to the sidewalk and passed a group of children dressed in the black coats and berets of the Mercy Orphanage singing merry songs, accompanied by the silent trombones of their breath.

Jeggard helped Rowland into the waiting taxi. "Telephone if you require our services further," he said quietly to Thomas.

"Thank you," said Thomas.

"Then," said Jeggard, "I bid you both farewell."

Thomas got into the taxi while Jeggard walked off along Front Street in the direction of his office.

THE TAXI HEADED SOUTHWEST, passing along the shoreline of Lake Ontario. The lake steamed like hot springs in the frigid morning air.

Rowland was alert, watching everything. "It's changed so much," he said. "The Toronto I knew is hidden by highrises. I always enjoyed thinking nothing would have changed here, that only I myself had changed."

Thick snow began to fall when they were several miles out of the city. In the middle of a farmer's field by the side of the road was a huge, bare tree with black fruit in it—crows, perched on the snow-covered limbs.

"They look like vultures," Rowland said. "In Manu, when you see vultures in a tree, you must always try and slip past without disturbing them. It's bad luck if they fly away." At that very moment, the crows scattered and disappeared into the thickening snow. "Ah, well," said Rowland, "one person's bad luck is often the best thing possible for someone else."

IT WAS QUITE LATE, around four in the afternoon, when they neared Camberloo. The snow was thicker. Spruce trees by the side of the road were stooping under the weight of it. On the outskirts of the town, street lights were stabbing holes in the murk.

"We won't be long now," said Thomas.

They soon reached King Street, where the store windows were specially illuminated for the season. Rowland drew Thomas's attention to one of them, where the taxi stopped at a traffic light. In the window was an ingenious display of a street scene covered in cotton-wool snow, with a toy taxi paused outside a tiny store. "Just like us," Rowland said.

Thomas was thinking about what that might mean when he noticed some passers-by who had also stopped at the traffic lights. Their faces were shadowed under their winter hoods, and for a moment Thomas could almost have believed their eye sockets were empty. He was surprised at the grisliness of the image. Travelling seemed to have warped his imagination in some way. He'd be glad to be home.

Just ahead, he could see the Walnut Hotel, its windows all lit up. It took up the entire corner of King and Queen, like a great ship anchored in an icy sea. The taxi dropped them off outside the foyer and immediately headed back to Toronto.

A ROOM HAD BEEN BOOKED for Rowland in the Walnut for the length of his stay. When he was comfortably settled in, Thomas excused himself. "I'll phone later and let you know the arrangements," he said.

"Are you going to your mother's?" Rowland said. "Shall I come with you?"

"No," said Thomas. "You'd better rest. You'll be seeing her tomorrow."

Rowland nodded. He looked around the room, a large, high-ceilinged room with soft lighting and a huge bed. "I'll read my notes for a while. I wonder what kind of dreams I'll have here," he said. "On Vatua, they say your dreams depend on where you are." He went to the window, pulled the curtains open and stood looking at the world below.

"Call room service for some food," Thomas said as he left.

From the lobby, he phoned for a taxi and soon one appeared, slithering to a halt at the entrance, its exhaust billowing back over it like a cat's tail. As he climbed in, he looked up at the second floor. Rowland was standing with his arms outstretched on the window frame. He might have been a giant insect, or a man crucified.

The city roads were a helter-skelter along which the taxi slewed and skidded its way. Unlike the driver who'd brought them silently from Toronto, this man began to talk immediately.

"You've got to be a real driver in this kind of weather," he said, nodding his round, bald head in agreement with himself.

"Is that so?" said Thomas, but not encouragingly, for he was tired.

"In last month's blizzard," the driver said, "a truck driver mixed up a railway crossing with the Victoria Street intersection."

"Blizzard?" Thomas said.

"You must have been out of town," the driver said. "We had an early blizzard three weeks ago. The snow didn't last."

Thomas calculated that he himself was probably cursing stifling heat at that very time.

"So this truck driver," the taxi driver said, "he made a left turn onto the tracks and drove along them for a hundred yards before he got stuck. He realized then he was on the railway line and got out to go for help. But while he was gone the six o'clock express came along and smashed into his truck, shunted it along the tracks for a mile and piled it into the overpass."

"Hmm!" said Thomas, for want of anything better to say.

"That's what I mean about this kind of weather," the taxi driver said. "Roads mixed up with railway tracks. Trucks mixed up with trains. You're not sure if it's solid road under you or not." He nodded his head. "Yep! Everybody loves the snow. It looks great—but it's dangerous."

"Like a lot of things," Thomas said.

– 3 –

HE LEFT HIS BAG in the hall of his mother's house and went straight into the library. Rachel was sitting in the floral armchair by the fire, a black-and-white cat on her lap, a ginger cat on the back of the chair. The eyes of the cats glared in the reflected light of the fire.

Seated at a table near the bookcases was a darker presence—Doctor Webber.

Thomas immediately went to Rachel. He was shocked at how much she had changed in the few weeks he'd been away. Behind the wire-rimmed glasses the eyes were as sharp as ever, but the flesh of her face was transparent, the little blue veins like live things that were coming ever nearer to the surface. Her hair, in a coil on her head, seemed even whiter than before. As Thomas bent to kiss her on the forehead, the two cats growled at him.

"Penny, Daisy, be quiet!" She tried to sound angry, but Thomas couldn't help noticing how much weaker her voice had become—it lacked substance, like a collapsing balloon. He went over and shook hands with Doctor Webber.

"I'm glad you're back," said Webber. He too looked more wizened than when Thomas had last seen him, though his lips glistened red in the reading light by the bookcases. His eyes were anxious.

AFTER THOMAS HAD EATEN some sandwiches and settled down with a glass of wine, Rachel and Webber began quizzing him about Rowland. Rachel was particularly interested in what he had to say about the two women on the island. She made him describe them in detail, and when he had done so as well as he could, she was silent, stroking the cat in her lap.

After a while she asked: "Does he seem happy?"

"I don't know," said Thomas. "Maybe. It's hard to say what's going on in someone else's mind." He'd often wondered about the sulky women and how they had made those unearthly noises when Rowland left. Perhaps they really loved him.

Doctor Webber had been listening. "He's had an odd kind of a life," he said, as though it was beyond his understanding. "But I suppose it's what he wanted."

"Was he surprised to see you?" said Rachel. "Did he wonder why I wanted to see him?"

"Yes," said Thomas.

"And?" she said. "What did you tell him?"

Thomas thought for a moment. "Let me see. I told him you wanted to know about the man who showed up at the door and called himself Rowland."

She was all concentration. "What did he say?"

"Nothing much," Thomas said. "He said he knew who it was."

"And?" she said, urging him on.

"That's it," Thomas said. "We didn't talk about it after that."

She shook her head at that. "You mean," she said, "you didn't ask him who it was? Or anything about him? Oh, Thomas, Thomas. Have you no curiosity?"

Thomas was thinking she was the last person to accuse him of that—she, who had lived for years with the man without even allowing him to tell her his real name. But he didn't quibble with her. "Anyway, Rowland can't stay too long," he said. "Two or three days at most. He's meeting his publisher in Toronto about a book on his work. Then he has to get back to his family."

"Make arrangements for him to come tomorrow after lunch," she said. Then she sat back, the most faded of the flowers in the armchair. "I'll go up to bed now. I'll need my strength."

Doctor Webber helped her out of the chair and upstairs. She climbed very slowly, both feet resting on each stair. The two cats led the way, glaring back at Thomas, the intruder.

DOCTOR WEBBER CAME BACK down after a few minutes. "I gave her one of her pills. She needs to sleep," he said.

Thomas was alarmed. "How is she?" he said.

"She's been quite ill," said Webber. "She wasn't too well even before you left. She didn't want you to know." He licked his red lips, making Thomas think of one of those medieval saints who would drink a daily glass of pus from the sores of lepers.

"Is she . . . dying?" Thomas asked finally. She had seemed to him somehow shrunken, as though in preparation for the final shrinkage.

"She's the type of woman who'll die only when she's finished everything she needs to do," Webber said. "You know your mother." He slowly blew out smoke, showing the purple-veined insides of his lips.

Thomas was thinking: *No, I don't really know her*. At times her mind to him was like a fish—whenever he tried to catch it, it slipped out of his grasp.

They sat for a while in the armchairs by the fire, sipping brandy, just as they had in the days before Thomas left on his journey.

Webber puffed at a cigar, pursing his lips, savouring the taste of it. "What about that island woman of his?" he said. "I had a feeling you weren't telling us everything."

Thomas told him about that night-time visitation to his bedroom in Rowland's bungalow and the roles of the two women, who certainly looked like the Consort and her daughter.

Webber listened intently. Once or twice his shoulders shook as he listened, as though he might be laughing. "What a fool the man is," he said. He meant Rowland. "To have given up a woman like your mother for a life like that. It's impossible to understand." He said this in the way of a man speaking about the woman he loves.

— **4** —

THOMAS TOOK A TAXI to his home, an apartment in a low brownstone building on Belview. He made a quick inspection tour; his plants looked well—they had been looked after by the superintendent. He ran his fingers along the books neatly ordered on the shelves; he glanced into the bedroom, tidy and black and white. He poured himself a brandy and sipped it slowly, looking out the window at the winter scene of skeletal trees and street lights illuminating the slanting snow. It would all have been very comforting if he hadn't just discovered how sick his mother was. He finished the brandy and phoned Rowland.

"I must have nodded off," Rowland said sleepily.

Thomas told him the arrangements for the next day, then remembered Rowland's earlier comment. So before hanging up, he said: "By the way, were you dreaming when I woke you?"

"As a matter of fact, I was," said Rowland. "I'd put my feet on the rug—it was a silky black rug. But it turned out not to be a rug at all. It was some kind of oil, and I started sinking into it slowly till it covered my mouth and nose and I woke up choking just as the phone rang."

"How unpleasant," said Thomas.

"Yes, indeed," Rowland said. "I hope you'll have more pleasant dreams."

"I never dream," said Thomas.

"Oh, yes, you told me that," said Rowland. "An old Shaman of the Himpolos of Middle Vatua said we do nothing else— that life's a dream. And that what we think of as our dreams are actually the only times we're awake. We get a glimpse of how mad the world is and go back to sleep right away."

NOT LONG AFTER, Thomas, exhausted, went to bed. But he couldn't sleep, unused, after travelling so long, to a bed that was immobile. He remembered the ships he'd sailed on, and the islands, and the trains. He must have fallen asleep at last, for all at once it was dawn. But the dim morning light wasn't accompanied by the shrieks of strange birds, the heralds of stifling heat and stinging insects and rapacious life and violent death. This dawn light was the cold light of the north and the morning was silent, except for the discreet tapping of snow on the windowpanes.

– 5 –

AT ONE O'CLOCK, they waited in the library for Rowland Vanderlinden's arrival. Thomas was standing at the window watching for the taxi. Mirrored in the panes, he could see the reflection of Rachel in the floral armchair, the flicker of the fire reflected in its turn in her glasses. Her two cats lay on either arm of her chair, their yellow eyes on him, an interloper from the predatory world that can't disguise itself from cats. Webber was sitting by the bookcases, a book open on his knee.

A taxi turned slowly into the icy driveway.

"He's here," Thomas said. He went to the door and opened it before the bell could ring.

Rowland's black winter coat and overshoes made him look like a penguin. His face was pinched, but he looked pleased to see Thomas. "I'm glad you're here. It's very cold," he said, as the door closed behind him. "Before the taxi came, I went for a little walk along King Street and I thought I'd freeze."

Thomas hung up the coat then led him into the library.

When Rowland saw Rachel, he smiled and went towards her holding out both hands. "Rachel!" he said. "How nice to see you." If he noticed how ill she looked, he didn't let it show. Thirty-five years of aging might already seem deathly ill enough. She leaned forward in her chair and stretched out her hands to him. He took her hands in his and pressed them. He bent over and kissed her on the cheek.

The cats were appalled at this behaviour of a total stranger and growled, then charged out into the hall, hissing at Thomas as they passed.

Rachel was inspecting Rowland's face, close up. "Your skin's smoother now—the pock marks have almost disappeared," she said.

"I'd almost forgotten them," he said, smiling.

"How on earth did you do that?" she said, pointing at his mouth. "The black teeth."

"That's a long story," he said. "I'll tell you about them later."

Doctor Webber, who'd been standing near, came forward, his hand outstretched. "You won't remember me," he said. "Jeremiah Webber. I worked with you once or twice when you were helping the Coroner."

Rowland shook his hand. "Of course," he said. "I wouldn't have recognized you."

Then he turned back to Rachel, who was still looking him over keenly. They looked at each other with an odd little gleam in their eyes, as though they were trying to superimpose the person in front of them on the one they had stored in their memories.

"Come sit by the fire," Rachel said. "You must be very unaccustomed to this weather. Thomas, pour some brandy."

THEY ALL SETTLED DOWN AGAIN, Rowland in the armchair opposite Rachel, his body hunched into the heat, Thomas at the reading table with Doctor Webber.

Rachel wasted no time beginning the interrogation. She asked Rowland to tell her everything about his life since they'd last met. He did tell her everything, almost exactly as he'd told it to Thomas on the train east—as though that had indeed been the rehearsal for this retelling. As he talked, she seemed, at first, less interested in what he was saying than in trying to comprehend this new Rowland who was saying it.

But she became very attentive when he spoke about his time in Quibo, and his love for Elena and her awful death. When he'd finished, the library was still, with only the tick of the clock and the occasional crackle from the fire.

"Poor Rowland," Rachel said with a sigh. "And yet, it's good to have had a great love in your life, isn't it? No matter how tragic."

"Perhaps, perhaps," he said.

Again there was a silence. Then he took a deep breath and carried on. He told her about how he came to settle on Vatua and about his life and studies there. He was quite open about the Consort and their daughter. He said his relationship with them gave him an invaluable entry into Tarawa society. "Of course, I'm very fond of them, too," he said.

"Thomas told us about them," Rachel said. "I'm sure they must miss you."

"In their fashion," Rowland said. "Yes, in their fashion."

DOCTOR WEBBER REFILLED THE BRANDY GLASSES. The black-and-white cat slunk back in and repossessed Rachel's lap.

"Well," Rowland said. "Now it's your turn, Rachel." He was all business. "I know you didn't bring me from the other end of the world just for a social call. What is it you want to know? What can I do for you?"

Rachel signalled to Thomas. "Bring the photograph," she said.

Thomas went to the sideboard in the dining room and picked up the silver-framed photograph. He brought it back into the library and gave it to Rowland, who studied it for a long time.

The picture had been taken by Rachel herself with a box camera in the back yard of the house. A man with close-cropped fair hair stood looking directly at the camera, smiling broadly. He was holding a baby—Thomas. The day was hot, with a sun-glare, and his shirt sleeves were rolled up, showing muscular arms.

"Well, well," said Rowland at last, looking up at Rachel.

"So you remember him?" she breathed.

"Of course I do," he said.

"He just showed up at the door one day. It was the best day of my life," she said softly.

Rowland looked at the photograph again, then at her. "Thomas said he died?"

"He was killed in the War," she said. "We were together for two years. We were very, very happy."

"I'm very glad of that," Rowland said. "Tell me about it."

And Rachel did tell him, lovingly, omitting nothing—even to that last morning when the fatal telegram came that broke her heart.

"How awful for you," Rowland said. He shook his head sadly. "And so long ago, too. I've often thought about him. I wondered what had happened: if he came here, if it turned out well."

Rachel raised herself a little in her chair.

"Now then, Rowland," she said, "I want you to tell me every-thing you know about him. Every single thing. That's why I sent Thomas to find you."

Rowland raised his eyebrows. "What I know about him?" he said. "What do you mean? What could I know that you don't? I only knew him a few weeks. You knew him for two years."

"No, I don't know anything at all about him!" Rachel burst out, frightening the cat, so that it leaped from her lap and ran out of the library again. "Don't you understand?" she said. "I never asked him anything. Even when he wanted to tell me, I wouldn't let him. That was part of the bargain. Then he was killed in the War and it was too late." She was looking at Rowland, pleading with him. "For years, I thought it didn't matter. Now I must know. Please try to remember!"

"You really mean it?" Rowland said. "You really don't know anything about him?"

"No," Rachel said. "I didn't even know his real name." She shook her head sorrowfully. "Do you know it—his real name?" She was full of hope, as though that answer in itself might be sufficient. "Do you remember it?"

"Yes, of course I do," said Rowland, looking at the photograph, then back at her. "He was called Will—Will Drummond."

She sat back in her chair and closed her eyes.

"Will Drummond," she said. She repeated the name, took possession of it, meditated on it. She softly mouthed the words over and over again, as if trying to make up for all the omissions, all the times she hadn't said it. Then she opened her eyes again. "Now, Rowland," she said, "tell me how you came to meet him. Tell me everything."

"It was such a long time ago," said Rowland.

"We're in no rush," Rachel said. "Just start at the beginning and tell us everything you can remember."

"Well, I'll try my best," Rowland said. He thought for a while. "Let me see. I left to go and do some work at the British Museum. Do you remember that? It was the last time we saw each other."

"How could I forget?" she said without any irony.

He smiled and went on. "I helped with cataloguing the findings of the Syrian Expedition . . ."

— 6 —

AFTER ABOUT A MONTH of exhausting work, it was time for Rowland to go back home. He wasn't especially looking forward to that, for decisions would have to be made. In addition, labour unrest was widespread that year and the ship he'd booked passage on back to Canada was strikebound in the docks at Liverpool. So he was forced to go farther north, to Scotland, where he might still find a ship.

The train to Glasgow didn't have many passengers and he soon found out why. It seemed to stop at every small station along the way. That didn't bother him, for he was able to work on his notes in peace. Anyhow, he'd never been that way before and he enjoyed the wild moorland landscape in spite of the grimy compartment window.

When the train crossed the border, it came to a region of ancient mountains worn down by æons till they were no more than rolling hills. After an hour it pulled into a little town with the sign MUIRTON on the station wall. The station was right beside what was obviously the main street—a typical row of grey buildings under grey skies: a bank, a church, a general store, a café and a hotel.

Rowland couldn't help noticing that, of the dozen or so people walking along the street, some were men with severe limps. One of them had to be assisted up the steps to the café.

While Rowland was watching, a well-built man with a duffle bag over one broad shoulder came into his compartment. He had a battered-looking face. He slung the bag onto the rack and sat at the far corner. Rowland presumed he was from Muirton and thought of asking him about the limping men. But he didn't seem very friendly, and when Rowland looked over at him, about to speak, he closed his eyes as if to sleep. The Conductor appeared shortly afterwards so Rowland asked him instead.

The Conductor seemed surprised at his ignorance. "Didn't you know Muirton's the town of one-legged men?" he said. He was only too keen to tell. "It happened ten years ago. The mine elevator was taking a load of miners to the bottom of the mine. The cable snapped and it fell to the bottom of the shaft—they say it was a thousand feet down. When it started to fall, the miners all used the standard safety procedure. Like this." He showed Rowland how it was done, reaching up and gripping the edge of the luggage rack with his right arm and lifting his right leg off the floor. Then he went on with his description. "When they hit the bottom, the leg they were standing on was crushed." He smashed his right fist into his left hand. "But that was what saved their lives. They were all given wooden legs." He smiled at Rowland, enjoying his audience. "Strangers usually notice the men limping when we stop at Muirton."

Just then one of the limping men came in to the station and hobbled to the ticket window.

"See?" said the Conductor. "Look at his boots."

The limping man was leaning on the wicket, chatting quite cheerfully to the clerk. Rowland could see that one of his black boots, his right, was worn and scuffed while his left was without even a wrinkle.

THE CONDUCTOR LEFT and the train got up steam and began to shudder forward once again. The man in the corner still had his eyes closed, though Rowland was almost sure he wasn't actually asleep. He wondered whether the man was a miner, for he looked rugged enough. But he wore a pin-striped suit and his chiselled tan shoes, though muddy, weren't a working man's.

After about fifteen minutes chugging along, the train slowed down and entered a tunnel. When it emerged it moved at a snail's pace through a pass between some high, bare hills. The Conductor came back in, looking for his audience. "We always have to slow down here," he said to Rowland. "The ground's unstable."

The train was creeping along the side of a hill. The ground fell away on the other side about five hundred feet to a plain that extended for three or four miles till it reached more hills.

"That's the Plain of Stroven," the Conductor said. "See, over there? That's what's left of the town. You get a great view of it from up here."

Rowland, looking down across the plain, could indeed see the remains of what had once been a town. In the middle of it was a great dark hole, like a huge drain into which many of the buildings seemed to have slid. Roads emptied into it, rubble and trees still clung to the edges. The houses a few hundred yards from the hole looked quite intact, though they seemed slightly tilted towards the abyss.

"What happened?" Rowland said.

"They don't know for sure," the Conductor said, "even though it was twenty years ago. It's too unsafe to go near it. Some people think the mining caused it. There've been mines here for hundreds of years. The ground's unstable all around."

"Was anyone killed?" Rowland asked.

"Not many," said the Conductor. "They had plenty of warning and the buildings began to shift twenty-four hours before the hole appeared." He looked at Rowland with a little humorous gleam in his eyes. "So, everybody that wanted to get away did get away."

Rowland took the bait. "Some didn't want to?" he said.

"That's right," said the Conductor. "Some of these people whose families had lived in Stroven for centuries wouldn't go. They stayed in their houses, and when their houses went into the hole, they went with them." He glanced over to see if the other man's eyes were still closed. "Miners!" he said softly. "They're crazy."

Rowland enjoyed hearing these things as much as the Conductor obviously enjoyed talking about them. "Carrick's not too far from the railway track, either," he said to Rowland. "Surely you must have heard about Carrick."

"No. Should I have?" Rowland knew the encouragement wasn't needed.

"I thought everybody in the world knew about Carrick," said the Conductor. "It's about ten miles west of Stroven. It's not inhabited any more either. A disease wiped a lot of the townspeople out." He paused for effect. "Yes, a disease. A weird disease."

"Really?" said Rowland.

"Yes, really." The Conductor smiled, making Rowland wait. Then he said: "The people talked themselves to death!"

Rowland asked him if he was joking.

"All I know is what I read in the papers," the Conductor said. "They say the people talked non-stop and couldn't stop talking and eventually died of exhaustion. They think it must have been the water that was poisoned with something, and that's what did it. But they still don't know for sure."

"Sounds incredible!" Rowland said. "Nothing like that ever happens in Canada."

"Oh, you're Canadian?" the Conductor said.

"Yes," said Rowland.

"Well," said the Conductor, "then I'm really surprised you don't know about Carrick. A Canadian was suspected of being responsible. Then he died too, so they never did find out."

The Conductor had to move on to other parts of the train. Rowland added Carrick to the list of things he'd find out more about. He looked over at his fellow passenger to see if he'd been listening to the conversation. But those eyes stayed determinedly shut, even though his eyelashes fluttered occasionally, making Rowland more certain than before that he was play-acting. He contented himself with making notes on what the Conductor had told him. He planned to do some research into these matters some day.

THE TRAIN ARRIVED IN GLASGOW. The other passenger took his duffle bag down from the rack and exited the compartment without a word. Rowland went to the station cafeteria and ate a cheese sandwich. Then he walked a mile or so down to the river, where the ships were docked. He saw a rundown-looking building, with an even more rundown hotel in it, like a rotten tooth in a mouthful of rotten teeth. The hotel was called the Hochmagandie. Rowland went inside. The hotel bar didn't seem especially respectable and was occupied mainly by sailors and women whose eyes were black with mascara. The receptionist was a tiny man with shifty eyes over a black leather nose-cone covering whatever was left of a nose.

Rowland booked a room. All in all, he stayed there for three days. In the mornings, he'd check out and, with his bag slung over his shoulder, walk along the miles of docks on either side of the river searching out ships bound for North America. But the strike that had driven him from England afflicted all the main passenger lines here, too, so each evening he had to check back into the Hochmagandie.

He now pinned his hopes on finding a freighter that would take him along as a passenger.

On the third day, a dreary Saturday, he'd spent hours walking the north bank. A sudden heavy squall sent him scurrying for shelter into a tavern on the windy corner of a sooty tenement building. It was called the Tartan Arms, its dirty sign like a bleeding wound in the soot.

Rowland went to the bar and had to make his way past a half-dozen men in the soiled dungarees of dock workers. They were gathered round a sailor who had drawn cheeks and yellowish skin. "Drink up," he was saying. "It's on me. Come on, mates, don't be shy." He was a small man and spoke in a high-pitched cockney whine.

Pints of beer were served to the dock workers.

"Cheers!" said the little man, holding up his glass. They all drank deeply, then he smacked his lips. "How good that tastes," he said. "I never thought I'd drink a pint of beer again, mates. I'm lucky to be off that death-ship, I can tell you."

The dockers listened politely to the man who'd bought their beer. Rowland listened too.

"As I was saying, we sailed from the West Coast of Africa," the sailor said. "We were half-way to the Cape Verde Islands, and that's when some of the hands came down sick. We thought it was some kind of fever. You expect fever if you've been in Africa. So we didn't worry about it. But this was altogether different. The sick ones were sweating a lot, then, after an hour or two, the sweat changed into blood. And blood started coming out of their eyes and out of their ears, and everywhere else." The sailor's voice became dramatic. "I'm telling you, mates, I saw it with me own eyes. And, blimey, within an hour or two they were all dead, every one of them. Yes, every single one of them."

The men in the pub sipped at their beer and nodded. They seemed a bit embarrassed because the way the sailor told his story was so stagy—even for an Englishman. But he was buying the beer, so they kept listening.

"Whatever that fever was," the sailor said, "it spread round the ship. Most of us started to sleep up on the deck where the air was fresher, and that helped. But then the Chief Steward came down sick, then the men who'd helped look after the ones that died. My pal, Joe Murphy, was one of them that croaked, and he was as tough as nails. There were fifteen died altogether. Some of the men wanted the skipper to head for the nearest port so's they could get off the ship. But he said no port would let any of us on shore. We'd just have to keep going till we got back here. So we did." He took another drink from his glass. "Now that I'm off her, I won't ever go back aboard. You've seen her anchored right out there on the river. She's got a new Captain now and the company's trying to sign up some men so's she can get on her way. She's still got to get to Nova Scotia with her cargo."

"What's the ship called?" This question was called out by someone who wasn't among the group at the bar.

Rowland looked round and saw to his surprise that it was the man from the train—the one with the battered face.

"The *Derevaun*," said the sailor without turning round. He laughed to his fellow drinkers. "It sounds like a curse, eh?"

"Are they still looking for men?" the man called out.

Now the sailor turned and looked towards him. "Sure they are," he said. "They'll take anybody crazy enough to sign up."

No one laughed, for the questioner didn't look like someone to laugh at. He finished his pint calmly and left, with his duffle bag over his shoulder.

Rowland now came over to the group at the bar. "Do you think they'd take a passenger?" he asked.

The little sailor seemed annoyed at the question. His story clearly hadn't been as frightening as he'd intended.

"How should I know?" he said.

"Where's she anchored?" said Rowland.

"You'll know her by the smell," the sailor said. He looked around at his hangers-on, but again no one laughed. They were not an ideal audience. "A mile downstream," he said grudgingly.

ROWLAND WALKED QUICKLY along the wet cobblestones. The man ahead of him, his bag slung over his shoulder, had a long stride. Rowland caught up with him. "Hello, again," he said. "I'm heading the same way."

The man just grunted.

They'd been walking in the rain and gusty wind for ten minutes before Rowland saw the freighter anchored out in the river with a black flag hanging from its mizzen. In a few more minutes he could make out her name—the SS *Derevaun.* She looked even dirtier than the other freighters they'd passed on the walk down the docks. She badly needed a paint job and some of her plates were dented like the toy of a monstrous dog.

On the quay, directly opposite the *Derevaun,* a stocky man with a fringe of red hair showing under his sou'wester sat on a bollard smoking a pipe. Leaning against the bollard was a painted board that read: QUARANTINE. In his waterproof gear, he seemed very much at ease in the raw weather.

"Are you from the ship out there?" Rowland said.

"Aye," the man on the bollard said, exhaling smoke. "I'm the Bosun. Are you looking for work? We're needing crew."

Before Rowland could answer, his companion did: "I need work," he said.

"Have you worked on a ship before?"

"No."

"What's your name?"

"Will Drummond."

"You look fit for hard work," the Bosun said. "You'll do fine."

"It's not a job I'm after," said Rowland. "I just want to get back to Canada. Are you taking passengers?"

The Bosun puffed and nodded. "Aye. We have some cabins for passengers," he said. Then he glanced at the notice-board. "I'm bound by law to tell the both of you the ship's been under quarantine. We had an outbreak of fever, but there's been no sign of it for weeks now."

He didn't ask Rowland his name.

THEY CLIMBED DOWN some greasy stone steps into a bulky tender. The Bosun seated himself in the middle and rowed them out into the river towards the ship. As they approached the glistening hull, Rowland became aware of a very unpleasant smell—like a sewer that had backed up. All the portholes on the lower levels had iron bars over them.

"Why the bars?" he asked the Bosun.

"She used to be a prison ship," the Bosun said. He reached out and grabbed the bottom of a rope ladder that dangled from the deck. He tied the tender to it and held it steady as first Will Drummond, then Rowland, his bag awkward on his shoulder, climbed aboard.

The Bosun himself, pipe in mouth, climbed slowly up. When he reached the deck he directed Will Drummond forward to the crew's quarters then led Rowland to the Purser's office to pay his fare.

"Welcome aboard," said the Purser. "You're the only passenger."

LIKE MANY OTHER FREIGHTER CABINS he'd spent time in, Rowland's cabin in the midships was no bigger than a seedy closet, badly needing a coat of paint. It had its own clammy smell, noticeable even in the pervasive stink of the *Derevaun*.

He'd barely settled in when he felt the vibrations of the engine and saw through the porthole that she was underway. For an hour, he watched as the dreary riverbank with its shipyards and slums slid by. He worked on his notebooks for a while, too. But his curiosity got the better of him and he went out onto the deck. He was familiar with the structure of these utilitarian vessels so it didn't take him long to find his way around. Amidships, he entered a dark corridor that led to a companionway. He descended several flights of narrow stairs and reached another corridor. He walked along it till he was halted by a heavy iron door. He turned the handle several times and pushed but nothing happened. Finally he leaned his shoulder into the door and swung it open.

An awful stench caused Rowland Vanderlinden to stagger and gag. A long gloomy corridor of barred doors with caged bulbs over them lay before him. Like a diver, he took a deep breath and plunged in. He reached the first barred door and looked. In the weak light, he discovered the nature of the cargo of the SS *Derevaun*.

In that first room, or cell, he saw a group of hairy forms making strange jabbering noises at the sight of him. As his eyes became accustomed to the light, he understood that they were chimpanzees, huddled together at the back of the cell. From there, he went to the next cell and the next and saw that they, too, had monkeys of every sort in them. Pinned to the wall outside the third cell was a printed list, some of the names familiar, some not: angwantibos, gorillas, baboons, macaques, gibbons, capuchins, siamangs, chacmas, lemurs, colobus, hanumans, guerezas, marmosets, spider monkeys.

Farther along the corridor, snorting sounds came from the cells. Rowland glanced into some of them and recognized sheep and goats and other animals. Again, there was a list: anteaters, zorils, babirusas, agoutis, pangolins, aurochs, capybaras, markhors, muntjacs, kinkajous, jabalinas, aoudads, chigetais.

From the end of the corridor, he could hear roaring and angry growls. The doors in that area were farther apart and the cells were much bigger. Inside some of them were tigers, leopards and cheetahs. The very last cell contained four lions, growling at each other because they were in the process of being fed. The keepers, who were themselves protected by bars at the rear of the cage, were using wooden poles pitted with teeth marks to push hunks of raw meat through an opening. The keepers, a man and a woman, wore dark coveralls. The woman had black hair tied back in a bun. The man saw Rowland looking in and nodded to him.

It was Will Drummond. They hadn't wasted any time in putting him to work.

FEEDING TIME FOR THE HUMANS on board the *Derevaun* began after night had fallen, by which time the ship had already left the calm, dirty water of the river and entered the ocean swell. That motion woke Rowland, who'd been having a nap. He realized it was time to eat and made his way to the dining room, where crew members from the off-duty watches were already eating. They paid little attention to his entry. Sitting at a corner table were Will Drummond and the woman who'd been with him in the animal cells. He saw Rowland and again nodded to him. Rowland took this as an invitation to join them, even though he could see they'd almost finished eating. They were both dressed in their coveralls, as though they still had work to do.

Rowland introduced himself to the woman.

"How do you do," she said very formally, without telling him her own name. She had a thin face and prominent cheekbones. Rowland would have guessed she was in her mid-twenties, but she had unaccountable wrinkles at the corners of cool green eyes.

While Rowland waited for his food they kept eating. At last she finished and put down her knife and fork. "Do you love animals?" she said to him in a very earnest voice.

Rowland was surprised at the question. "I have respect for them," he said.

Those green eyes didn't change, but he had a feeling she was satisfied with his answer.

"They're the only honest beings to inhabit this planet," she said. "It's a great privilege for us to associate with them."

Just then the steward brought Rowland's meal. Will had finished eating and he took their plates away. The woman stood up and so did Will.

"It's back to work for us," she said, and off they went.

THE FOLLOWING NIGHT, Rowland went to dinner a little earlier and joined them again. This time, she put out a small, thin hand. "My name's Eva Sorrentino," she said.

Rowland asked her how she came to be working with the animals.

"They're for zoos," she said.

He was surprised to hear that, considering what she'd said the night before. "Isn't there some contradiction," Rowland said, "between having a high regard for animals and capturing them for zoos?"

Will Drummond, who'd been concentrating on his food, now looked up. He, too, was listening attentively.

Eva shook her head vigorously. "My father said that was their only hope of survival," she said. "He believed that before a hundred years were gone, the only representatives of most species would be the ones preserved in zoos." Her father, she said, was a member of an Italian family whose business it had been, for almost a century, to procure animals for zoos. He had married an Englishwoman and taken the business to England, where Eva was born. Her father instilled the love of animals in her, for which she'd always be grateful. "Poor father," she said, shaking her head sadly.

"What's wrong with him?" Rowland said.

"He's dead," she said.

"Was he one of those who died in the earlier part of the voyage?" Rowland said.

"Yes, he was," she said. And she began to talk about the ill-fated voyage of the *Derevaun*.

— 7 —

A GROUP OF NORTH AMERICAN ZOOS, wishing to expand their African collections, engaged Alfredo Sorrentino to lead an expedition to West Africa. Eva begged him to take her along with him.

He agreed. Reluctantly. She found out why, during three months of misery.

Africa turned out not to be the Paradise she'd always imagined from her reading. From the moment she set foot on its soil, she suffered. Though she wore trousers and a long-sleeved shirt like the male members of the expedition, the mosquitoes and wasps and other stinging creatures seemed to seek her out especially. For one particular week each month, every blood-loving insect within miles hovered about her and made her life a misery.

To make matters worse, they had barely begun trapping animals when she came down with such a severe form of malaria she feared her bones would break to pieces from the violent shivering. Alfredo, anxious to complete his work, left her at a village of the friendly Benolo people to recuperate.

"Don't drink water that hasn't been boiled," he said. "Remember the Guinea Worm!"

She'd seen some of the Benolo children infected with that abomination trying to reel the worms out of their bellies on little twigs. So she assured her father she'd be very careful and rest up.

But her stay at the village wasn't as restful as it might have been. The Benolo women would barge in at all times of the day to stare at her and touch her white skin and strange clothes. When she went into the bush near her hut to empty her bowels, it became a spectator sport for the entire tribe. In spite of everything, however, she began to feel better. She was feeling quite fit when, much earlier than expected, Alfredo's team emerged from the jungle with their quota of animals filled in record time.

After a few days' rest, Alfredo hired fifty Benolo men to help with the transportation of the animals. They loaded them, in their bamboo cages, onto hitched pairs of dugouts and ferried them down to the estuary of the river.

Eva was taken immediately out to the *Derevaun,* where she could stay in relative comfort while the hardest part of the task was performed. The ship was anchored in the deep water half a mile off shore, beyond the breakers, and the animals had to be brought out there. For three days, she watched the cages being rowed across the breakers by the Benolo and hauled up onto the ship. It was exhausting and dangerous work. All things considered, the operation went very well.

The only mishap came on the last day when a cage containing seven capuchin monkeys was lost in the surf. The two rowers were also drowned.

That same night, the Benolo Chief and his Shaman came out to the ship to talk to Alfredo. Eva watched as they stood on the deck, their tribal tattoos and animal pelts odd against the mechanical winches and nautical apparatus, engineered in factories a world and an æon away. The two Benolo talked heatedly to Alfredo for a while then slid down a line into their canoe and headed for the shore.

Eva asked her father what was wrong.

"They say the drownings are a sign some of the animals were reincarnations of the Benolos' ancestors," said Alfredo. "The Shaman told me to release them all or he'd put a curse on us."

"Then let's do as he says," said Eva. "Let's leave them here, where they belong."

Alfredo looked at her as though she wasn't thinking straight after her illness. "Never," he said. "It's all superstitious nonsense. Remember what I told you: we're saving the animals from extinction. That's what counts in the long run."

The next morning, the *Derevaun* upped anchor and began steaming away from that muggy shore. But even above the noise of the engines, drums could be heard, booming out landwards. From the deck, Eva, Alfredo and some of the deckhands saw a group of Benolo tribesmen beside a bonfire on the fringe of sand. In front of them, the Shaman was dancing a strange, convulsive dance, pointing his juju sticks towards the departing ship.

The Captain of the *Derevaun* joined Eva and Alfred by the rail. "What the devil are they up to?" he said, looking towards the beach.

"I've no idea," said Alfredo.

Eva kept silent.

THREE DAYS OUT, the sickness struck.

One of the crew who helped look after the animals was the first to come down with it. At lunchtime he was sitting at the table, joking and speculating with some of the others about what they'd do with all their money when they got back to civilization. At three in the afternoon, he collapsed on the deck and seemed to have trouble controlling his lips. *"Ma face ish shore,"* he kept saying till someone understood him. That evening when Eva went down to visit him, he was unconscious. By then, blood was welling out of his mouth, his nose, his eyes. Soon it was oozing out of his pores like sweat. An hour later, he was dead.

Shocked by what she'd seen, Eva went immediately to her father. "Maybe you should tell the Captain about the Shaman," she said. "We could still take the animals back."

"Don't be silly," Alfredo said. "Anyway, the Captain won't turn back, but the crew might just be superstitious enough to throw the animals overboard if they hear about it. You don't want that on our conscience, do you?"

Eva certainly didn't.

THE SHIP'S DOCTOR, whose two admitted specialties were Scotch whisky and tropical diseases, was at a loss as to what had killed the sailor. So he was no help the next day when one of the deckhands began complaining of pains in his face. This was followed by unconsciousness, the effusions of blood and subsequent death. Then a stoker started to display the same symptoms and died in due course. The Doctor said he'd never heard of anything so virulent and that everyone should be careful: the sufferers should be regarded less as patients than as enemies armed with a killer weapon. He was afraid even the slightest contact with them might be deadly.

The Captain gave orders for the immediate disposal of the bodies. Some members of the crew, muffled in heavy-weather gear for protection, threw the dead men, with their blankets and all their possessions, overboard.

That night, the Doctor himself began to feel unwell. He was philosophic about it and told the Captain he'd medicate himself with the only drug he really trusted—Scotch. He was found dead the next morning in a pool of his own blood.

For several nights thereafter, Eva had a nightmare about a mammoth beetle. These beetles were twelve inches long—she'd seen them during her stay with the Benolo. Slow-moving, hideous-looking insects, they were perfectly innocent leaf-eaters with kindly eyes, and the Benolo children used to keep them as pets. The mammoth beetle of her nightmare, however, had evil eyes and would creep into the bunk beside her, crawl down her belly and suck her blood.

She'd had that nightmare the morning she heard that Alfredo was ill. When the Captain told her, she insisted on seeing her father. But Alfredo had begged the Captain under no circumstances to allow Eva near him. Accordingly, the Steward had been ordered to padlock the cabin door.

She was able to call to Alfredo through the door and he was able to call back, his voice faint and distorted with pain.

"Goo'ba, goo'ba! Loo' afta tha anamash!"

She could do nothing but stand outside his door and weep. He died later in the morning and his body was thrown overboard.

Five more crew members died that week. But some men who'd shown the early symptoms began to recover. The Captain said that in his opinion there were two possibilities: either the strength of the disease had diminished, or those who remained alive were too strong for it. Eva, who had ceased to be visited by her nightmare, wondered about a third possibility: that the *Derevaun* had now outrun the Benolo Shaman's curse.

But she thought it might be better to keep that to herself.

— 8 —

"SO," ROWLAND ASKED Eva Sorrentino after her account of the sickness that afflicted the *Derevaun*, "what do you think caused it? You don't really think it was a curse."

"I don't know," she said. "But I'm glad the animals are safe and will soon be in their new homes." She looked at Will, and those wrinkles in the corners of her eyes were deepened by a smile. "They seem to like Will. He's a natural with animals."

Will, who'd listened to her story with great interest, just shrugged. "I enjoy them," he said.

"Well, I have to admire both of you," Rowland said. "The smell down there's awful. How do you stand it?" He suspected Eva would have a ready answer, and she did.

"I don't even notice it," she said. "If I don't notice it, it doesn't exist. What about you, Will? Does it bother you?"

He was a little more wordy than usual. "Smells?" he said. "They can't do you any harm."

Eva smiled at him again.

— 9 —

THREE WEEKS OUT OF GLASGOW and the god of seas was smiling on the *Derevaun*. The voyage towards the New World had been as uneventful as the voyage away from the Dark Continent had been horrific. She was nearing her destination. From her motion, Rowland could tell she had left the deep ocean behind and begun to cross the Continental Shelf. The shallower seas were a little choppier. At the rails, he watched a September iceberg a few miles to starboard. He could even feel the chill of it in the breeze. The Bosun, who tolerated him now, told him to enjoy such sights while he could. "We're coming into the region of fogs," he said. "You won't be able to see much for the next few days."

Already, far to the west, Rowland could see a rolling grey wall, its edge glinting in the sun, stretching from ocean to sky. Towards it the *Derevaun* steamed.

By noon that day, the ship had penetrated the flanks of the greyness. The railing Rowland leaned on dripped with dew. The bass rumble of the engines, which till this point in the voyage had been scarcely noticeable, now became dominant. It was accompanied by a chorus of animal howls rising through the open portholes of the lower decks.

The *Derevaun*'s foghorn now began its melancholy bleat every three minutes. Lookouts were doubled to watch for icebergs and other ships. The Bosun came and stood beside Rowland for a moment, the smoke from his pipe now indistinguishable from the general greyness. "This is a ship's graveyard," he said, gesturing towards the invisible sea. "Who knows how many thousands of vessels have foundered in these waters?"

Rowland, peering down, could make out the whitecaps of the waves lapping around the ship like the hooded ghosts of all the men who'd drowned here over the centuries.

When he went for lunch, the dining room was quiet, most of the sailors being on watch. Eva and Will ate quickly, for the animals were tense and needed comforting—especially the gibbons, which whooped nervously every time the foghorn sounded. Eva told Rowland she'd heard that whooping sound from gibbons once before, when she was ill in the Benolo village. "The gibbons could see army ants on a rampage," she said. "That gave the villagers time to build a circle of bushfires to keep the ants away. Later on they left out baskets piled with fruit for the gibbons to thank them for the advance warning."

"Well, there are no army ants out here in the ocean," said Rowland.

WHEN HE WENT OUT on deck again, it was just after two in the afternoon. He immediately noticed how warm the foggy air had become—as though the *Derevaun* were sailing in a huge steam bath. He went up the stairs to the wheel-house; its door was propped open. The Bosun and the Captain himself were at the rails peering into the fog, which now seemed even thicker.

"Why is it so warm?" Rowland said. "Is it because of the Gulf Stream?"

"I've sailed these seas a thousand times," the Captain shook his head, "and I've never come across anything like this." He was an elderly man, dragged out of retirement to finish this voyage.

The Bosun puffed at his pipe. Then he cocked his head. "Listen," he said. "I don't hear the animals any more."

Rowland listened. It was true. The whooping from below decks had ceased. Now the only sound was the deep hum of the engines.

And something else, something very faint.

The Captain looked alarmed. "Signal the engine room: Stop Engines!" he called in to the man at the wheel.

The trembling of the engines ceased. From the invisible sea around, they could hear a hissing—the kind of hissing, Rowland thought, a million snakes might make. Yet even as he listened, the sound was becoming louder—no longer the hissing of snakes but a more familiar sound, the gurgle of water boiling. And the air seemed warmer, too. He even thought he could feel the heat of the deck through the soles of his shoes. Yes, it was as though the ocean had become a huge cauldron of hot water and that water was now beginning to bubble. From the rails, he couldn't see the water because of the fog, but he could hear that bubbling sound all around them.

"Start Engines: Full Speed," the Captain shouted to the man at the wheel. To the Bosun he said: "The quicker we get away from here the better." The ship trembled as the engines came back on again, but now it was impossible to hear them amidst the gurgling. The Captain, his weather-beaten face anxious, took his place at the rails alongside Rowland and thus was in time to see the conclusion to this strange phenomenon.

The *Derevaun* began to rise up. At least, Rowland was sure he could feel the sensation of being lifted up, though he couldn't see anything because of the fog. He held on to the rails, for the ship was shuddering its entire length and tilting as it rose into the air. The lifting lasted for perhaps ten seconds.

Then the *Derevaun* dropped.

That dropping broke her in two.

– 10 –

ROWLAND VANDERLINDEN PLUNGED DEEP into a sea that was as warm as a hot bath. He kicked upwards with his shod feet till his head emerged into air that smelled so putrid, he choked and went under. Again he came to the surface, coughing the water out of his lungs, breathing in the foul air. He toed off his shoes and swam as hard as he could. His eyes were clouded and he couldn't clear them to see where he was, but he swam and swam till he was exhausted, choking in the stench. He felt hands grip his shoulders and pull him out of the water.

"You all right?" It was Will Drummond's voice.

"Yes," Rowland said. He blinked till his eyes cleared and he saw he was on a slatted wooden raft with a fringe of rope around it. "But my notebooks are in the cabin."

"You're lucky you're not with them," said Will.

Eva Sorrentino was lying on the raft too, her eyes closed, her clothes smeared with engine oil. Will Drummond, who had pulled them both aboard, wore no shirt. He had a paddle in his hands.

"Is Eva all right?" Rowland said.

"She's all right," Will said. "She's had an awful shock. She's better off sleeping for now. Keep an eye out for anyone else." He began rowing the clumsy float.

Rowland saw that Will's body was badly scarred by old wounds of some sort. But he had other things to think about. He looked around. The fog, or the steam, or whatever it was already seemed much thinner now. Less than fifty yards away, he could clearly see the *Derevaun* with her prow and her stern in the air, the point of the V well underwater with his cabin and his notes. Debris floated all around—broken timbers, ropes, decking, crates, spars, all shining with oil.

Behind one of the crates, Will had noticed some splashing and he paddled the float in that direction, thinking it might be a survivor. It was, in fact, a zebra, covered in oil. When it saw them, it swam towards the float, its eyes wild with fear. It managed to get its front hooves aboard and tried to heave itself up, almost tipping the raft over with its weight. Will lifted his oar in the air and smashed the zebra on the nose to fend it off. Rowland held on to the raft with one hand and clutched Eva's arm with the other, for she had begun to slide into the sea. Will kept striking out at the zebra till it gave up its efforts and swam away.

Will nevertheless kept on searching all around the stricken *Derevaun*. But they could see no other signs of life. The two legs of the V were becoming shorter and more upright, the broken ship groaning loudly in its unnatural posture.

"We'd better get away from here now," Will said at last.

The raft had begun to move slowly away from the ship towards the open sea when a curious thing happened. An oily arm reached up from out of the sea and grabbed the left arm of Eva Sorrentino, which was trailing overboard.

Rowland thought it must be one of the crew, a survivor at last. But the head and shoulders that emerged from the water belonged to one of the apes, its brown eyes looking at them pathetically. Will again used his paddle and slashed at the ape's head till it began to bleed. The animal released its grip on Eva and splashed away. Three deep scratches marked her arm where she'd been held, but she remained unconscious.

IT WAS ALMOST SUNDOWN and Will had paddled about a mile from the *Derevaun* when her two extremities finally snapped together like scissors and slid into the depths. Now the raft kept floating in a westerly direction, only partly helped by the paddle. As darkness fell, Will stopped paddling entirely and nestled beside Eva to keep her or perhaps himself warm, for he had no shirt. Not long after that, from away to the east, they were startled by a great gurgling sound, as though a giant bathtub were draining. For a while after, the air smelled foul. Then it cleared away, and all sounds ceased except for the slap of waves against the raft. There were wisps of fog, but this time it was a cool, northern fog. The water that sometimes lapped over the edges of the raft was as cold as it ought to be, the chill water of a chill northern sea. Reassured, Rowland himself at last fell asleep.

– 11 –

COLD WATER SLAPPED Rowland Vanderlinden's face. He spat the salt and the sleep out of his mouth and looked around. The night sky was covered in bruises from its losing battle with the dawn—the sun was peering over the eastern wall of the world. It reminded Rowland of the bloodshot eye of an old Magus he'd once met in a village on the fringes of the desert—the old man used to rub ashes in his eyes to make himself look even more frightening.

Rowland began to shiver, but not at that memory. He was wearing only a shirt and trousers and the sea-breeze was cold. He envied Will and Eva, lying at the other end of the raft, wrapped together like lovers.

Will's eyes were open. "Can you hear something?" he said quietly.

Rowland listened. "No," he said.

"Listen again," said Will.

Rowland listened. Nothing but the slap of the waves against the raft. Then he heard it—a distant, menacing growl. "Oh, no!" he thought. His heart beat faster as he took hold of the paddle, his eyes straining as he searched the water, looking for the source of that ominous sound. Again he heard the growl, coming from the direction the sun hadn't yet illumined. He heard it again, and again and again, rhythmic and precise. That growl was the sea's greeting to a sandy shore. "Breakers!" he said.

Eva had opened her eyes now too. She and Will disentangled and they all peered into the gloom. There it was, only a few hundred yards away—the black outline of an island against a horizon of ocean that was already less dark.

"It's not very big. We'd better make sure we don't drift by," said Rowland. He gave Will the paddle. "You steer," he said and slipped overboard. The cold of the water shocked him for a moment, but he clutched the fringe of rope and kicked out with his stiff legs, propelling the raft ever so slowly towards the shore. He swam this way for ten minutes or more.

Then something thick and hairy, something nightmarish, curled itself round his thighs. His legs scissored wildly in his panic and he tried to scramble aboard. "Will!" he shouted.

Will Drummond hunched over him, the paddle high, ready to strike whatever it was that had him in its grip. Then he put down the paddle. "It's all right," he said. "Your legs are tangled in seaweed, that's all."

Rowland believed him, for he could now feel his feet touch bottom. The raft lodged against some rocks, where the sea was waist-deep. Will helped Eva overboard and all three of them waded the last fifty yards to the beach and staggered across the sand to some dunes that were in the grip of scraggy bushes. They found a hollow out of the breeze. The sun was higher now and the air was already warming. Cold and wet, they sat down.

A BLACK-AND-WHITE DOG came leaping into the hollow, saw them, and ran away with a yelp of fear.

Rowland got to his feet, balancing himself against the unaccustomed sway of the land. He looked in the direction the dog had run but could see no farther than the high dunes. "I'll go have a look," he said. "Maybe it has an owner."

Will also tried to get up but sat down again quickly, wincing with pain. He hitched up the right leg of his trousers. There, just below the knee, was a deep cut, six inches long. The knee itself was badly swollen. "I'll just sit for a while yet," he said.

Eva spoke for the first time. "It looks bad," she said. Then she looked at her own left arm and fingered the livid scratches there. "I don't remember getting these," she said.

Rowland would have told her how Will defended her from the ape, but he feared she wouldn't appreciate the way he'd done it. "You two stay here," he said.

HE SAW THE WHITE STRUCTURE of a signal light on the first headland. Just fifty yards behind it, on a hill behind the high dunes, was a clapboard cabin, its chimney stack painting little white daubs on the blue morning sky.

As he approached, the black-and-white dog came running towards him, then ran back to the cabin and stood at the door, barking. Its bark was high-pitched and nervous.

Rowland kept advancing, the dog kept barking.

The door of the cabin jerked open.

"Robbie! Quiet!" shouted a stocky little man in rumpled clothes. He wasn't old but bald with a fringe of black hair and a scraggy grey-black beard. He was shocked at the sight of Rowland standing there, but extremely polite. "A visitor!" he said. "Well, well! Are you all right?"

"I'm not alone," said Rowland.

– 12 –

HERBERT FROGLICK, the little bearded man, accompanied Rowland to the beach and helped support Will back to the cabin. It was really just one cluttered room, so getting Will from the door to the bunk required careful navigation between heaps of thick books and scattered papers. Much of the floor space was taken up by a large table covered with charts and pencils and compasses and protractors. Froglick swept a number of papers off the bunk, adding to the debris on the floor.

In all this time, he'd asked no questions, only given directions in a loud voice. When Will was at last deposited on the bunk, the little man went to a wall cabinet full of medicine and took out disinfectant and bandages. He cleansed Will's leg quite expertly and bound it. He sat Eva on the wooden chair— the only chair—beside the table and disinfected the scratches on her arms. "This island's called Wreck Bar," he said at last. "It's an MMO—a Maritime Meteorological Outpost. I tend to the signal lamp and record the weather and the tidal patterns in this area."

He now went to the cooking area in the corner and made a pot of coffee and sandwiches of bread and tinned beef. The three survivors ate hungrily. Rowland told him about their voyage, the fog, the strange lifting up and dropping of the ship, the escape on the raft.

Froglick listened with great interest. "Very strange," he said when Rowland had finished. Then he told them he'd experienced something peculiar the night before too. He'd been walking on the beach with Robbie around seven o'clock, just before sunset. From far out to sea, he'd heard a deep booming sound such as he'd never heard before. Robbie was terrified. A few minutes later Froglick saw a wave bigger than usual sweeping in. To be on the safe side, he retreated to the higher dunes. The wave came and went, and the sea settled down. He went to the beach again and saw that its entire length had been dyed a yellowish colour and that thousands of fish had been cast up, dead or dying. Just as unusual was the smell—a pungent stink. "The next tide washed away almost every trace," Froglick said. "But that smell was unmistakable—it was sulphur. I believe your ship must have sailed directly over an underwater volcano just as it was erupting. You've experienced something very rare

in the annals of Meteorology. Yes, you've been very fortunate."
He said this with obvious envy.

Rowland wondered what kind of man he was. "How long
have you worked here?" he said.

"Seven years," said Froglick. "A ship brings supplies four
times a year."

Rowland looked around. There were no luxuries in the
cabin, and they'd already discovered that the nearby dunes
served as a washroom. "You're a scientific hermit," he said.

Froglick seemed quite flattered. "I'm very happy here," he
said. "But you won't need to concern yourselves about being
here too long. As a matter of fact, the supply ship's due to arrive
here tomorrow. They'll take you to Halifax."

WHEN NIGHT FELL, Froglick lit an oil lamp that hung from
the ceiling and again disinfected the wounds. Will said he was
feeling much better and gave the bunk to Eva. Her scratches
looked angry, and she winced as Froglick cleaned them tenderly.

Afterwards, he went out to check the signal lamp. When he
returned, he put more wood into the stove, then took out a
bottle of brandy from a corner cupboard and poured them
each a quantity in tin cups. He sat against the wall with
Rowland and Will and told them about his meteorological
duties on the island, the chief of which was his annual report
on weather anomalies and any other natural phenomena
worth observing. "This matter of the eruption will be of great
interest at the Control Centre," he said.

The night wind was howling eerily outside. Robbie
hunkered against his master's knees and would sometimes

whimper back, for the sound was at times so human it was on the verge of being intelligible. As though, thought Rowland, it was the sad call of the mariners who'd perished in these seas.

Aside from Froglick, they weren't a talkative group. Perhaps it was the effects of the brandy, for Rowland was suddenly numb with exhaustion and barely listened. Will's head fell back and he dozed against the wall. Eva lay gazing at the ceiling for a while, then closed her eyes and was soon asleep. Around nine o'clock, Froglick gave out blankets and turned off the lamp.

THE NEXT MORNING, when Rowland awoke, he went outside for a walk. The sky was overcast and the wind was very strong. The pounding of the waves made the ground under him vibrate so that the island didn't feel that much different from a ship. When he got back to the cabin, Froglick had bathed the wounds of Eva and Will and had made some coffee and sandwiches. "The ship will be here by noon," he said.

Eva was over at the bunk, talking quietly to Will. After a few minutes she came to Rowland, tears in her eyes. "I'd like to talk to you," she said, "outside."

Rowland went with her out of the cabin. She closed the door firmly behind them and spoke. He couldn't help noticing how attractive she looked in the morning light, even though her eyes were wet and her lips quivering.

"Are you going on the ship?" she said.

"Of course I am," he said. "We don't want to be stuck here for another three months, do we?"

She put her hand on his arm and looked at him with great intensity. "I like you, Rowland," she said. "You know that?"

He wasn't quite sure what she was getting at. "I like you too, Eva," he said.

"Then why don't you stay on here?" She said this in a desperate way.

"Stay on here?" he said. "Why would anyone want to do that?"

"I'm not getting on that ship," she said. "Or any other ship. I swore if I ever reached solid ground I'd never leave it."

"Then why don't you ask Will to stay?" Rowland said. "You know he's the one you really like."

"I did ask him," she said. "He won't stay. He says this place reminds him too much of where he came from and he'd be miserable here."

Rowland was more touched than amused by her admission that he was only her second choice. "Then why don't you go with him?" he said. "Wherever he's going, you two might be happy together."

She shook her head. "Never!" she said. "I can't face going on a ship again."

"Not even for love?" Rowland said.

"Not even for love," she said. She took a deep breath. "Well, that simplifies matters." She opened the door and went back into the cabin followed by Rowland. Robbie greeted her, wagging his tail enthustically. Will watched from the bunk as she went to Herbert Froglick, squatting on the floor drinking his coffee from a battered tin mug.

"Froglick," she said.

"Yes?" he said. He was very shy when she spoke to him.

"I'm staying here," she said challengingly, as though she expected an argument. "Do you understand what I'm saying? I'm not going on the ship."

He said nothing, so she kept on.

"I'm staying here," she said. "I can keep this place tidy. I can cook. There must be lots of other animals on this island—birds and rodents and whatnot. I'd like to find out about them too."

Still he said nothing, so she changed tack. "Do you mind if I stay?" She said this coaxingly, gently, the way she'd approach a shy, reluctant animal.

"No," he said, quietly for once. "I wouldn't mind at all."

She smiled, and her eyes softened in a way Rowland hadn't noticed before, even for Will. Perhaps it was a phenomenon witnessed only by her animals.

Everyone was smiling. Will, on his bunk, Froglick and Eva, too. Rowland himself couldn't help smiling at all that smiling. Looking at Eva, with her new softness, he could almost have envied Froglick.

LATER THAT DAY, the relief ship arrived and anchored a few hundred yards off shore. Supplies were landed and a written statement about the sinking of the *Derevaun* was elicited from Eva. Then the other two castaways were ferried out to the ship. Will was helped down into a cabin but Rowland stayed on deck. As the ship got underway, Herbert Froglick and Eva Sorrentino stood on the beach, watching. She wasn't tall, but she was a head taller than Froglick. They waved for a while then turned inland towards the cabin, accompanied by Robbie.

Rowland wondered what would become of them. It was true, he knew, that the most unlikely of unions often seemed to thrive, while the most promising in appearance often contained some hidden core-rottenness that was fatal to endurance. He watched the pair disappear behind the dunes, knowing it was very unlikely he'd ever see them again, or ever know how their story worked out. Finding out how stories worked out necessitated putting down roots, staying long enough, even a lifetime if necessary, in one place. He was already sure that his own was the only story he'd ever see to a conclusion.

– 13 –

CAMBERLOO HOSPITAL HAD SEEMED RELATIVELY SILENT, as hospitals go, while Thomas Vanderlinden told me about the meeting of Rowland and Will, and about the sinking of the *Derevaun* and the survivors. I'd been enthralled. Now, as he picked up his oxygen mask and took some deep breaths, reality intruded in the form of all the usual hospital sounds from the corridor outside.

I was curious, though, about why Rowland had insisted on telling Rachel about Eva Sorrentino's obvious attraction to Will Drummond. When Thomas put down his mask I asked him about that.

"I wondered about that myself," he said. "Maybe it was because he thought she should know Will was attractive to other women. That he had other choices. She certainly listened to every word."

At that moment, in came the sterile figure of the duty nurse, carrying a tray full of phials and needles.

"Time for medication," she said. "The doctor's coming in to see you after that."

"I'm getting near the end," Thomas said to me.

Did he mean of the story-teller or the story? I didn't want to think about that. "I'll be back tomorrow," I said. "I can't wait to find out what happens next."

PART FOUR

WILL
DRUMMOND

We carry within us the wonders we seek without us: There is all Africa and her prodigies in us.

—SIR THOMAS BROWNE

AS USUAL, THE NEXT MORNING, I sat for an hour or two in the garden, trying to think about *The Kilted Cowpoke*. And, as usual, the sight of that gap in the hedge reminded me of another one of those occasions when Thomas and I had chatted there.

"I don't suppose you've read Basilius Medicus?" he'd said, without much hope that I had. "He was one of the most prominent Spanish physicians and essayists of the mid-sixteenth century. His contention was that the body is a mirror of the mind, and that in the mind, therefore, lies the cure for all physical ailments."

I'd tried to look alert.

"His treatise, *Exteriorum Expositio*, begins with the most obvious examples," Thomas said. "For instance, most of us would agree that the physical phenomenon of the smile is a reflection of the mind's having perceived the humour in something." He looked very pointedly at me. "Or, if you yawn, it's because your mind isn't interested in what someone's saying— the yawn's a sign of boredom."

I'd just stifled a yawn so I blinked hard and nodded.

"For Basilius," said Thomas Vanderlinden, "that was only a starting point. He went much further. He claimed that every single physical ailment is a direct emanation of the mind of the sufferer. So, if you caught a cold, or malaria, or dysentery or any of the multitude of human illnesses that afflicted the world at that time—even bubonic plague—they were all reflections of your inner state. Conversely, he argued, through your mind you ought to be able to heal your body."

To show I'd been listening, I said: "Many people blame bad health on mental stress."

He paid no attention whatever to my comment but talked about the ancient theory of the Humours, whereby the four major bodily fluids could somehow be harmonized to bring health. He drew a parallel with acupuncture, which defied western understanding of the physiological processes of the body. He spoke about psychology and its great figures, Jung and even Freud, with their theories of how the Unconscious affects human behaviour in the most fundamental ways.

I tried to look interested. "What if you fall off a ladder and break your leg?" I said. "I can understand how falling off the ladder might be because your mind was elsewhere. But once you've broken your leg, even if you admit it was because you weren't paying attention, how can your mind cure it?"

"You've come up with the question Basilius asked himself," Thomas said. "Like many doctors at that time, he had to go to battlefields to find people with awful injuries so that he could try out his theories. At the Battle of Hessebellerin in 1562, he had himself appointed Surgeon General. One of the things he noticed was that the rate of healing of wounded soldiers seemed to depend exclusively on their states of mind. Those who were optimistic actually speeded up the process of healing exponentially. Those who were pessimistic, even if they were strong physically, died in very short order."

"But the wounds themselves," I said, "surely they were caused by the guns and arrows of the enemy, not some internal mechanism. What did he have to say about that?"

"Nothing," said Thomas. *"He became completely opposed to all further research in the matter."*

That really woke me up. "What?" I said. "Isn't that more or less the same kind of thing that man you spoke about the other day—Matthew of Paris—said about travelling? Isn't it a complete cop-out? Isn't it perverse, in fact?"

Thomas nodded. "These original—or, as you call them, perverse—types of thinkers aren't to be dismissed lightly. Basilius became more attached to protecting the mysterious qualities of the mind than to exploring them. He came to believe mysteries are sometimes preferable to knowledge. Perhaps he was right."

WHEN I ARRIVED at Camberloo Hospital that afternoon with my coffee, Thomas had been resting with the oxygen mask on his face. He looked more pinched than usual. I told him I'd been sitting in the garden that morning and that he'd soon be back there himself. But I could see he had even less interest in small talk than usual. He took a few deep breaths from the mask and put it away. Then he focused his eyes again on that day when Rowland had at last met Rachel.

– 2 –

IN THE LIBRARY of Rachel's house, no one had interrupted Rowland as he'd talked about how he'd first met Will Drummond.

But Thomas could see his mother was getting restless. She'd listened carefully to the account of the sinking of the *Derevaun* and of the stranding on Wreck Bar and of Eva Sorrentino's proposal. She wanted Rowland to tell her more about Will himself. "Didn't he say anything about his life before you met him?" she said. "I was hoping you'd know something about that, too."

"I'm coming to that," Rowland said, smiling at her impatience. "As a matter of fact, it wasn't till we'd got to Halifax after leaving Wreck Bar that he told me anything about himself. They'd put us up in an old hotel to wait for the Inquiry into the sinking. Everything I have to tell you now happened while we were there. We had to wait a few days and we talked a lot, mainly comparing notes about what happened on the *Derevaun*. But as Will got to know me, he opened up a little more."

"Please, please tell us what he had to say," Rachel said.

Rowland took a sip of brandy. "He wasn't a man for embroidering things," he said. "He just told the plain facts, and you usually had to guess what he was thinking. One thing's for sure, he'd had a hard life . . ."

THEY WERE IN THEIR ROOM in the Maclaren Hotel. It was a rainy night. They'd eaten some fish and chips and were sharing a bottle of cheap whisky. Rowland had been telling Will all about his own life and the reasons for his trip to England and, now, his return to an uncertain domestic situation.

Perhaps it was the whisky, but Will was more relaxed than usual and it wasn't hard for Rowland to coax him into talking about his own life.

He came, he said, from the Uplands region, near where Rowland first saw him on the train. He was born in a little mining village called Tarbrae, in a miners' row house. His father had a surface job at the mine, classifying coal, because he had black lungs from too many years at the coal face. When Will was very young, he'd already be in bed when his father came home from work at night and stripped to the waist and washed himself at the kitchen sink. His wife would dry him off in front of the fire. She had a nervous condition and didn't have much to do with anybody else except her husband and son. They didn't talk much. Will never heard either of them so much as hum a tune, so he was surprised to hear other people whistle and sing as though music was natural to them.

When he went to Tarbrae School, Will wasn't much of a scholar. Like all the boys there, it was taken for granted he'd be a miner when he turned thirteen. And that's exactly what he did, along with his schoolmates.

The first time they had to go down on the mine elevator, they weren't keen. They all knew about the one-legged men in Muirton. But they had to get in anyway. They went down so fast and slowed up so suddenly, Will thought his stomach would come out of his mouth.

They were five thousand feet underground and it was so warm they had to take off their coats.

"Now you know what Hell's like," the foreman said to the apprentices. The tunnel was dark, but there were oil lamps every twenty yards so they could see enough not to trip on the rail tracks that carried the coal. The men kept on their hard hats—the apprentices didn't have any yet.

They started to walk to the coal face—the foreman said it was a mile away from the bottom of the shaft. Will thought that would be no trouble, even though the tunnel was five feet high. But even at thirteen he was five foot eight, and that meant he had to walk with his head and shoulders stooped. After about five minutes, he started to get pains in his back from the effort of bending. It got to be so bad he thought he'd be sick.

Somebody shouted: "Look out!"

Will got such a fright, he jerked his head up and smashed it against the roof of the tunnel. So did the other apprentices.

The miners had a good laugh at that. It was a trick they played every year on the apprentices before they got their helmets. By then Will was sweating and the pains all through his body were awful. Some apprentices were crying. The foreman called them cry-babies and told them they'd be fired if they didn't keep moving.

That was the longest walk Will ever took, even if it only lasted half an hour.

THE APPRENTICES DIDN'T HAVE TO do any work that first day. They'd only to watch what was going on and see what they'd be doing for the rest of their lives. At first they watched the proppers, the men who put up the wooden posts that held the roof up. Then there were the fanners: they carried canaries in cages and kept the tunnels clear of gases that could cause an explosion. The foreman told the apprentices how easy it was to die down there. Everybody had to rely on everybody else.

The hardest workers and the strongest were the men at the coal face. Most of the time they were on their knees, drilling holes for the dynamite, then hacking out the coal. Everybody's wages depended on them.

Will had no idea what time of day it was, but the hours soon passed and the miners began the long walk back to the elevator. All the apprentices dreaded that. Will had stiffened up during the day and thought he wouldn't be able to do it. But the knowledge that they were going home helped, and he was able to put up with the pain. The foreman said it would take a week or two for the newcomers to get used to that crouched walk.

When they got to the elevator at last, they shot to the surface like a rocket. It was great to stand up straight and breathe in the fresh air. Will's father met him and was as pleased as punch.

WILL WORKED IN THE TARBRAE MINE six days a week for five years. The seasons didn't matter, for there was only one season underground—a dark, hot summer. Even when he slept, there was no escape—he would dream he was down that mine. Generally, Will's life seemed nothing but darkness and sweat and coal dust and itching throat and bruised limbs. Sometimes they laughed and kidded around at work, but at the back of their minds was the worry about gas and explosions and maybe being buried alive. Will supposed all the miners felt the same way he did, but they never talked about it, even when there was an accident. What choice did ordinary working men have?

Anyway, he found out that terrible things could happen above ground in the fresh air, too.

One rainy Friday, Will and his father left for the mine at half past four in the morning, as usual. His mother was upset about something—she often was, they never knew why—and his father patted her arm as they were leaving just to cheer her up.

She stood at the window with the curtain pulled back, watching their departure. Her black-and-white cat, Mindy, was sitting on her shoulder.

At three-thirty in the afternoon, father and son came home from work. The rain had stopped but it was a dull day, one of those days that didn't seem much brighter than a tunnel ten thousand feet underground. When Will's father opened the door, he knew something was wrong, for he couldn't smell any cooking. They had a quick look inside. Mindy was asleep on the chair, but there was no sign of Will's mother. They tried the neighbours, but they hadn't seen her either.

They split up and looked all over the town, then Will went up into the moors. He met Hayworth, a bow-legged shepherd with two collies. Hayworth said hours before he'd seen a woman walking up in the moors near where he was herding.

"It was up by Tibby's Bridge," he said.

Will knew what that meant.

He went back for his father and they both went up into the moors. They couldn't go fast, because of his father's bad lungs. The old bridge was about a mile east, among the hills. It crossed a deep ravine with a fast stream at the bottom—a great place for trout fishermen from all the little mining towns in the hills. But as far back as anyone could remember, it had always been a great place for suicides, too.

Will got to the bridge and looked over and saw his mother right away. She was lying on the rocks and the moorbirds were pecking at her. He climbed down and chased the birds away. Then he hauled her back up over his shoulder. She wasn't nearly as heavy as a sack of coal. His father was in an awful state, wheezing and trying to wipe the blood off her face with his handkerchief.

Will carried her back down to Tarbrae, and three days later she was buried, without much fuss. She'd always kept the house in good order and cooked nice meals, his father said. He said she used to be very lively before Will was born.

TARBRAE WAS JUST LIKE all the other mining towns in the region—it had no shortage of widows. So within a year, Will's father was walking out with another woman. She was a waitress at The Stag and was energetic and talkative. Her own husband had been crushed, along with three other men, in a cave-in years before. Her children were grown.

Will knew his father wanted to marry her, so he thought he might as well get married himself. He asked Jenny Stewart, a girl from his class at school he'd gone out with a few times, and she said yes. They got married and set up house in one of the miners' rows, and it wasn't long before she had a baby. It was a boy, and they called him Will, too.

So, Will Drummond was set for life.

THAT FIRST DECEMBER after he got married was a cold one— snow every day and a north wind. Will didn't mind too much having to go underground; at least it was warm down there. His father had married his waitress by then, but he would come by Will's house in the mornings and they'd walk to work together, as usual.

One morning in the middle of the month, his father said he'd be going underground with Will, instead of staying on the surface. That was because they'd reached a fresh seam of coal and he had to come down to classify it.

So they went down in the elevator together, then walked the two miles to the coal face. It was hard for his father, with those bad lungs, and they'd stop every five minutes and let him wheeze and cough for a while. They stopped once beside the opening of an old tunnel and he told Will that was where he used to work, years ago, before the bad lungs.

They eventually got to the coal face and all the men took a break while he examined the coal.

He'd only been at it five minutes when they heard a thud from a long way back up the tunnel. They knew it was an explosion from where there shouldn't have been an explosion. The foreman told them all to keep very quiet and listen. At first Will thought maybe everything was going to be all right, then he heard a kind of popping noise in the distance, the kind of pop they'd hear from the local gamekeeper's guns when he was out shooting the grouse.

"It's the props! They're snapping!" one of the older miners said.

They all knew what that meant. The roof of the main tunnel was caving in and it was coming their way. The popping was getting louder and faster. There was no place to go: only the coal face was behind them.

Will's father grabbed his arm.

"Run for it, Will!" he said. "Run for that tunnel I showed you. It goes through granite. Maybe it won't collapse!"

Will didn't like the idea of leaving him there. Nor did he like the idea of running back towards that popping noise. But it was either that, or just wait to be crushed. So he started to run, and some of the others ran behind him. The popping got louder and louder, and now he could hear the rumble of the roof caving in up ahead. He was bent over double and scared and running into a wind caused by the collapse. His ears were bursting with the pressure and he thought he was done for, then he saw the opening of the cave a few yards away and dived in. Some of the others tumbled in behind him just in time. A noise like an express train went past them in the main tunnel and they were left lying in the dark and the dust. All they could hear was a rumbling that got fainter and fainter till it sudddenly stopped. The props in this side tunnel were creaking as though they were ready to collapse too. They were all coughing from the dust they couldn't see. Then, after a while, everything was quiet except for the sound of their breathing.

THERE WERE SIX MEN in that side tunnel for three days before they reached them by boring in from a tunnel in a disused mine that ran parallel. They were hauled up to the surface through an old shaft. Jenny was waiting for Will. The waitress from The Stag was waiting for his father. Will told her how they were saved because of him, even though he couldn't run himself with his bad lungs.

She looked at him as if she hated him.

THE GOVERNMENT INSPECTOR closed the Tarbrae mine forever. Forty-nine men and boys had died in the tunnel and he said that was enough. There was too much gas and the ground was too unstable for any more mining in the area. That was a death sentence for Tarbrae—it would be a ghost town before long, like a lot of places that had run out of coal.

Most of the men started looking for jobs right away in other mining towns in the Uplands. But Will had had enough of the mines. Leaving Jenny and the baby with her parents, he went to Glasgow to find work.

THAT WAS THE FIRST TIME he'd ever been in a city. He couldn't believe how dirty the fogs were and how dead the river was and how so many people could live so close together. It was strange, after living all his life in a place where everybody knew everybody else, not to know anybody at all. The only lodging he could afford was in a room shared with four other men at the top of a tenement. It was on the south side of the river where there were street gangs and knife fights and robberies. The police were seldom seen.

Jobs were hard to find and usually only temporary. Will took anything he could get. For a while, he hauled bags of coal, but the owner paid so little he could hardly afford the food to give him the strength to carry the bags. Then he worked at a cooperage where they made whisky barrels. He could drink as much whisky as he liked, but he didn't get much money. He thought he'd struck it lucky at last when he got a full-time job at an iron foundry, cleaning out the gas furnaces. He soon found out why the job had been so easy to get: he'd only been there a week when his whole crew was overcome by gas fumes and had to be dragged out unconscious. When he woke up, he was as sick as a dog for three days. But the foreman liked him and said he'd take him on as a tender of the vats of molten ore to replace a man who had carelessly fallen in. Because the job was so dangerous, the wages were good, and Will stuck at it for three months, saving up money to send to Jenny. Then came a strike at the shipping yards. Ore wasn't needed any more and the foundry was shut down.

THINGS WERE TOUGH after that. Will was hungry most of the time. Then he found a few hours' work cleaning up at Duffy's Travelling Fair while it was in a park at the east end of the city. The very day the Fair was about to move to another town, one of the regular men quit and Duffy asked Will if he wanted the job. There wasn't much money in it, but he'd have a bunk in a trailer and plenty to eat. Sometimes there were women. And he'd see the country.

Will accepted.

HE SOON GOT USED TO LIFE with the Fair, cleaning up after the horses, swabbing out the beer tents, mopping the fortune-teller's booth, stoking the brazier in the fire-eater's booth. Sometimes, indeed, there were women. All in all, he was kept busy.

Occasionally, whenever he had time at the end of a day's work, he'd go to the boxing tent and watch the fights. It was the usual thing: Challenge The Champions For Two Rounds—Win Five Pounds. Duffy himself looked after it and didn't mind if Will came in to watch so long as he didn't take up one of the seats. Duffy acted as referee at the bouts and always dressed up in a white shirt with a black bow tie. He'd been a boxer himself. His nose was bent and his left eye was dead.

The "Champions" weren't really champions, just good enough boxers in their day. They were both big men in their late thirties. Gentleman Jaco Acker was black—a rare sight for that time—and on the flabby side. Crusher Jones was white and also on the flabby side. Aside from the difference in colour, they could have been brothers with their flat noses, cauliflower ears and scarred eyebrows. Even when they talked they sounded alike, for their words didn't come out right from all the punches they'd taken. On top of that, they'd both been married and left by their wives.

Duffy told Will he wished they would act more ferocious in public. In private they were both easygoing and even-tempered. Crusher was forever reading, and Jaco's hobby was house plants—his trailer was full of them.

WHILE THE TENT WAS FILLING UP for the bouts each night, the Champions would get into the ring and spar with each other. Seeing men their size move around like dancers and the easy way they'd slip punches should have been enough to put any challengers off. But there were always enough drunks or show-offs to volunteer. Will never saw any of them last the two rounds.

He'd been working a month when the Fair set up in Bellsvale, an industrial town on the edge of Glasgow. There, Duffy made him a proposition. He said it was good for business if a challenger occasionally won a bout. Will looked big enough to be convincing, so he wanted him, from time to time, to act as the challenger.

Will was worried someone might realize it was a fix.

Duffy assured him that was unlikely. And anyway, it was really just show-biz and there wasn't anything wrong with it. He'd let Will have time off work to do a bit of rehearsing with the Champions. And he'd give him a pound each time he went in the ring.

Will needed the money, so he agreed.

ON THE THIRD NIGHT in Bellsvale, Will went into the ring for the first time. The tent was packed and he had to wait, for there were two legitimate challengers before him.

The first of them was a thin man covered in tattoos who got in to face Gentleman Jaco. He was wiry and fast and tried to keep out of Jaco's way. Though the crowd booed him for being a coward, he almost got through the first round. Then, just before the bell, Gentleman Jaco got him in a corner and gave him an uppercut and that was that.

The second challenger looked the part. He was a big, ginger-haired Irishman, flushed with drink. He came running straight at Crusher and threw some heavy punches. Crusher took them on the gloves and let him keep on charging all through the first round. The Irishman was breathing heavily at the end of it. At the beginning of the second round, he rushed at Crusher again. But Crusher just stepped out of the way and gave him a short punch to the belly. The Irishman dropped to the floor, vomiting, and couldn't get back up.

Now it was Will's turn against plant-loving Jaco.

The first few seconds of the first round, Will thought he'd forgotten the rehearsals, for Jaco hit him in the face, making his nose bleed. Will put his hands up over his face, so Jaco punched him a few times in the chest almost stopping Will's breathing. The crowd was shouting for more but Jaco backed off then, let Will get a few shots in and winced as though they hurt.

The second round went much the same way. Near the end of it, just the way they'd rehearsed, Will punched Jaco in the face and he fell back against the ropes, looking really stunned. Will was exhausted but kept his feet and arms moving till the welcome final bell. The audience seemed convinced and cheered loudly when Duffy made a big deal of handing Will five pounds.

AFTER THAT, WILL "WON" the prize in many towns across the country. At first, he was constantly afraid there might be someone from the audience who'd seen him "win" before. Nothing happened. So he stopped worrying and concentrated on trying to improve his boxing, or, at least, his acting skills.

WILL HADN'T BEEN TO TARBRAE for more than six months. At last, he had some money to take home to Jenny. The Fair stopped in Galahead and he asked Duffy for a couple of days off. He caught an early-morning train via Edinburgh to Muirton. It was a typical Uplands day with a grey sky and a drizzle as he walked the seven miles to Tarbrae. When he got there, he could see that the main street was deserted and a lot of windows were boarded up. Not too many chimneys had smoke coming from them.

He knocked at the door where Jenny's parents lived.

Her mother opened the door. She'd always been kind to him but now she just looked at him coldly.

"Is Jenny here?" he said, thinking maybe they'd had a falling-out or she'd gone to live somewhere else.

"You're lucky her father's not here now or he'd kill you," she said. "She never heard a word from you and now she's been dead a month. If you want to see her you'll have to go up to the graveyard."

"Dead?" said Will. "Dead? And what about little Will? Is he all right?"

"No, he's dead too," she said. "Jenny got pneumonia, then he got it. Just as well, too." She slammed the door in Will's face.

Will did go to the graveyard, but he didn't go in. He stood for a moment, then turned and walked back to Tarbrae to catch the train back to Galahead. The odd thing was, he wasn't one bit sad. More relieved. That made him feel guilty, so he tried not to think about anything at all.

WORKING AT THE FAIR, it wasn't hard to find women. They'd hang around looking for work, or food. Most of them were homeless, runaways from something awful. Duffy sometimes gave them odd jobs, cooking or cleaning.

A month after Will came back from Tarbrae, when the Fair was being set up in Golsway, a town just north of Aberdeen, one of those women showed up. She looked like a Gypsy she was so dark, with brown eyes. She didn't speak English, but Duffy figured out her name was *Vatua,* an odd word she said several times when he tried to communicate with her. He gave her a job as a cleaner. One of the other barkers knew Spanish, but she didn't seem to understand him. Others tried bits of French and German and Italian, but she shook her head. Some

Gypsies were camped near the town and Duffy asked their Chief to come and try to talk to the girl. But she didn't understand the Gypsy tongue either.

Three days later, when the Fair left town, she tagged along, and Duffy didn't mind—she was a good worker. She picked up some English phrases but didn't seem interested in learning much more than that. She was like a cat, the way she knew her own name and a few more words, and that was enough.

January came in with heavy snow, and Vatua started to hang around Will. He was lonely, and before long, she'd moved into his trailer. She hated the cold weather and would wrap herself round him all night to keep warm. He sometimes talked to her about himself and about Jenny and the dead baby, even though she didn't know what he was saying. She'd sometimes talk to him, too, and he could only wonder what it was that made her laugh sometimes, and sometimes cry. They didn't understand each other, but it was very soothing, as though the words didn't matter as much as the way they were spoken, and the person they were spoken to.

Some other things about her were very unusual for a woman. She had a tattoo around her right ankle of a snake swallowing its tail. Will pointed to it and she said something that didn't make any sense to him.

Then there was the six-inch hunting knife she kept in her purse. He supposed that, wherever she came from or whatever she'd been through, it was a necessary thing to carry.

A FEW MONTHS LATER, the thing that was never supposed to happen, happened.

The Fair was set up in Lethian in a park overlooking the Firth, and Will was to appear in the ring. After a couple of regular bouts had gone by, Will challenged for the money. Gentleman Jaco was the opponent, and he did the usual good job of making Will look better than he was. At the end of the bout, the crowd clapped loudly when the challenger's hand was held aloft by Duffy and he was given the five-pound prize.

Will was climbing down from the ring when he heard a loud voice from the back of the tent.

"It's a swindle! I saw him do it before!"

It was the drunken Irishman who'd lost to Crusher in Bellsvale, the very night Will began his career.

Some of the crowd may have believed the Irishman, but before they could think of doing anything, Duffy and Crusher grabbed the troublemaker and threw him out of the park.

Duffy came to Will's trailer later. "It was bound to happen sometime," he said. "You haven't done anything wrong." He could see Will was unhappy. "We'll just keep you out of the ring till we get to England. Everything'll be fine there."

THAT NIGHT, WILL AND VATUA WENT OUT, as they often did after the Fair closed, to a little pub that looked over the Firth. Will had a pint of beer, Vatua didn't have anything. She just sat and looked around. She always seemed to enjoy that, though Will had no idea what was going through her mind. They left the pub at midnight and were walking along the dark street when three men came out of the shadows and faced them under a street light.

"Hey, you!" one of them said.

Of course, it was the big Irishman. His friends were as big and as mean-looking as he was.

"Let's see how tough you are when the fight's not fixed," he said.

The three of them dragged Will into a nearby close. The other two held him while the Irishman punched him in the face over and over again. Will felt his nose break. Then they let him drop to the ground and they began kicking. He felt some of his ribs snap. Vatua was shouting at them—he could hear that—but they just kept on kicking. They kicked and kicked and kicked. By the time Will passed out completely, he was sure they'd damaged him so badly there was no possibility he could live.

He was found unconscious the next morning and taken to the Lethian hospital. In his moments of awareness he felt he was nothing but a bleeding wound with a mind attached to it, and he wanted to die. Freedom from pain was just a short leap away. But every time he was going to jump, something in him would rebel. After a few days, the pain was bearable.

At first, he had no idea how he'd come to be in such a state. It was while Duffy was visiting one day that the whole thing came back. He asked for Vatua and Duffy said she was dead. The night Will was attacked, she'd got her knife out and stabbed the Irishman over and over. One of the others grabbed the knife from her and stuck it into her chest. She was found the next morning lying dead beside Will.

As for the three men, they were easily caught by the police. The Irishman was so badly cut he probably wouldn't live to be hanged.

WILL DRUMMOND WAS IN A BAD STATE for three months before he started to recover. When he was fit again, the Fair had moved to England and he didn't want to go back to it. He found odd jobs in Glasgow—even hauling bags of coal to get his strength back. He took a last trip up to Tarbrae and this time went in to see the graves. They, like the rest of the grave-yard, were covered in weeds—no one lived in Tarbrae any more. Then he took a last walk over the hills and caught the train at Muirton.

"THAT'S THE TRAIN you were on," Will Drummond said to Rowland in their room in the seedy Maclaren Hotel.

Rowland remembered very well that day when he'd first seen Will. They'd been through so much together since then. "I didn't think you'd noticed me," he said.

"I did, all right," said Rowland. "I just didn't feel like talking."

They were silent for a while.

"So, will you head for Panama after the Inquiry's over?" said Rowland. "That was your plan, wasn't it?"

"I'm not sure any more," said Will.

"I'm glad to hear that," Rowland said. He'd been considering certain possibilities. For the moment, he kept them to himself.

ON THE THIRD DAY of their stay in Halifax—a Friday—the Inquiry into the sinking of the *Derevaun* was held. Only a few hours had been set aside to investigate the loss of a merchant ship whose cargo was of doubtful worth. In the late afternoon, Rowland and Will, wearing the clothes they'd been given by the

Sailors' Aid, were summoned to the offices of the Maritime Commission. They walked there under a cloudy sky and on arrival were brought into the Board Room, a high-ceilinged room with its own little cloud cover of pipe and cigarette smoke. On the walls were gloomy paintings in ornate frames of various dead Admirals. At a long table sat the Commissioners themselves, three elderly men in uniform.

Rowland and Will were shown to chairs facing the Commissioners by a younger officer, who then sat down with a notepad to record the meeting.

The High Commissioner, seated between the two others, wore a heavily brocaded uniform. He called the meeting to order. He was a bent-shouldered man with a tight mouth, extraordinarily large ears and a rather abrupt way of talking. After the swearing-in, he told them the Commission had heard that morning from the Captains of the various ships that had searched the scene of the disaster. It appeared that there were no survivors except for the three who'd reached Wreck Bar.

After this introduction, Eva's statement was read into the record. Then the High Commissioner appointed Rowland to act as spokesman ("to avoid duplication of verbiage"), unless he and Will had conflicting views of any matter raised. He said the Inquiry must conclude in exactly one hour, so Rowland should give a *brief* (he said this emphatically) accounting of his presence on the *Derevaun* and his impressions of the sinking.

Rowland told how he and Will had been looking for a ship in Glasgow and had heard about the *Derevaun* and its problems on the African voyage. He talked about the circumstances of their joining her. Finally he described the voyage across the Atlantic and the sinking.

The High Commissioner listened, occasionally glancing at the clock on the mantel. When Rowland was finished, he nodded approvingly. Then he asked some questions in his pointed manner. "The master of the ship—was he competent, in your view?"

"I'm not sure I'm able to make such a judgment," said Rowland. "All I can say is he seemed so to me."

"Odd behaviour? Signs of derangement?" The High Commissioner was very stingy with his words, Rowland thought, as though he had trouble squeezing them out of that tight mouth.

"Not that I could see," said Rowland. "All I know is he'd been brought out of retirement to finish the voyage."

The High Commissioner, at that point, said he had no more to ask. The Commissioner to his right stirred. He had unruly grey hair plastered with oil.

"Tell us more about the fever on the voyage from Africa," he said. "Talk about that."

"Well," said Rowland, "I know some of the crew blamed the animals."

The Commissioner nodded, encouraging him. He didn't seem to want the same pithy answers as the High Commissioner. "Go on," he said.

So Rowland told him everything he'd heard from Eva about the Shaman's curse as they were leaving the African Coast, about the subsequent fever and how contact with the animals seemed to be at the root of it.

"How interesting," the second Commissioner said. "Well, I have no further questions."

The High Commissioner checked the clock. There were still twenty minutes to go.

The third Commissioner cleared his throat. He had a big nose with broken veins, a man who looked as though he enjoyed his rum. "Now," he said, "what about the weather conditions?"

"At the time of the sinking?" said Rowland.

"Of course," said the Commissioner.

Rowland described in detail the heat, the fog, or maybe it was steam, the strange smell that day. He told how, after they'd landed on Wreck Bar, the resident scientist there, Froglick, had said that such conditions were the result of an undersea volcanic eruption.

The third Commissioner addressed his colleagues. "I read a report last week from a sailing lugger in that same region," he said. "When it raised its nets, they were full of thousands of codfish that looked as though they'd been freshly boiled."

The second Commissioner nodded. "Yes, I read that," he said. "They were given to the Charity House. But no one would eat them. They said they tasted like sulphur."

There was silence in the hearing room except for the sound of the clock.

Then the High Commissioner spoke again. "Five minutes to five," he said. "We're doing very well." Then he turned to the officer who'd acted as Secretary and ordered him to write a *brief* (emphatically, once more) official account of the hearing. "So far as this Commission is concerned," he said, "the master of the *Derevaun* was blameless." He shook his head. "Who ever heard of such a case? Jungle beasts on ships! Volcanoes under the ocean!" He looked at Rowland. "*Wrong things in wrong places,*" he said to sum it all up. He shook his head again so vigorously Rowland marvelled that those big ears didn't flap.

Now the High Commissioner looked at Will. "Have you anything to add? You have exactly one minute."

"No," said Will.

"Good," said the High Commissioner. He looked at the clock on the wall, watching the second hand climb towards the hour. At the exact moment it reached its zenith, he pushed back his chair, stood up and said: "Commission adjourned!"

– 3 –

WHEN WILL AND ROWLAND LEFT the Commission building, it was raining quite heavily. They hurried to a nearby restaurant and ate fish and chips, then went to a bar. This would be their last night together, and they were both conscious of it. They sipped their drinks silently for a while.

"Now you can go home," said Will. "I envy you."

This was the moment Rowland had been waiting for. "I'd like to put a proposition to you," he said. "I've been thinking about it for some time—something that might be quite attractive to you. Something that might be good for the two of us. And for someone else." He thought for a moment. "It would be a sort of . . . social experiment." He then outlined his scheme in some detail.

Will shook his head. He said he wouldn't even consider it.

"I just want you to think about it, that's all," said Rowland. "Just think about it and give me your final answer tomorrow."

The time was now around eight o'clock.

"The night's still young," said Rowland. "This'll be our last night. Let's celebrate."

THEY WENT OUTSIDE and stood under the awning of the bar to keep the rain off. Just across the street, they saw a sign in red bulbs: CLUB INFERNO. A taxi drew up outside it and four people got out and went through the door.

"Let's give it a try," said Rowland. They bent their heads into the rain and sprinted across the cobblestones.

Gloom and the smell of beer greeted them inside the door. Most surprisingly, considering that Rowland had just seen four people enter, there seemed to be no patrons. The few tables scattered around were quite empty except for ashtrays. They could see a bartender busy behind the bar. Rowland and Will stood uncertain at the doorway till the bartender saw them. "Come on in, boys!" he called.

They went over to the bar.

"You boys looking for some fun?" the bartender said. He nodded towards a green felt-covered door through which they could faintly hear music and the hubbub of voices. "That's where the club is," he said. "You pay me a dollar and I let you in."

"Why not?" said Rowland. "If nothing else, we can have a few drinks."

INFERNO WAS THE RIGHT NAME for the club, Rowland thought—if by inferno was meant dim red ceiling lights, loud music, a tobacco haze, the mingled smells of perfume, beer, fried fish and the sweat of too many people in a confined space.

A waitress led them to the remaining two seats at a candle-lit table with two other couples already seated. They were the four Rowland had seen get out of the taxi. The men were in sailors' uniforms. The faces of the two women were so white and their eyes so dark they looked to him like death's heads in some old painting.

They all drank beer and watched the floor show on the tiny stage. A man in a bow tie stepped out from the wings and announced each act. There were ballad singers of various sorts and a comedian who wasn't all that funny. Then the jazz band began playing loudly and Rowland signalled to Will that perhaps they ought to go elswhere. But just then the band stopped playing and the ceiling lights of the club dimmed even more, leaving only the spotlight shining on the stage.

The man in the bow tie came out. "And now, ladies and gentlemen, what you've all been waiting for, the highlight of the evening. I give you: Shaddock the Wondrous!"

He left to some light applause and Rowland saw a very thin man with a bald head, wearing only black shorts, shuffle onto the stage. His body was so pale, it might have been white-washed. He was carrying in his right hand an ordinary-looking blue tin basin, the kind used to wash dishes, and in his left a glass jug filled with water. He looked pathetic, and some of the audience, including the death's head next to Rowland, giggled.

Shaddock the Wondrous looked around the audience, quite

at ease, knowing he was going to do something that would surprise them. Carefully, he placed the basin right under the spotlight and the jug of water beside it. Then, very gingerly, as though it were full of hot water, he stepped into the basin. He carefully straightened himself till he was perfectly upright, then he stretched his hands out like a man on a cross.

For a while, it looked to Rowland as though nothing was going to happen, and there was some impatient murmuring among the audience. Then they noticed the man's legs begin to turn black at the shins; they saw that the blackness, all the more startling because he was so white, was rising slowly up, as though his body were a sponge, as though his flesh were absorbing some kind of black dye from the basin. This dye mounted higher and higher till all his body was black, then the dye spread out over his arms to the tips of his fingers. As it rose slowly up his neck, he closed his eyes. The dye climbed over his chin and, within seconds, his face, his entire head was black. His bald head was a black ball.

Shaddock the Wondrous stood there for a moment, quite still.

Then he opened his mouth—a round, pink orifice in all that darkness. And now the blackness began to pour into his mouth, like a river rushing into a sinkhole. At the extremities of his body, at his spindly legs, at the tips of his fingers, whiteness began to reassert itself. It seemed to be taking over faster than it had receded.

With revulsion, the audience understood.

The blackness was alive. It consisted of millions of little black insects that had crawled up out of the blue basin till they covered every inch of the body of Shaddock the Wondrous. Now that great tide of insects was pouring into his mouth—he was swallowing them.

From all around Rowland came cries of disgust.

Shaddock the Wondrous kept swallowing till only his face was covered—then it too was all white again. He opened his eyes, closed his mouth and stepped out of the basin. He seemed in a hurry. He lifted up the jug of water, threw his head back and poured it down his throat. He kept his head back for a moment, then went back to the blue basin and leaned over it. He opened his mouth and his frail body began to heave as he vomited the blackness out of himself, millions of insects shining wet, plummeting into the basin once more.

After the last dribble, Shaddock the Wondrous shook himself and straightened up. The audience applauded. He smiled, bowed several times, then picked up his basin and his jug and went back into the wings.

"I'VE NEVER SEEN ANYTHING LIKE THAT before," Rowland said to Will, who was shaking his head in disbelief.

"I've seen it done," said one of the sailors at their table. He was with the death's head next to Will and he was a little drunk. "They do it with ants on one of the islands down near Vatua. They eat honey and that attracts the ants into their mouths. Then they drink salt-water to chase them back out."

"*Vatua?*" said Will, suddenly interested. "I knew somebody called Vatua. Where is it?"

"It's an island down in the southern seas," said the sailor. "It's a dump, believe me."

Will persisted. "Do the women have tattoos on their ankles?" he said. "A snake swallowing its tail?"

"A lot of them do," said the sailor. "Why?"

Will didn't answer. He shook his head at Rowland, marvelling at what he'd heard. "That's where she must have come from—you know, that girl I told you about who tried to save me," he said. "We thought it was her own name. I wonder how she came to be so far away from home."

The sailor went on talking. "They've a lot of funny ideas down there," he said. "The last time we stopped in for a load of corpra, the Bosun got stung by a rockfish." He turned to the death's head, showing off his knowledge. "There's no cure for that, you know." Then back to Rowland: "You just swell up and burst if you get stung by a rockfish. The Vatuans said we should kill him and get it over with, that you shouldn't let a friend die like that. Well, anyway, we didn't do anything. He was no friend of ours." He laughed in an unpleasant way.

Rowland was still thinking of the performance by Shaddock. "And why do they swallow the ants?" he said, even though he could see the death's head was getting annoyed at her sailor for talking to others.

"It's supposed to cure sickness," the sailor said. "They believe the sickness goes into the ants and that's how to get rid of it."

"Does it work?" Rowland said.

The death's head had taken the sailor's arm and was trying to get him to pay attention to her.

"I don't know," said the sailor.

Rowland found the information about Vatua fascinating. He'd never heard of it before. Now, he had a premonition it might become important in his life. "Where exactly is Vatua?" he asked the sailor.

But it was the death's head who answered. "Find your own sailor!" she said venomously.

Just then, the man with the bow tie came back on stage to announce upcoming acts. The sailors and their escorts whispered together for a moment, then all four of them staggered from the club without another word.

– 4 –

THE NEXT MORNING, over their last breakfast together, Will and Rowland talked for a while about the odd way in which Will had at last found the truth about the girl at the Fair.

"The world's a strange place," said Rowland.

"And sometimes an awful place," said Will.

They thought about that for a while. Then Rowland asked him if he'd come to any decision about the proposition they'd discussed the day before. "I need to have an answer now," he said.

Will was silent for a moment. "I suppose I've nothing to lose," he said. "I'll give it a try."

Rowland raised his orange juice and they clinked glasses across the table.

In this way the bargain was sealed.

AT NOON, THEY WALKED TO THE STATION in a thin rain and a chill breeze—perfect weather, Rowland was thinking, for farewells.

From the station's Post Office, he telegraphed Rachel while Will bought his ticket. When the final call for boarding was made, they parted with a handshake at the platform.

Will had no sooner climbed into his carriage than the doors were slammed shut by the Porters and the Great Western puffed and squealed into motion and set out on its long journey. Rowland watched it disappear, then went back to the Maclaren Hotel.

– 5 –

IN THE LIBRARY of Rachel Vanderlinden's house in Camberloo, everyone was silent. Rachel's eyes behind her glasses were beady with concentration.

"That," Rowland said after a while, "is more or less all I can tell you. I never saw Will Drummond again. I left for India myself a few days later. But most strange for me is how that name—Vatua—became so important in my own life. That was the first time I'd ever heard it."

Thomas himself had found the entire narrative revealing. So his father had been a coal miner, a boxer, a not-very-ordinary ordinary working man, who'd arrived at his mother's door one day and taken the place of her husband and had gone and got himself killed because of love. He had only the vaguest of memories of the man with the fair hair and the deep voice who'd long ago carried him in his arms.

He glanced over at Webber, who was smiling benevolently at Rachel, his lips redder than usual from the brandy. Had he always known she'd brought a stranger into her house, the father of her child? Thomas wondered. The knowledge that she'd done such a daring thing might even have made her more attractive to him.

Rachel spoke at last. "So he'd been married before!" she said—as though, of everything she'd heard, that was what had impressed her most. "I always wondered."

"You didn't even know that?" Rowland said. "You knew none of these things?"

She shook her head. "He told me nothing," she said. "I wouldn't let him tell me anything."

Thomas felt like a spectator at some enigmatic play.

"Why not, Mother?" he said. "It doesn't make any sense."

This was an unusual outburst from him, but Rachel ignored it. She was interested only in that private conversation with Rowland.

"When he first appeared at my door," she said, "I didn't understand what was going on. Then, even when I realized what was happening, I didn't think it would work. But it did, it did. Yes, it really worked. I intended to ask him everything later. Then, when he was killed in the War, I thought it was better just to preserve things as they were. But in the last few years, I've regretted more and more that I'd never let him tell me who he really was. I couldn't bear the thought of dying without knowing. That was when I sent Thomas to look for you."

"Don't you think your son ought to know the truth now?" Rowland said.

She looked at Thomas and smiled. "I suppose so. I meant to get around to it eventually. Why don't you tell him, Rowland?"

"Very well," said Rowland. "You see, Thomas, it came out of one of my trips to Africa, long before I met your mother. I spent some time there studying a tribe with a peculiar custom. They were called the Bizwas. The husbands were always recruited from distant villages by the elders and were never allowed to tell their wives anything about themselves or where they'd come from. The marriages seemed to work very well."

Thomas was trying to fathom the absurdity of what he had heard. "So, that's where the idea came from?" he said. "This primitive tribe was where you got the notion of sending Will Drummond to my mother's door, a total stranger, to take your place?" He was exasperated, especially because he could see his mother still had a little smile on her face. "I must say," he said to her, "I'm astonished you let him persuade you."

"Persuade *me?*" Rachel said. "You've got it quite wrong. It wasn't *his* idea. It was *my* idea."

Thomas was speechless.

"I told Rowland, before he left for England, that I envied the Bizwas," she said. "At least there would always be some element of surprise left in their marriages. When Will Drummond appeared at my door a few months later, it didn't take me long to figure out what was going on. And indeed, letting him in that morning was the best thing I ever did. Thank you for that, Rowland."

Thomas was silent, still trying to absorb what he'd heard.

"Oh, Thomas!" Rachel said. "You're always so stuffy. For you, excitement's something confined to a book."

To that, Thomas could think of no reply.

"And what do you think now?" Rowland asked her. "Now

that you at least know something about Will. Does it match the man you knew?"

"Yes, in a way, it does," she said. "The funny thing is, I don't really think it would have mattered *what* you told me. He loved me and I loved him. And in the long run, that's really all that counts."

As she made this final remark, she sat back in her chair, satisfied and exhausted.

Webber got up and went to her. "You've had quite enough for today," he said. "Time for bed now."

She made no objection. "Will you come again tomorrow, Rowland?" she said.

"Of course I will," he said. "But then I have to be on my way."

Webber helped her upstairs, and when he came back down Thomas poured fresh brandies. They chatted to Rowland for a while about life in Vatua and about the long journey involved in getting there and back. Nothing more was said about Will Drummond.

Around nine o'clock, Rowland couldn't stop yawning, so Thomas called a taxi. He dropped Rowland at the Walnut and went back to his apartment. He thought about his mother and Will Drummond for a while, then inwardly shrugged. He was convinced he'd never know why she'd done such an odd, erratic thing. He went to bed and was soon in a deep sleep.

– 6 –

THE NEXT DAY, Thomas had to go to the University and deal with History Department matters that had accumulated during his absence, so he wasn't there when Rowland visited Rachel. Doctor Webber had left them alone too, so that they could talk in private. They'd talked all day long and, apparently, at the end of it, she'd tried to coax him to extend his stay a few more days. But Rowland had said he needed to go back to Vatua. When he left that night for the Walnut, they'd parted affectionately, knowing they'd never see each other again.

Thomas himself went to the hotel the next morning to say goodbye. A taxi was already waiting to take Rowland to Toronto, where he'd arranged to visit the University Press that afternoon. It was a cold morning and still snowing lightly, but the roads were passable.

"Remember," said Thomas as they stood a moment in the lobby, "go to Jeggard's office after you leave the publisher's. He has your tickets and travel arrangements. Macphee will be looking out for your arrival."

"Thomas," Rowland said, "you've been very kind to me and a wonderful travelling companion." He blinked, and Thomas thought his eyes were a little moist. "I do hope we'll meet again. Perhaps next time you visit me, you'll stay a while?" He asked this as though he wanted to believe such a thing might ever happen.

They went out to the taxi and shook hands. Even that brief exposure to the frigid air had made Rowland's hand cold and his face pinched and yellow.

The taxi slithered off down King Street in a cloud of exhaust. Thomas supposed that Rowland, used as he was to final partings, would quickly put this one out of his mind. As for himself, he was surprised at how empty he felt.

THE FOLLOWING MORNING, Jeggard phoned Thomas to tell him Rowland Vanderlinden was safely on the train to Vancouver.

"What about his visit to the University Press?" Thomas said. "Did he say anything about it?"

"He didn't keep his appointment," Jeggard said. "He looked quite ill and said he was feeling under the weather. He wanted to rest up instead for his journey."

— 7 —

DEATH, WHICH HAD ONCE BEEN AN EXOTIC to Thomas Vanderlinden, was about to become quite domesticated.

Six months after Rowland's departure, a big brown envelope arrived at his apartment by special delivery as he was drinking his morning coffee. In it was a note from Jeggard saying that he'd received the enclosed letter from Macphee and was forwarding it to Thomas immediately.

Thomas examined the other, smaller, white envelope, stained from distance and humidity—or, perhaps, sweat—and bearing a big triangular stamp with the word VATUA over a palm tree. It was addressed, in block capitals, to Jeggard. Thomas lifted it to his nose and imagined he could smell cigarette smoke from it. Inside was a brief letter signed "Alastair Macphee." The handwriting was surprisingly neat and precise for a man who drank so much, and the message was equally precise:

Dear Jeggard:
    This is to inform you of the death of Rowland Vanderlinden.

When he returned from his trip to Canada, he was very ill. The journey up to the Highlands had to be delayed so that he could recover from the voyage. He stayed at the local hotel for several months.

As soon as he was able to travel, I accompanied him safely back to his bungalow. He asked me to be sure to write you about his arrival, so that you in turn might inform those interested in his welfare.

I was halfway down to the coast again when the news of his death came by drum telegraph.

Sincerely,
Alastair Macphee

Thomas read the letter again. He wasn't so much shocked at Rowland's death—he'd known all along that he must be more ill than he admitted—as at his own sense of loss. In the course of their journey together, he'd become attached to Rowland. He couldn't help admiring his persistence and enthusiasm in his search for whatever it was he was searching for.

Later in the morning, he went to his mother's house and gave her Macphee's letter.

She read it and wept.

– 8 –

SIX MONTHS LATER, on a snowy Saturday morning in December, the phone rang in Thomas's apartment, and he picked it up with an unaccountable feeling of dread. It was

Doctor Webber, at his mother's house. "Can you come over right away?" he said. "She's very weak."

When Thomas arrived by taxi, the maid let him in before he could ring the doorbell. "You're to go straight up," she said.

As he climbed the stairs, he was very apprehensive. The pictures on the staircase wall caught his eye—a set of miniature landscapes she'd bought more for the symmetry of their frames than anything else. Now he was aware of a certain menace about those about dark mountains swathed in angular trees.

Doctor Webber—a thin, black scarecrow this day—was waiting for him at the top of the stairs outside the open bedroom door. Most unnerving to Thomas, his eyelids were red with weeping. "She doesn't have very long," said Webber.

This cliché, applied to the person Thomas loved most in the world, was like punch in the stomach.

Together they went into the bedroom. It was very warm, the window curtains drawn, the only light coming from the bedside lamp. The shadowy furniture in the corners might have been discreet mourners. Thomas and Webber went over to her bed.

She was wearing her silver-rimmed glasses, but her eyes were closed. Two little candles were tied together in a cross on her breast and that puzzled him; she'd never been a religious woman.

She opened her eyes and held out her right hand. "Thomas, thank goodness you've come." Her voice was weak but distinct, her hand was papery light. She saw him glancing at the candles on her chest. "They're supposed to ward off pain," she said. "Rowland once told me it was the custom in one of those strange places he'd been to." She now took a very tremulous breath. "I've been thinking about him a lot lately.

There's something I want you to know, Thomas," she said. "I ought to have told you long ago."

Doctor Webber began to back away. "I'll leave you alone," he said.

"No, no," she said. "Stay here." She smiled at him. "Dear Jeremiah—the best friend I've ever had."

This was the first time in all his life Thomas had ever heard her speak Webber's first name.

"Now, Thomas," she said, "I don't have time for subtlety, so here it is: Rowland was your father. You're Rowland's son." She said it again, in case he hadn't understood: "You're Rowland's son. The real Rowland. Not Will Drummond."

"But, I thought . . ." Thomas said.

"I was pregnant the month Rowland left for the British Museum," she said. "If I'd told him that, he'd have stayed. *But I didn't want him to.*" She let Thomas think about that. "I only wish I'd told you long ago," she said. "But I thought it was for the best."

"Rowland didn't have any idea?" Thomas said.

"No," she said. "I should have told both of you when he was here. A father should know his own son. You've always been just like him in so many ways, you know."

Thomas was so surprised at hearing that, he could think of nothing to say in reply. Her eyes were closed now but her hand, light as a butterfly, still held his.

She opened her eyes again.

"Will you forgive me?" she said.

"Of course," he said.

"Thank you, Thomas," she said so quietly he could barely hear her.

She focused her eyes on Webber, who'd been standing there all along without saying a word, and her lips moved but no sound came from them. Her eyes closed again, but a little smile stayed on her face. A moment later, a long sigh came from her and she was deathly still.

RACHEL VANDERLINDEN WAS BURIED TWO DAYS LATER, in a light snow, beside her father at Mount Hope Cemetery. She'd made three requests: that, twenty-four hours after her death, Webber should sever her carotid arteries to ensure against her waking up after the burial; that she be buried wearing her glasses; that the ceremony be private. The wishes were honoured.

Thomas and Webber stood together in the cold wind at the cemetery. James Best, who'd been a funeral director for forty years and for whom any show of genuine emotion would have been quite unprofessional, saw to her interment in a businesslike way. Webber and Thomas Vanderlinden were themselves well schooled in the matter of self-discipline. They successfully appeared quite unmoved as the coffin containing someone they both loved deeply was lowered into the frigid earth.

– 9 –

THOMAS SAW DOCTOR WEBBER on two more occasions after that funeral. The first time was at the lawyer's office where they heard the reading of Rachel's will. Webber seemed, impossibly, thinner than ever, even his lips beginning to lose their ripeness. For him, the will contained no surprises. She left him all he'd requested: a few photographs and some keepsakes.

The rest, aside from a sum of money and some furniture for the maid, went to Thomas.

As they were leaving the office, they spoke for a few minutes.

"Did you always know Rowland was my father?" Thomas said.

"I suspected it," said Webber. "But we never spoke about it, ever. She preferred it that way."

Thomas wasn't surprised. "The funny thing is," he said, "if Rowland was my father, that means I have a sister, too." He remembered, as he often did, that night in Rowland's bungalow. "Or, at least, a half-sister," he said.

THE SECOND TIME THOMAS SAW WEBBER was three months later. The Doctor himself was lying in a coffin at Best's. Dead, he looked healthier than the last time Thomas had seen him— even his lips had been rouged to their old colour. But basically, he was just an old, thin, dead man. He was cremated holding a photograph of Rachel to his breast, as he'd requested. And, as he'd requested, Thomas went straight to the cemetery and sprinkled the ashes over her grave.

– 10 –

IN CAMBERLOO HOSPITAL, Thomas Vanderlinden lay back against the pillow. I watched as he took several deep breaths from the oxygen mask. The revelation that he himself was the son of Rowland had certainly surprised me. I wondered what could possibly come next. He looked about to say more, but just then a nurse came into the room with some pills for him.

"Enough for today," she said to me.

"Should I come back tomorrow?" I said to Thomas. "I have a thousand questions."

He gave me a little smile. "I have a thousand answers," he said.

THAT NIGHT, MY WIFE MANAGED to sneak away from her trial preparations on the Coast and we talked for a few minutes on the phone. I told her briefly the latest developments in Thomas Vanderlinden's story. She was most surprised that Rachel hadn't told the two that they were father and son. It would have been good for father and son to acknowledge each other, she pointed out.

I said what shocked me most was that it was actually Rachel's idea to have a stranger sent to her.

My wife wasn't as indignant about that as I'd expected.

"Isn't true love all about knowing someone inside and out?" I said. "I mean, doesn't real love begin when the mystery's over? And anyway, aren't women supposed to be less interested in mystery than security and all that sort of stuff?"

"I suppose you're right," she said, but didn't sound convinced.

– 11 –

THOMAS VANDERLINDEN DIED that very night just before midnight. I didn't find out till next day when I went to pick up a coffee for my visit and some instinct made me call the hospital from the wall phone outside Tim Hortons. Through the doughnut-shop window I could see the customers, chatting to each other, reading newspapers, munching doughnuts, all of them with things to do, places to go. I was watching them as the duty nurse told me he'd died peacefully in his sleep.

I hung up the phone and stood for a while. I would miss Thomas. In the short time we'd been acquainted, I'd come to like him a good deal. I thought I knew the kind of man he was: a scholar, a spectator who lived on the fringes of others' exciting lives and whose own life was relatively dull.

I could hardly have been more wrong.

PART FIVE

THOMAS
VANDERLINDEN

They change to a high new house,
He, she, all of them—aye,
Clocks and carpets and chairs
        On the lawn all day,
And brightest things that are theirs . . .
        Ah, no; the years, the years;
Down their carved names the rain-drop ploughs.
                —THOMAS HARDY

– 1 –

A WOMAN HOWLED at the funeral.

IT WAS TWO DAYS AFTER Thomas Vanderlinden's death and
the service was being held at Mount Hope Cemetery. I don't
like funerals and didn't really want to attend. But he'd specifically asked his lawyer to invite me, and I didn't know how to
refuse a dead man's request.

So I drove to the cemetery, which, like most cemeteries, was
once on the outskirts of the town so that people wouldn't have
to be reminded constantly of mortality. But Camberloo has
grown and grown until it now cautiously encircles the old
graveyard. Many of the old families who settled the town
almost two centuries ago were buried here, their final sleep
now ruined by the roar of machines they could never have
imagined. The graveyard oaks that were once taller than most
buildings those old folks had ever seen are dwarfed by even the
least impressive apartment towers.

I got out of my car and walked in through the north gate
past a mix of old and newer gravestones—those founders of
Camberloo have been joined here by thousands of latecomers
from around the world, all equally "landed immigrants" at
last. Some of the dead here were born in countries where it's
the tradition to put photographs of the deceased on their
gravestones. The faces of many of them have become as
ghostly as their owners now presumably are. As for the oldest
gravestones, I could barely make out the names on them. The
stones seem no longer to commemorate individual deaths so

much as Death itself. Some graves had fresh flowers on them, and that made me think of Thomas Vanderlinden, tending his flower beds in the mornings. My acquaintance with him hadn't even lasted as long as the life of one of his hardy annuals.

Thinking such melancholy thoughts, I gradually worked my way through the cemetery and joined the small group assembled at the Vanderlinden grave. Aside from the bald undertaker—BEST'S FUNERAL SERVICES on his breast pocket—there were four gravediggers. A woman in black was there too. She was quite tall, her face covered by a veil, so I couldn't tell how old she was. There was also a chubby clergyman wearing a dog-collar with the undertaker's logo on it—the in-house clergyman, I presumed. I was surprised, for I hadn't thought of Thomas as a conventionally religious man. The clergyman smiled and nodded to me when I joined them. His left eye was bloodshot and had a slight upward cast, so that he kept one eye constantly on Heaven.

The gravestone itself was made of some kind of dark marble. The only name on it was the incised family name, *Vanderlinden*. A gleaming mahogany coffin lay on two wooden supports beside the grave.

"Let us now commence," the clergyman said and began reading the words of the funeral service. When he came to the words "Thy servant Thomas———," he had to look at the stone to remind himself of the last name. His earthbound eye then glanced over at the veiled woman apologetically. "I didn't know the deceased personally," he murmured. "I'm sure he was a good man."

When he'd finished reading, he gave a signal, and the gravediggers took hold of the silk-tasselled ropes and started lowering the coffin into the ground.

THAT WAS WHEN the howling began.

It wasn't really so much a howling as a high-pitched whine, the kind you hear from a telephone wire. It was coming from the woman behind the veil. The sound was so eerie that people attending another burial, fifty yards away, were looking over at us. The undertaker and the clergyman seemed quite uncomfortable too, but the gravediggers paid no attention. They kept on lowering the coffin without so much as a glance at her. No doubt, in the course of their work, they'd seen everything.

I was wishing I'd followed my instincts and stayed home.

When the coffin reached the bottom of the grave, the ropes slackened and the howling stopped. The woman took off her glove, picked up a piece of clay and threw it down onto the coffin. It struck with a dull thud. The clergyman read a brief prayer then closed his book with finality and smiled. The gravediggers picked up their long-handled shovels, ready to begin their work. The undertaker, the sun glinting on his bald pate, nodded to them, then took the woman's arm and led her from the graveside, followed by the clergyman. As I slipped away, I could hear the earth thumping down heavily on the coffin.

I'D ALMOST REACHED MY CAR when I heard footsteps right behind me.

"Thank you for coming."

I turned reluctantly, knowing who it must be. She had taken off her veil. She looked as though she was in her thirties, with a noticeable jaw, blue eyes behind wire-rimmed glasses and fair hair. She was quite tall and solid: a competent-looking woman, with a big black purse. She put out her gloved hand and shook my hand firmly.

"I'm Thomas's daughter," she said. "Miriam."

That was certainly a surprise. I'd taken it for granted that Thomas Vanderlinden was one of those adults who never have children and retain a certain childishness of their own.

She read my mind, or my face.

"I'm sure he didn't mention me," she said.

We were standing on the sidewalk near my car, the sun was beating down on us and I didn't know what to say.

"You probably thought I was a madwoman?" she said. "I mean, making that noise?"

I denied it, but I could see she didn't believe me, for she laughed—a nice laugh that lit up her face.

"It just came into my head at the last minute," she said. "I thought he'd like the idea of it. He once told me it was something mourners in ancient Smyrna used to do. The noise was supposed to drive the souls of the dead out of their bodies, on the off chance they didn't want to leave." She smiled. "I was hoping it wouldn't drive everyone else away too."

I relaxed, knowing she wasn't a madwoman.

"I think he'd have liked it," I said. "But I was surprised at seeing a clergyman. Thomas never struck me as a religious man."

"Best's phoned last night and said he was part of the funeral package," she said, laughing her nice laugh. "My father always liked tradition, so I thought, why not?" Then she said: "Could I buy you a cup of coffee?"

"Great," I said.

WE SAT IN THE COOL of the Donut Palace on the corner of Camberloo Square. I watched her as she talked. She had the kind of face you grew to like the more you saw her. Her eyes behind her glasses were like little blue ponds. Sometimes, when she was being very serious, they'd darken the way water does when clouds get in the way of the sun. In the astute way she looked at you, I thought I could detect her father most. I discovered she was a social worker in Toronto, married, with children of her own.

"I phoned Father every week," she said. "He told me you were his new neighbour. How do you like the house?"

"Very much," I said. "I like everything about it. So does my cat."

She laughed at that.

"Except for the basement," I said. "She won't go near it."

She gave me an odd look when I said that but talked about her father again.

"He told me he enjoyed talking to you."

"We used to chat in the mornings out in the yard," I said. "I really only got to know him well when he was in hospital."

"What did he tell you about himself?" Her blue eyes seemed to me honest and fearless.

"Well," I said, "he didn't actually talk much about himself. But he did talk a lot about his parents. It was quite fascinating."

"Please," she said. "Tell me."

So, I began at the beginning. I gave her a rough outline of everything he'd told me in those last days in the hospital: about Rachel and her relationship with the stranger who came to her door; about Thomas's journey to find Rowland Vanderlinden; about the revelations concerning Will Drummond; and finally about Thomas's discovery that he was Rowland's son. She listened to all I had to say with great interest, nodding from time to time at certain parts of the story, as though she'd heard them before.

"So that's about it," I said when I'd finished. "It was really incredible. But he never actually said that much about himself. For example, I'd no idea he had a family of his own."

"He had his secrets, all right," she said.

"Really?" I said. I was enjoying her company and she seemed to want to talk. So I said: "I'd love to hear about them."

We ordered another cup of coffee and she began to talk about the Thomas Vanderlinden I didn't know.

– 2 –

AFTER RACHEL VANDERLINDEN'S DEATH, Thomas had remained a bachelor for some years. Then, in his mid-forties, he met Doris Petzel. She was a quiet woman who worked in a used bookstore but was more interested in books as objects than in reading them. She was forty by then, always meticulous in her clothing and appearance, and she had reached that stage when she assumed she'd be a spinster forever. She did have a sort of family: five cats who dominated her life and her apartment—in fact, simply put, she was their servant.

Thomas asked Doris Petzel out to dinner several times and did most of the talking, mainly about his research. She was a good listener. Sometimes, too, they shared silences that were bridged only by the clatter of the restaurant dishes and the murmur of other diners. She was a woman who was comfortable with silence.

Three big surprises were in store for Doris Petzel: the first was when, within six weeks of first asking her out, Thomas proposed; the second followed immediately when she heard herself accept; the third was just a month after their subsequent marriage, when she found herself pregnant.

By then, of course, she and the five cats were living in the Vanderlinden mansion. When she told Thomas about the pregnancy, he immediately went to his study and, within a few minutes, emerged carrying a smouldering dish. From it, a sweet, sickly smell arose.

"I've had this prepared for some time," he told her. "It's a recipe from ancient Persia I found in Herodotus. When couples discovered they were going to have a child, they'd fumigate their house with civet and myrrh for thirty days. The smell's supposed to ensure that the child will be universally loved."

To please him, Doris put up with the awful smell for thirty days. The five cats wrinkled their nostrils with disgust at it. In due course, Doris gave birth to a daughter, Miriam. But far from being universally loved, she was loathed by the five cats: they snarled and hissed whenever Doris fed her, or even touched her.

Naturally, the cats had to go.

MIRIAM GREW into a contented, self-possessed child. By the age of five, she understood and accepted the nature of the household she'd been born into. Her father was more interested in his studies than in domestic life and often worked late in his office at the University. Her mother stayed at home but was always well groomed, her make-up perfect even at breakfast.

Doris had no more to say for herself then than she had before she married. One day, when little Miriam was around five, playing in the yard with a school friend, she saw her mother watching her through the kitchen window. The children were chattering the way children chatter.

Later, Doris asked her about it.

"What do you talk about?" she said.

"I don't know," said Miriam. "We just talk."

"Do you just keep saying the same things over and over again?" Doris said. She seemed to believe that conversation was some kind of a trick her daughter might teach her. Miriam, of course, couldn't help.

On other occasions, Doris would weep helplessly, and it was Miriam who would comfort her, hugging her and cooing: "There, there. Mummy'll be all right."

Nothing in particular seemed to set off Doris's tears, but on one occasion she confessed to Miriam that it was the memory of her cats. She said she couldn't forget the accusing looks they gave her as they were bundled away in a truck to be disposed of.

"I feel so guilty," she said.

"Why?" said Miriam.

"If I hadn't had you, they wouldn't have had to go," she sobbed. Then she realized what she'd said and was stricken with such extra guilt at having blamed her daughter that Miriam had to spend a long time soothing her.

WHEN MIRIAM WAS FIFTEEN, she had a frightening dream. In the dream, she came home from school and found the house completely empty, all the furniture gone and no sign of her parents. She awoke in a state of panic and was relieved it was only a dream.

At breakfast, she told her parents about it. Doris, of course, had nothing to say. Thomas was very interested: he told her how, in the Renaissance, great stock was placed on dreams. They were taken as omens of things to come, though nowadays that idea was somewhat discredited.

Miriam asked him if he ever had ominous dreams.

He said perhaps he did, but if so, it didn't really matter, for he could never seem to remember them. No sooner did he try, he said, than they fell apart, fragile as roses when you picked them.

MIRIAM DREAMED VARIATIONS OF HER DREAM about the empty house several times thereafter, but she didn't take them as omens. She came to the sensible conclusion that there was only the most tenuous link between the world of dreams and the real world. Nor did she worry about the lack of communication between her parents. Didn't the parents of most of her school friends often seem to ignore each other too? Anyway, she was certain her parents loved her—though they'd never have said it outright—and that was what mattered most to her.

AT EIGHTEEN, MIRIAM APPLIED to the University of Toronto and was accepted. She'd never been away from home and was looking forward to living on her own in a University residence.

On a Wednesday morning at seven o'clock, three weeks to the day before her departure, she was awakened by Doris bending over her.

"What's wrong?" Miriam was alarmed.

"It's your father," said Doris. "He didn't come home last night." Despite the fact that she seemed distraught, she'd meticulously applied her make-up before waking Miriam.

Miriam got out of bed and the two of them sat, considering what they should do. They phoned Thomas's office, to no avail. Miriam was for calling the police, but just then the phone rang and she picked it up, hopefully.

It was Thomas's lawyer.

"I'd like to come and see you and your mother at nine o'clock this morning," he said. "To discuss your father's absence."

The lawyer did arrive at nine and quickly explained the situation. There was nothing sinister about it. Thomas had simply moved out. He'd been planning his departure for some time and had decided to make the move before Miriam left for University, knowing she'd be able to deal with the practicalities before she went.

Indeed, it was not to Doris but to Miriam that the lawyer showed a thick file containing detailed financial arrangements.

"Overall, it's very fair," he said. "Your allowance will enable you to continue your education quite comfortably. In addition, your mother will have a very generous settlement and she'll retain possession of the house for as long as she lives. Your father and I tried to anticipate every contingency." He said this as though he expected to be congratulated for his part in the matter.

Miriam didn't feel at all like congratulating him.

"Was it another woman?" She asked this on behalf of her mother.

The lawyer seemed disappointed at the question.

"I don't believe so," he said. "But that's neither here nor there. My function is to deal with the distribution of property and finances. Personal matters are outside my ambit."

THAT WORD "AMBIT" ECHOED in Miriam's brain after the lawyer left. She remembered how Thomas, earlier that very summer, had come to the dinner table late. He'd been reading and put the book beside him on the table.

"What a nice cover," Miriam said, for the book was old and leather-bound with gilt ornamentation.

"It's about Cyrius the Ambulist," Thomas said. "Have you come across him?"

"No, I haven't," she said.

"He was one of the most fascinating of the ancient Stoics," Thomas said. "He believed that attachment to earthly things is what makes life, as well as death, unbearable. So, at an early age, he left his home in Damascus and began walking around the countries of the Middle East, never using the same road twice. For forty years he walked all day long, every single day, stopping only to defecate and to sleep. And, of course, ultimately, to die."

"How weird!" Miriam said, as she often did about matters that seemed to interest her father.

"The followers of Cyrius," Thomas said, "walked along with him and recorded his sayings for posterity. You see? Here's one of his most famous axioms." He handed Miriam the book. There, in bold print on the opening page, were the words: **"Whatever the wise man loves, he walks away from."**

– 3 –

NOW, IN THE DONUT PALACE, I could only shake my head. But after a while I did say something.

"Well, well," I said.

Miriam sipped her coffee, enjoying my reaction.

"Of course, I'd no idea *he* was going to imitate Cyrius!" she said, smiling her nice smile. "But he did. That was twelve years ago, now."

"Where did he go?" I said.

"Not far," she said. "But it might as well have been a thousand miles. We were to communicate with him from then on only through his lawyer."

"You must have felt very hurt," I said. "You must have missed him."

She smiled.

"Not really," she said. "I suppose he'd always been sort of missing—as though a major part of him had never really been at home with us. Anyway, we couldn't do anything to stop him. He wasn't breaking any law. We couldn't have forced him to come back even if we'd wanted to." She thought for a while. "Actually, I've always believed the reason he told me about Cyrius the Ambulist wasn't so much to warn me that he was thinking of leaving. I think it was to let me know indirectly that he loved both me and Mother, in his way. I never really doubted that. Then again, you must have noticed he always liked citing precedents. I sometimes wonder if he would have done it if it hadn't been done before!"

Looking at her, I wondered how two such parents could have produced such a daughter, so wise, so good-humoured. Perhaps she'd reacted to her parents—as many children do—by becoming their opposite: practical, rather than bookish, like her father; active, rather than passive, like her mother. But for that howling at the funeral, I'd have thought her the most down-to-earth of people.

"How did your mother react?" I said.

"Much as you'd expect," she said. "She seemed stunned at first, so I talked her into getting some cats. She got three of them and right away they took up all her attention—she dedicated herself to being their servant. I think, when all's said and done, that's the kind of woman she was: she didn't mind being used."

"A Dutch Wife!" I said.

Miriam looked puzzled but kept talking.

"She died eight years ago," she said. "I was living in Toronto permanently by then. Father moved back into the house and looked after the cats till they died." She shrugged.

"After that, there's not much more to tell. Naturally I'd no idea he was ill. His lawyer called me to let me know he'd died. I was upset at first that I didn't have a chance to have a last talk with him. But I wouldn't be surprised if that was the way he wanted it."

She thought about that for a while, then those blue eyes focused on me again.

"I think," she said, "that's why I'm able in my work to deal with dysfunctional families. I mean, that's what our family was—dysfunctional, in a civilized sort of way. I'm sure it's a very common syndrome."

We ordered one more cup of coffee.

"So," I said, "all those things he told me about his own parents: you'd heard all that before?"

"Oh, yes," she said. "He used to tell me about them often when I was a little girl."

"So it's all true?" I said.

"Of course it is," she said, frowning. "He may have been many things, but he wasn't a liar."

"I didn't really mean that," I said. "I just mean it all sounded so exotic."

"Exotic to an outsider, perhaps," she said. "I never thought of it that way. Isn't it funny how your *own* family never seems all that exotic. Especially things you've heard since you were a child."

"Maybe so," I said.

"By the way," she said, "a while back, you said my mother was a 'Dutch Wife.' What did you mean by that? She wasn't Dutch. Neither was my father, really—except for the name."

I told her it was Thomas I'd heard use the phrase several times. That it wasn't always flattering and could mean a woman who wasn't much more than a piece of bedroom equipment.

"Well," she said, "in that case, I'm sure there are more than enough Dutch Wives to go around. And Dutch Husbands, too, for that matter."

While I was trying to figure out what that meant, she sipped the last of her coffee and glanced at her watch. "I really have to get back to Toronto. It's been very nice meeting you." She took a pen from her purse and wrote a phone number on the back of a napkin. "Next time you're coming to town, give me a call. I'd love for you to meet my family."

We left the cool of the Donut Palace and went out into the heat of the midday sun. We shook hands and went our respective ways. I had no doubt we'd meet again.

— 4 —

ONE MORNING A FEW WEEKS LATER, I was at home in the library struggling with *The Kilted Cowpoke*. I'd been at it for hours and felt like a break, so I got up to stretch my legs and look out the window. Just then a black Mercedes pulled up on the street outside. A stocky man in a pin-striped suit, carrying a briefcase, got out and came up the pathway. I opened the door before he could ring and he stared at me with the unblinking, red-tinged eyes of a bulldog.

"I'm Scott Campbell, the late Professor Vanderlinden's lawyer," he said and put out his hand. His grip was light for

298 THE DUTCH WIFE

such a fierce-looking man. "I'd like to speak to you for a few minutes."

I brought him into the library and we sat down.

"I'll come to the point right away," he said. "This building's to be sold in the New Year. In Professor Vanderlinden's will, he says you can stay here till then, rent free." He pulled a document out of his briefcase. "I've drawn up a memo to that effect."

I didn't quite understand.

"The building? Professor Vanderlinden? You mean Thomas? What did he have to do with it?"

"He owned it," he said.

"Really?" That was a surprise. "I assumed he just rented the other side, like me."

The red-tinged eyes didn't flinch.

"No," he said. "He was your landlord. He owned the whole building. It used to be one big house till it was split up, years ago. He and his family stayed in the other side and rented this side out."

I was just absorbing this, wondering why Thomas never mentioned it, when Campbell surprised me again.

"Actually, when he separated from his wife it was a bit like Musical Chairs." He said this without any sign of humour. "He just moved into this part of the building. Then when she died, he moved back next door again."

I couldn't believe what I'd heard. I asked him to repeat it and he did: that Thomas Vanderlinden's separation from his wife amounted to moving only a few yards away.

Campbell continued to heap surprise on surprise. He gave me the whole history of the place. It had been bought by Judge

Vanderlinden at the turn of the century, when he was involved in the circuit courts. He had a reputation for promptness—clocks everywhere, even in the bathroom. He'd intended to retire there, but died at his work. The house went to his daughter Rachel, Thomas's mother. As a source of income, she'd had it split into two parts. Thomas, in his turn, inherited it from Rachel.

"So, naturally," said Campbell, "when he separated from his wife, he just moved into this side."

I searched those red-rimmed eyes for any sign of amusement, in vain.

"But what was the point in separating, then?" I said. "How could he avoid seeing the woman every day?"

"He saw her, all right," said Campbell. "But they communicated only through the lawyer. He never spoke to her directly for the rest of her life."

I was trying to absorb all of this. Thomas Vanderlinden was a much stranger man than I'd ever suspected. I was still puzzling over the fact that he hadn't told me I was actually his tenant when Campbell spoke again.

"She actually died in the basement," he said.

"What?" I said. "Who?"

"His wife," he said. "It seems she went down to the basement after one of the cats, and while she was down there the bulb blew. They found her a few days after. Her mind was a little delicate, you know."

Again, I was startled.

"After that," said Campbell, "Professor Vanderlinden moved back in and began renting this side out again. It became vacant just at the time you were looking for a place." The red eyes glared. "I instructed his agent to encourage you to take it."

The house agent, Victoria Gough—she had been so anxious that I should rent the place. I'd been surprised at how cheap it was.

"Why me?" I said.

"I had you checked out," said Campbell, his eyes, if possible, wider. "The Professor always liked to know who he was renting to. His previous tenants were an accountant and his wife. They were very tidy and very quiet. The Professor thought it might be nice to have a writer for a neighbour." The bulldog eyes bulged again.

"Why didn't he tell me he owned the place?" I said.

"He was a thoughtful man," said Campbell. "I'm sure he didn't want you to feel obliged in any way."

I was nevertheless beginning to feel quite paranoid.

"By the way," Campbell said, his eyes bulging so much I feared they might drop out of his head, "did you meet his daughter at the funeral?"

"Yes, I did," I said. "She didn't mention anything about the house either."

"That's good." He said this as though he had just ticked off an item on some mental agenda.

– 5 –

CAMPBELL'S VISIT LEFT ME WITH NO DOUBT that Thomas Vanderlinden had manipulated my life and would have enjoyed my discovery of that fact. I remembered a conversation

I'd once had with him. It was on one of those beautiful summer mornings in the back yard when I was having an awful time with *The Kilted Cowpoke*. I remarked to Thomas that nothing could be less pleasant, on such a day, than being stuck at home, sweating out sentences.

"Ah well," I said. "I suppose I've no one to blame but myself."

That cliché seemed unusually interesting to him.

"Not according to Franciscus Hispanicus," he said. "He believed we have *nothing* to blame ourselves for."

Of course, I'd never heard of him.

"He was one of those sixteenth-century mystical philosophers," Thomas said. "He was burned at the stake."

"Was that because he didn't believe in Free Will?" I said.

"You mean, you do?" he said with a little smile.

MY WIFE FINALLY CAME BACK for good from the West Coast and we did stay on in our now rent-free abode and I did get *The Kilted Cowpoke* finished. The Scottish dialect was abandoned, but those kilts and sporrans remained.

In mid-December, just after the first snow, FOR SALE signs went up on the front lawn, and a variety of potential buyers came to look the building over. My wife was at work, and during the inspections I usually went for a coffee. One morning, I asked the real estate agent if I could have a quick look at Thomas's side before his clients arrived. He gave me the key and in I went.

Thomas's side of the building was for the most part a reverse-image of the part I'd lived in for the last six months. Not just the location of the various rooms—no, the two sides were replicas of each other even in the details of décor and colours: the same dark carpets with their faded geometrical designs; the same gloomy mahogany furniture, with the knobby sideboard standing in exactly the same place; the same eccentric bathroom with multiple shower-heads, privy on a platform—complete with a rusted-out clock with the hands fallen off, lying together like twigs at the bottom of the crystal. Even the library seemed to have the same set of books that were in my side. Where pictures had once hung on the wall, there were only the same ghostly shapes.

As I was leaving, I passed the basement door and the hairs on my neck stood up. I peeked in and switched on the light, but I didn't go down the stairs. The earth floor smelled as earthy, the dark corners mocked my timidity. I switched the light off, shut the door firmly and went outside into the cold, fresh air.

– 6 –

THAT WAS TEN YEARS AGO.

This present March, I was sitting on the balcony of our latest apartment, sipping coffee, glancing through the *Camberloo Record*. On the back page was a brief report on an accident on the highway south of Toronto. A certain Miriam Vanderlinden-Smythe, daughter of the late Professor Thomas Vanderlinden, had been killed, along with her entire family—her husband and two children—in a collision between their car and a truck.

I was saddened. I'd only met Miriam once, at her father's funeral, but I'd liked her and regretted never having got in touch with her—even if it was only to ask if our meeting at the funeral had been purely accidental. Or why she didn't think it worth mentioning that when her father left home, he only moved next door.

Then again, who can make sense of what other people do? Often it's hard enough making sense of what we do ourselves. I remember saying something of that sort to Thomas, but, of course, he didn't agree. He just quoted a couple of memorable lines from some old poet I'd never heard of:

> Thy neighbour's life hath e'er a plot;
> Thine own hath never one.

I didn't argue. But, to be honest, I wasn't even sure what the lines meant till some time after his death.

It was a late summer's evening, and my wife and I were climbing Barden Hill at the southern edge of Camberloo, where the city suddenly becomes country. The hill isn't all that high, but old—one of those drumlins formed by a deposit from one of the Ice Ages, a billion years ago, or whenever it was. Perhaps, as hills go, a billion years isn't that old. But Barden Hill isn't much of a hill, either: getting to the top is less a climb than a sweaty, mosquito-attracting walk.

That particular night was warm and cloudless. When we got to the top, we had a clear view of the Milky Way spread out across the skies. Looking earthwards, to the north, we could see all the street lights of Camberloo, with Regent Street dominant, intersected by innumerable lesser streets and avenues.

But when we moved just a hundred yards along the crest of the hill, my wife drew my attention to something strange. From where we'd stood at first, Camberloo had looked all laid out in an orderly, human way. But from here, the order was completely disrupted. The city had become a sparkling chaos, just like the chaos of stars above.

That was when I remembered those lines Thomas had quoted and I thought I understood what he'd meant. That your own life is a chaos to you—you're inside it and you're so overwhelmed by the detail, you despair of ever finding any consistent order or meaning in it. Whereas an outsider—an observer of your life—is able to move about and, with any luck, might be able to find an angle to view it from and make some sense of it, might be able to spot the tendencies and symmetries and coincidences you yourself can't possibly see.

– 7 –

COINCIDENCES, COINCIDENCES.

Six months ago, the Vanderlinden property came up for sale again—and this time I decided to buy it. The two sides of the original house, separated for more than half a century, had been reunited by the previous owners and completely renovated. At the front, the western entrance had been expanded, the eastern door had been bricked off. Out back, the hedge over which I used to talk to Thomas Vanderlinden had been excised to make an unbroken expanse of lawn.

The changes to the inside of the house weren't, to my mind, for the better. The dark-brown wainscotting and the lovely old mahogany furniture were gone. The walls throughout were now covered in eggshell-blue paint. Other things were simply disconcerting: the rooms that had been on either side of the partitioning wall were now doubled in size—I felt as if I were walking right through a mirror. The library, which before I had thought quite large enough, now seemed so massive I felt myself dwarfed by it, and even more overwhelmed by all those books I'd have no more excuse for not reading. Another thing I regretted: the quirky bathrooms off the two main bedrooms had been conventionalized. The raised toilets had been lowered, the multiple showers replaced, the rusted clocks removed.

When we eventually took possession, our cats (three of them now) enjoyed roaming through the house after the confinements of apartment life, and we sometimes lost track of them for hours. But we could always be sure they weren't in the basement. In that regard, the younger cats took their cue from Corinna—twelve years old now, with grizzled whiskers—and always steered well clear of the basement door. Even my wife wasn't keen on going down there. That was my fault; I hadn't been able to resist telling her how Thomas's wife had died.

I, on the other hand, did have to go down from time to time to check the plumbing or the electrical fuses. The door had been changed by the renovators, so there were no scratches on the back of it, but the stair was still creaky. The basement itself was doubly cavernous now that its dividing wall had been removed. The caged ceiling bulbs were just as gloomy as before, so the corners were in semi-darkness. You could barely see that there had once been an equivalent little stairway at the far side; it had been dismantled and the door above it walled over. The size of the place and the earthy smell of it always made me think of one of those little cemeteries you see at dusk beside country churches.

NOW THAT WE LIVED THERE permanently, I even had a recurrence of the nightmare I used to have—of the beautiful creature lurking behind that basement door, waiting to destroy me.

It must have been around midnight when I heard the noise and got out of bed, quietly, so as not to wake my wife. I went downstairs and crouched in the darkness outside the basement door. I knew exactly what was coming and my heart was battering. I could hear the creature stealthily climbing the creaky stairs. When the doorknob slowly began to turn, I got myself ready to pounce. The door opened and there it stood in all its beauty (I knew it was beautiful, even in the darkness) for just a moment. Then I shoved it back and slammed the door against it. I had absolutely no doubt it would have destroyed me if I hadn't.

− 8 −

AT ANY RATE, it wasn't long after having the dream again that I began to consider seriously the feasibility of making a book out of the Vanderlinden story. Maybe I thought telling the story would lay the ghost to rest, I don't know. But the idea of doing it must have been in my mind somewhere, all along—that was why I'd kept notes of my various conversations with Thomas.

"It's just like *The Rime of the Ancient Mariner*," I said to my wife. "You know—the bearded old man who can't die in peace till he's passed on his story. And I'm the wedding guest chosen to hear it, and all that stuff. I feel sometimes as though *I'm a part of someone else's plot* and Thomas made sure I rented the place so that he'd end up telling me his story."

"But you've always said you prefer making up your own stories," my wife said.

"Yes, but this one is so interesting," I said, "it outdoes fiction. Even the things he didn't tell me, like the fact that when he separated from his wife he moved next door. It's astounding."

"You really believe it's all true?" she said.

"Before I write a word," I said, "I'll check up as much of it as I can. It's a pity his daughter's dead. She vouched for him. She said it was all true."

My wife sighed.

"Women don't always tell the truth, you know," she said.

"Not even the women I like?" I said, trying to butter her up.

"Especially not those," she said.

IN THE WEEKS FOLLOWING that conversation, I set out to reassure myself about the basic facts of Thomas Vanderlinden's story. I dug up my notes from our talks and did a little research. Here's a sample of the results:

1) *Rachel Vanderlinden:* I found her listed in the *Provincial Registry* of 1920 as the daughter of the eminent Judge Ebenezer Dafoe. Her marriage to Rowland Vanderlinden was recorded, too.

2) Will Drummond: I could find no references to him. On the other hand, Scottish newspapers of the period were full of sensationalist reports on such matters as *The One-legged Miners at Muirton; The Abyss at Stroven; The Talking Disease at Carrick;* and *The Mackenzie Family Atrocity.*

3) Doctor Jeremiah Webber: He was cited frequently in *Ontario Medical Records.* He figured prominently on Medical Boards in the community of Camberloo for more than half a century.

4) The Jeggard Agency: It was no longer in existence but was mentioned in several old issues of *The Police Journal* as a reliable source of investigative information. Apparently Jeggard himself, now dead, had once been a member of the Force.

5) The Sorrentino Family: This Italian family was lauded in early ecological journals. But I also found references to their work even in quite recent monographs (e.g., *Of Apes and Italians,* by the well-known activist Alfredo Romano). Their far-sighted attempts to preserve exotic animals, early in the century, were said to be truly remarkable.

6) The Loss of the S.S. Derevaun: Many national newspapers reported the ship's foundering without mentioning the matter of survivors. In *The Abridgement of Maritime Commissions* I came across a report that the ship's officers were exonerated, *post mortem,* of all blame.

7) Herbert Froglick: He published one rather dry, academic piece entitled, "Sunami-type Occurrences off the East Coast" *(The Journal of Marine Meteorology).* It was full of graphs and technical matters based on many years of observations made on Wreck Bar. It was quite unreadable to a layman; but I was thrilled to find this note at the end: "To my co-researcher and beloved companion, *the late Eva Sorrentino,* this article is dedicated."

8) John Forrestal: In *A Cultural History of Latin America* by J. M. Barthez, a paragraph is devoted to the Quibo Museum. The politically correct author, while rejoicing that the era of foreigners as Curators is long since past, commends the work of "such early administrators as the North American John Forrestal." I could find no information on his wife and daughter.

9) Rowland Vanderlinden: He is listed in the most recent *Canadian Almanack of Anthropology* as a "former honorary affiliate of the National Museum." He'd been erroneously reported as killed in action in the War. He'd published numerous articles (including "Fetishistic Devotion Among the Arborean Boma") and received the prestigious Haas Corporate Endowment to pursue his research indefinitely. One of the perks of the Endowment was that the University Press would publish the holder's research (presumably that was why Rowland had intended to visit the Press during his visit). I then made a sad discovery in a special Preface to an old issue of the *Universal Journal of Field Anthropology* (vol. xxx): The *Journal* issued a heartfelt plea to working anthropologists to see to the publication of their research in a timely fashion. It cited a tragic case in point. *"After his death in Manu, the anthropologist Rowland Vanderlinden was ritually cremated—a signal honour for an outsider—-by the Tarapa tribe among whom he'd spent much of his career. Ironically, as part of the ceremony, all of his notebooks—a lifetime's invaluable observations—were added to the funeral pyre."* The *Journal* noted that information on this incident had been garnered from a certain Alastair Macphee, an agent for the Pacific Information Bureau.

10) Alastair Macphee: I immediately contacted the *Pacific Information Bureau,* whose Head Office was in Wellington, New Zealand. I hoped I might be able to phone Macphee, or even meet him. The Human Resources Department for the P.I.B. told me, however, that he had retired long ago. For at least a decade, his monthly pension had been forwarded to various remote islands. Several years ago, the cheques began to be returned, uncashed. Macphee himself was presumed dead.

11) Rowland's Consort and daughter: This was the least fruitful line of inquiry. Apparently the custom in the Manu Highlands was for widows and orphans to be adopted by other members of the tribe and to change their names accordingly. Since I'd no idea of their original names anyway, I abandoned the search.

12) Thomas Vanderlinden: Out of curiosity, I paid a visit to the History Department at Camberloo University, where he'd been on the faculty for thirty-five years till his retirement.

The Chair of the Department was a plump, nattily dressed man who said he only vaguely remembered Thomas as an old-fashioned scholar who'd dabbled in the Renaissance: *"He was one of those amateurish types who managed to survive in academia at a time when standards weren't so rigorous as nowadays. I can't imagine why anyone should be interested in him."* I smiled (inwardly, of course). Thomas had once referred to this same Chair of History as a "total pisspot." He'd seen my surprise at his use of such language and assured me it was a perfectly respectable term of abuse—in the sixteenth century.

13) *The Bizwas:* This was perhaps the most astonishing discovery. I came across an article in *Anthropological Investigations* (vol. lxvii), from more than half a century ago. It was written by Rowland Vanderlinden himself and is illuminating.

A Bizwa Custom

One night, the District Commissioner and I were invited to the dining hut as guests of the tribe and were greeted by the Chief, who was a woman. Like most Bizwa women, she was quite tall and muscular with a shaved skull. Her all-male councillors were at least a head shorter than she was.

The Commissioner greeted her on behalf of the Government and presented her with a roll of silk.

Now dinner was served: pieces of roast meat and jugs of honey beer were set on mats. I didn't eat much, but I found the beer delicious and drank plenty of it. I had an adequate grasp of

*the various dialects of the region so I was able to converse with
the Chief. She was an intelligent and good-natured woman.*

*Emboldened by the beer (and in spite of the Commissioner's
warning), I asked her about a man I'd seen earlier that day tied
to a post in the middle of the village. He'd been smeared with
honey and was being attacked by thousands of vicious wasps. She
said she was sorry that had been my introduction to the usually
very placid lives of the Bizwas. It had always been the Bizwa
custom to intermarry their women with men from distant
villages. This particular man originally came from a village
twenty miles upriver and married one of her subjects. The man
had broken one of the major Bizwa taboos:* the taboo against the
husband revealing his past life to his wife. *Just yesterday, he had
been overheard telling his wife about his life in his home village.*

*The pair were dragged before the Chief. The husband confessed
it was all his fault. He said it took him almost a year to persuade
his wife to allow him to break the taboo.*

*The Chief had no choice in the matter. The man was sentenced
to be smeared with honey and tied to the stake. Some nests of the
most vicious jungle wasps were set nearby. It would take several
days before their stings paralyzed him completely and he died.*

*His wife was pregnant, but because she was a native of this
village, an even more terrible fate was reserved for her. This very
night, she would be driven out of the village into the jungle when
darkness fell. As everone knew, the jungle was infested with
night-demons.*

*I asked the Chief why the taboo existed. She believed it must
have some spiritual root, hidden in antiquity. That it was sound
common sense, as well as the tribe's tradition, was good enough*

for her. She was astonished when I told her that, in the society I came from, complete disclosure between married couples was regarded as vital. She doubted such a society could prosper.

Just before nightfall, the feast ended and farewells were made. As with most of these tribes, the Bizwas don't allow strangers to stay in the village overnight for fear of contamination. We, accordingly, went down to the river and boarded the Government launch. Darkness had just fallen and the crewman was about to start the engine when I asked him to stop. He and the Commissioner and I listened. The usual night sounds were stilled, and we could hear quite plainly from the nearby jungle the fearful shrieks of a woman.

WELL, GENTLE READER, as you are by now aware, *this* is the book about the Vanderlindens. I thought writing it would get them out of my system—like getting rid of Guinea Worms, I suppose. But it didn't work, and I'm glad of that. Just the other morning I was sitting out in the back yard with my coffee. I heard a noise and looked up, half expecting to see Thomas Vanderlinden at the gap in the hedge with a question ready for me: "Have you by any chance read . . . ?" Of course, there was no longer any hedge—or any Thomas. But I realized then how much I miss him. He always enjoyed hearing about my dreams. And that's the way I remember him now—like a dream, delightful and dangerous, as all the best dreams are.